IGNITED BY LOVE

BY LOVE SERIES

MARY O FLOURNOY

Captive 8 Publishing

COPYRIGHT

DEDICATION

To my family and friends who stood by me when I wanted to throw my laptop out the window. I love you.

CONTENTS

Chapter One   1
Chapter Two   11
Chapter Three   19
Chapter Four   27
Chapter Five   35
Chapter Six   41
Chapter Seven   52
Chapter Eight   60
Chapter Nine   68
Chapter Ten   78
Chapter Eleven   85
Chapter Twelve   95
Chapter Thirteen   106
Chapter Fourteen   113
Chapter Fifteen   121
Chapter Sixteen   130
Chapter Seventeen   138
Chapter Eighteen   148
Chapter Nineteen   157
Chapter Twenty   167
Chapter Twenty-One   176
Chapter Twenty-Two   184
Chapter Twenty-Three   194
Chapter Twenty-Four   204
Chapter Twenty-Five   212
Chapter Twenty-Six   220
Chapter Twenty-Seven   228
Chapter Twenty-Eight   235
Chapter Twenty-Nine   242
Chapter Thirty   249
Epilogue   254

CHAPTER ONE

Rocky

I TRIED TO RELEASE MY DEATH GRIP ON THE WEAPON. I REALLY DID.
Those tiny black words on the innocent, thin, fibrous, good-for-the-environment trees cut deep. A paper cut wasn't supposed to hurt so much, but this one killed me.

Because it was important.

Life and dreams important.

So much so my heart beat a techno rhythm inside my chest, and nausea danced in my stomach as visions of my shop being yanked out from under my feet due to the fucking series of complaints swarmed me.

How could those innocuous symbols hold such much power over someone's livelihood?

It was fucking terrifying.

First, the zoning complaint and now these bullshit ones. A noise ordinance and nuisance complaint and traffic and parking issues which could lead to the Environmental Protection Agency's involvement. Just what I fucking needed on top of the city coming down on me, the EPA's unwanted attention.

So with each step Feldspar's Vice Mayor, Kevin Reynolds, took toward my office door—even if it was a beautiful custom glass door etched with swirly sapphire letters spelling *Sterling Custom Auto*—my fist clenched tighter and tighter around the documents.

And the noose around my neck shrank the closer he got.

Because if Kevin's highly inferred matrimonial suggestion for saving my shop was real, then death was imminent.

His.

Literally.

Mine... It felt like a million lacerations slashed through me. My father's dream, my dream slowly leaking from each cut.

It wasn't that Kevin wasn't a good-looking man. He absolutely was with hair the color of wheat but as soft as cotton—unfortunately, I knew what it felt like—and his sparkling blue eyes that twinkled when he set them on you. That alone made a woman take notice. His attire? Yeah, he rocked the retro Ward Cleaver suit, tailored in a trendy way. And his mannerisms? Complete gentlemen.

It was an appealing package if you wanted to be June Cleaver waiting on him hand and foot with no other ambitions.

Ambitions like I was currently standing in.

My late father's legacy. My dream come to life. Everything I worked to achieve since he died, and it was all at risk.

A shot of fear blasted through me, and my hand spasmed around the offending noose of papers, releasing them. They fluttered onto my desk, and I choked back the hysteria lodged in my throat that even my beloved chocolate that it landed on couldn't remove. No effing way was I going to let Kevin take away my livelihood, my dreams, or my life with some trumped-up series of bullshit complaints.

He stepped into my office, and his sky-blue eyes scanned my face. "You look a little tired, Raquel."

In more ways than one. Not that I'd tell Kevin. Any sign of weakness, no matter how little, and he'd pounce. I glanced down at the papers—case in point—and back at him.

I really needed chocolate.

"What can I help you with?"

"I came by to see if you had time to talk. I'm sure we can resolve the zoning grievance before tomorrow's city council meeting. I was hoping we could sit down and talk, just the two of us, and figure all this out. Come to an agreement that suits everyone. It seems like all this is getting out of hand."

His serene smile, topped by his absurd statement, sent my blood racing through me like a geyser, where the only thing I could hear was the roar in my ears.

Come to an agreement? Was he genuinely insinuating what I thought he was? Me at his side, and all this would disappear? He wouldn't. Would he? It was always so thinly veiled that I couldn't be sure. Angry chills traveled over me at the audacity he had to use his position of authority to *persuade* me to his way of thinking or my livelihood, my life would suffer.

The world around me disappeared, and the only thing I was aware of was Kevin's isn't-everything-great smile.

No, it fucking wasn't.

But I was frozen in fear, staring at that ludicrous expression. I was scared I wasn't woman enough to run the shop my dad started. I was scared I wasn't woman enough to oversee a typical male-run business. I was just plain scared that I wasn't woman enough.

"Raquel?"

Kevin's grating voice pulled me out of the draining pool of dread, forced calm into my cells, and gave me the restraint to not kick Kevin's butt right out of my office.

"This," I pointed to the various violations on my desk, "is very much the definition of out of hand. This," another jab at the offensive papers, "very much indicates a boatload of seriousness. And not something that will simply disappear," one more angry jab that jolted the used chocolate wrappers into the air, "if we come to an agreement."

He remained focused on the sheets of paper on my desk as confusion replaced his earlier carefree attitude.

Had I read him wrong? Was my fear making me believe the worst in him?

Then, I saw *him*.

Tall. Taller than Kevin, who was no slouch. He easily topped Kevin by at least three inches, maybe four. His shoulders were massive, inches from fitting between the door frame, and stubble hid his jaw. Stubble I just *knew* would leave evidence of his touch. Marks I desperately wanted to mar my skin. My body shivered uncontrollably at the prospect.

Now, *he* was a man who could make a woman forget chocolate.

"Raquel?"

I struggled to pull my gaze from the newcomer's bourbon-colored eyes and woodenly shifted my attention to Kevin. The wrinkles between his eyes told me he wasn't again pleased with me.

"Maybe I shouldn't have kept you out so late at the mayor's birthday party." The confusion creases remained firmly in place on his face.

What?

"I believe you should close the shop and do something more suitable for your sensibilities."

My sensibilities? As in home and hearth sensibilities? Or children-rearing sensibilities? The words coming out of his mouth were like cold water poured over me—jarring.

"Mr. Reynolds, can I do something for you *automotive-wise?*" It was more than a job, more than a business to me, a fact Kevin did not comprehend.

He scanned my face. "I see you need a little more time. I'll sincerely await your presence tomorrow for our date."

"No need. Mr. Quincy and I will see you at City Hall for the *council meeting* where all the complaints against Sterling Custom Auto will be addressed."

Not.

A.

Date.

"Raquel, there is no reason to include your attorney in these proceedings. I could quite easily dismiss all this zoning business if you'd take the time to meet with me."

He *was* implying if I dated him, then he'd veto the crap out of the violations.

My hands curled into fists with the desire to punch Kevin. A feat I barely struggled not to follow through with. No reason to include Mr.

Quincy? He was talking about my deceased father's legacy, not some dilapidated shack that caused an eyesore in Feldspar's historic downtown. As for meeting with him? I'd rather jam a spark plug in my eye while attached to a live battery than give up my father's shop, much less marry Kevin and become his Stepford Wife.

My silent count of ten didn't do anything to lessen the itch to throttle Kevin. Damn the potential customer.

It took me to the count of twenty and a vow I'd sic Mr. Quincy on Kevin and his highly illegal proposal.

"Mr. Vice Mayor, the answer is still no. It will remain no," I leaned toward Kevin, *"forever."* Okay, maybe I hadn't fully throttled my desire. My chest expanded as I sucked in a massive breath in an attempt to regain my composure. "If there is nothing else, I have a customer waiting." I glanced at hunkalicious, who hadn't moved from his spot by the door, scowl and all.

Kevin's nod was slow and reluctant. "I genuinely wish you'd reconsider going home to rest. It is evident our late weekend did not sit well with you. On that note, I will bid you a good afternoon, hoping to ease some of your stress." He faced the newcomer and said, "Good day, sir."

The sullen but handsome stranger jerked his chin up in acknowledgment.

The jangling of the bell above the door confirmed Kevin's departure as I focused on the handsome man before me. His scowl only intensified his lusciousness. It made me want to reach out and pet him until he softened under my touch. However, a quick inspection of the rest of him made me realize flaccid wasn't what I wanted. His feet were encased in well-worn hiking boots planted shoulder-width apart. Moving up, I saw his jeans were as worn in as his boots, with the denim around his knees faded from use and...

I jerked my eyes up, and my cheeks blazed. Here I was, checking out a potential new client right in front of him—no need to worry about Kevin making me seem unprofessional. I was doing a bang-up job all by myself.

A hint of a smile graced his lickable lips.

Whoa.

A rush zipped through my body. A barely there twitch of his lips, and I was ready to jump him.

"Welcome to Sterling Custom Auto. How may I help you?" There, that sounded professional—nothing like the desire coursing through my body.

"Mornin'. I have an appointment with Rocky to discuss the restoration of my car."

His voice resonated through my body like the bass in a timeless jazz tune and warmed me like a smooth shot of bourbon.

Oh boy, I truly needed to stop my mind from associating sex with this man and concentrate on professionalism.

I swallowed to moisten my suddenly dry mouth. "Your name and vehicle?"

"Max Hudson. I have the convertible '67 Cadillac DeVille."

Not potential. An actual customer.

I walked around my desk and extended my hand. "It's great to meet you, Mr. Hudson. I've spoken with your brother, Paul, regarding your grandfather's car. She's a beauty."

A warm, calloused hand engulfed mine, and sparks shot directly to all my womanly parts.

Great.

Now my body was wholly participating in my waking sex dream.

Pulling my hand away, I tried subtly wiping it on my jeans, hoping to smother the embers that danced through my body. Because with that one simple touch, I knew I'd never want chocolate again if I had the pleasure of experiencing the completely uncensored Max package.

"It was, is. I'm hoping Rocky can make it so again."

A chill slowly swept through me at his words. I shouldn't have been surprised. He wasn't the first man who glazed over me in search of a man—looking for Rocky.

"Well, I have no doubt we'll be able to get your baby back in pristine order. Shall we go check her out?" I fell back on years of training, plastered on a professional smile, and headed toward the side garage door with a pitstop at my desk for some much-needed confectionery delight.

Screw the optics to the customer. After my morning, I could only handle so much without my edible vice.

I opened the door, waiting for Max as he stood there and contemplated whether he should follow. This introspection wasn't unusual. It was one of the normal responses I received from my male customers. Not quite sure if they should follow the little lady out, and if they did, thinking I was taking them to meet Rocky or insisting they speak with Rocky before they ventured any further.

My skin bubbled with irritation, and my heart squeezed as another man dismissed me. Being female and young, twenty-six years young, this feeling happened too frequently. I sucked in another deep breath and exhaled my disappointment as I waited for Max to decide.

Max chose option number one as he made his way to me. Not waiting for him to reach me, I entered the cubby area that separated the office from the actual workspace. The entire length of the cubby area was windowed so you could watch the progress of any vehicle. Each bay was staggered so that you could see each bay with tool stations placed in intervals. Yes, chocolate was a tool, too. So, no matter what station you were at, you had access to whatever tool you might need.

It also allowed us to watch Clay as he stepped back from his build, pointed at Bruno, and busted into a badass air guitar performance to the rock music blaring through the shop. This interaction was one of the many reasons I loved the cubby area—to watch the guys enjoying themselves.

Dad set up this area for different reasons. First, it allowed customers to view their babies' progress before entering the work zone. Second, it was a place where he could discuss the projects with everyone and anyone. Last but not least, it also served as a place where his employees could grab a break from whatever pesky automotive issue bothered them at the time.

It wasn't their official break room. No, that was in the back, away from all the hustle in the shop. Dad was a firm believer in separating business from personal. So, when his employees were off the clock, they were *off* the clock—even if it was for ten minutes.

Mom, Ash, and I agreed with Dad. So after he passed on, Mom and

Ash took control of the shop while I finished my business degree, and they kept all of Dad's rules and systems in place. It wasn't broken, so why change it?

"That's some shop."

"Yeah, she's a beauty all right." I tilted my head toward the bay in question.

His bourbon eyes gazed down at me. Who knew eye color would want you to take a sip of...

"After you." Max opened the door and waited for me to walk through.

I broke the contact and felt my cheeks pinken again. Good Lord, Rocky, get a hold of yourself.

I hightailed it to the DeVille, nodding at the guys as I passed them. I fell in love with the Caddy when she first came in—rust and all. Her lines, edges, and curves—gorgeous.

"She's looking better already," Max commented as he walked around her.

I ran a hand along the hood. "Yeah. Once we stripped her of everything, we gave her an overdue bath to see what we were working with. She wasn't as bad as we initially thought. The rust was pretty stubborn and refused to leave. It took a little work, but once we got it all off, we got all the dents and scratches out pretty quickly. From there, sanding her was easy." It's like she was working with us to get back in shape as fast as possible.

"Why didn't Rocky start the priming then?" he asked.

"We don't start that process until the remainder of the work is almost complete. There is too much activity inside and out of the DeVille before that type of preparation can occur." I bent down to the partially disassembled engine—since most of it was missing—picked up the shiny carburetor and stood back up. I held it toward Max and said, "For example, this baby here was filthy. Grease and dirt caked on it with a family of spiders nestled inside. The latter made me drop it atop the still-assembled engine." I shivered at the memory of the little guys running around the inside of the hood. "So, we err on the side of caution."

I had his full attention. The intensity in his eyes smoldered me as I watched him work out what I had just said. I knew from experience he was trying to figure out if I genuinely worked on cars or not.

Max eyed me across the hood. "How did Rocky do all this work by himself in such a short time?"

"Well, this gal helped. She didn't fight me—too much." I wiped some dust off the hood with the rag from the tool bench.

"*You?*" The incredulousness in his one word grated on my nerves.

"Yes, me." I gave him the respect he didn't give me, bent down, and placed the part back, which hopefully gave him the time to regroup from his disbelief. I eyed the box of chocolate on the rack and debated whether or not I should grab a piece as another option to delay some time.

Or as a way to keep my mouth shut instead of giving Max an earful on his sexist ways.

"I was told that Rocky would be working on my car." He didn't give up.

"And I am. However, I won't be the only one handling your baby. We work as a team and float between all our builds." Even though I was used to this type of response, having it come from Max bothered me more than usual. Something I'd have to ponder later. "If you come around to this side, I can go over what I've found regarding the engine spread out here, and then we can come up with some scheduled times for you and your family to stop by and check on her."

Max walked around the DeVille and stopped by the tarp across from me. "Sorry, I didn't know you were Rocky. I was..." He looked down at the engine parts before he looked back up and said, "I can't spin or excuse what I thought."

"Thanks." I was at a loss for words. His apology was a first for me. Every other man made excuses. None of them ever outright admitted they were being a misogynistic ass for thinking it and coming from Max—my whole body somersaulted in joy.

We spent a good thirty minutes reviewing the work I had completed and scheduled regular check-ins. The entire time, I struggled to focus on Max's questions and my answers. I'd catch myself watching his mouth move, thinking I'd love to taste his lips, or staring at his eyes, wondering if they darkened when he was sexually excited.

And his fingers? Every time he pointed at something, I'd imagine what their thickness would feel like inside me.

Max truly tested my business etiquette, and I questioned whether I'd be able to handle all the checkups with him in attendance.

So, when he finally left, I shoved a chunk of chocolate in my mouth and thought maybe I would include a vibrator in my chocolate fest tonight.

CHAPTER TWO

Max

SITTING IN MY OFFICE AT HUDSON FLIGHT SCHOOL, I THOUGHT about kicking Paul's ass for not telling me about Raquel. A simple heads-up would have sufficed. But, instead, he let me walk in there and make a fool of myself. The little shit deserved at least a solid smack upside the head for the omission.

"Hey, Max. What's up?" Paul's baritone resonated in my ear.

Fuck the pleasantries. "Why didn't you tell me Rocky was female?" Even to my own ears, I sounded like a sexist ass.

"Because her gender doesn't matter." Paul paused. "Or does it?"

Normally? It wouldn't matter, but this wasn't a normal situation. And neither was Raquel, not that I would tell Paul that, though.

"If she can mislead her customers with something as simple as this, then what else is she hiding? How do you know she can genuinely get the job done?" I squeezed my eyes shut and tried not to imagine Raquel getting *any* job done.

Naked.

On the hood of the DeVille with her thick hair spread out around her, one hand cupping her generous breast. The other hand glided down to her core as she opened her legs, exposing herself to me.

"Max!" Paul's shout penetrated my fantasy of Raquel.

"I'm..." I cleared my throat. "I'm here."

"What the hell is going on with you?"

Great question. I had one goal—give my dad back his '67 DeVille before... But, instead, I found it rusting away in someone's cornfield, missing practically every*fucking*thing. Finding someone to quickly restore it to its original condition was a miracle. But to be confronted with the other stuff?

"Why did you pick this shop? How sure are you about the quality of the work she does?"

"It's a highly-rated shop. We were lucky Rocky was able to fit us in." Paul's voice dropped as his concern overtook him. "What exactly happened?"

"A dissatisfied customer plus ordinance issues."

"What?"

I stared unseeing at the pile of papers on my desk. "When I arrived, I ran into an asshole outside the entrance. He warned me against utilizing Sterling Custom Auto, stating they would only steal my money while handing me a subpar product. He suggested running the other way, fast. Not even two minutes later, I entered the office and was confronted with Dick Number Two. This one wants Raquel home, barefoot and pregnant. To top it off, Dick Number Two states Sterling Custom Auto has some sort of violation, which he will address at the council meeting tomorrow. How solid is the contract you signed?" And what could I do to discover what was happening with Raquel's shop? "Plus, she has chocolate all over the shop. It's like a damn chocolate factory exploded in there."

I heard nothing but silence on Paul's end.

"You there?"

"What exactly does Rocky look like?" I could hear Paul's smirk.

Why he was smiling, I had no idea. "What do you mean? I thought you met her when you signed the contract?"

"No, I met with Bruno when I signed the contract. I never met Rocky." He was definitely smiling.

"What the hell are you smiling about?" There wasn't a single thing funny about any of this.

"Max, I do believe you have the hots for Rocky." Paul's chuckle vibrated through the phone.

"Fuck you."

Paul's laughter bellowed through the phone into my ear. It took more control than I wanted to admit to not hang up on him, but I knew he'd be on the horn with Cole and Vic the second I did.

Damn nosey brothers.

"When do you go back?" Paul spoke through his dying laughter.

"Why?" My body tensed as leeriness spread through me.

"Because I'm going with you. I can't wait to meet Rocky."

He sounded way too happy for my own good.

"We scheduled regular check-ins. I'll email everyone the dates and times later." I hesitated. Not sure if I should admit anything to Paul. "But I plan on being at the council meeting tomorrow."

"Oh, I'm absolutely coming with you."

"The fuck you are." For some reason, I didn't want Paul near Raquel.

"Oh, yes, I am. I gotta see who's got my big brother's nuts all twisted." I didn't think he stopped smiling during the whole conversation. "Don't even think about leaving me. I'll follow your ass."

Damn it. I knew he would too. "You know what? That's a great idea. Then we can confront her about the zoning issue and get out of the contract." I smiled because it worked out great. "You're a freaking genius, baby brother."

"Yes, I am. Thank you."

I ignored the sound of Paul's smugness. "Who was the second option for shops? We need them lined up to move Granddad's car over."

"There wasn't a second shop."

"What do you mean there's no second shop?" If Paul pushed me to state why, I wouldn't be able to give him an answer because there is no way I'd admit Raquel was hitting all the right buttons.

A quiet seriousness poured through the line. "We want the best for Granddad's car, and we want it done quickly for Dad. We're not going with second best because you got the hots for the owner. Granddad, dad..." Paul cleared his throat. "Sterling Custom Auto is the only damn choice."

"Damn it." I squeezed my eyes shut.

"Besides, I looked into a dozen or so shops in the area and out. None of them come close to Sterling Custom Auto's reputation. And, if you pushed me to choose a second, we'd have to transfer the car seven hours away *and* wait over a year for them to fit us into their schedule." Paul didn't let up.

"If she's so damn good, then how can she fit us in?" Why was I pushing so hard on this? I didn't give a fuck a woman was doing the work.

"I asked her the same thing because I was surprised too. She comes *that* highly rated. She said a customer backed out—and no, she didn't tell me why—and that left a slot available. More importantly, you need to trust that I'll do the right thing for Granddad's car and that I'd never do anything to jeopardize this for Dad." Paul fought his corner and chastised me for doubting him, rightfully so. "Now you wanna tell me what your problem is because I know it's not that a female is working on the car."

Nope. Because Paul was right. Raquel drew me and until I figured out why she did, I wasn't going to give my little brother any ammunition to fuck with me. "If she can mislead us with something as simple as a name, what makes you think she won't mislead us on something regarding the DeVille?" I sucked in a breath because I was being a Grade-A Jackass. "I just don't want anything getting in the way of the restoration. It's too important."

"First off, she didn't mislead us. If you had looked at any of the information I sent you, you would have known she is Rocky. And do I fucking have to repeat it? You should trust me and my judgment." Paul's usual jovial self vanished.

"Sorry, man. I just..." Needed to clear my head. "I'm just in a sour mood and taking it out on you. No excuse, but I was a dick."

"Yes, that you are." Fucking little brothers. "Now, tell me, what's got your nuts all twisted?" Awesome little fucking brothers.

"Nothing. I'm just thinking about Dad and his heart, and I need the DeVille to bring him some happiness." I didn't completely lie to Paul.

I heard Paul blow a breath out. "Yeah, I feel you. Trust me, Rocky will restore the car to pristine shape in no time. Dad will love it so much we won't be able to get him out of it." He did his best to alleviate some of my concerns.

"You're right, and not just about Dad. About Raquel too." I put aside my irritation and conceded to what I already knew to be true. My absolute trust in Paul to do the right thing for our dad meant trusting Raquel was the right person for the job.

Even if I wanted to bed her.

"I know. Like you said, I'm a genius." Paul chuckled.

The dickhead didn't even wait for a response.

The papers swam before me as visions of my meeting with Raquel danced through my head. Her composure—even when she slightly cracked, when Dick Number Two tried to push her into making a hasty decision—remained level-headed and professional. The calm, capable way she handled the various auto parts and the obvious excitement when she discussed all the phases of the restoration. And the slight reddening of her cheeks when I caught her staring at my body.

No doubt about it, there was definitely a spark between us.

Dad's name popped up on my cell screen, interrupting my cyclical thoughts of Raquel.

"Hey, Dad. How are you doing?"

"I'll tell you how I'm doing. I can't find ten minutes without Lucy or you boys on me."

Dad wasn't upset with me. No, he was in a sour mood because his nurse ensured he didn't veer from the doctor's restrictive regiment after his heart attack. But, more importantly, without any allies in us boys, he couldn't even get one of us to sneak him a treat or two.

"It's your damn fault. You raised us to be mule-headed."

Dad snorted. "I raised you all to mind me and look where that got me. Damn it, Max, would it kill you to bring me a burger from Harper's? You were in Feldspar this morning checking up on the Cadillac.

You couldn't stop and bring me back a damn burger on your way home to Granite Creek?" he bitched.

"Yes, because it *might* kill you. The doctor clarified that you had to change your lifestyle to beat this back and stick around longer. So, do what Nurse Lucy says and stop bitching about it." No fucking way was I taking any chances. I couldn't imagine not having Dad around. He made sure we stayed a family after Mom left. He was the rock in our family. "And I was there checking on the DeVille, not for a meal at Harper's."

"All right, Max, don't get your panties in a bunch. I'll do what Lucy tells me, but I want you to know if I choke on the *salad*—" spoken as if it was a bowl full of prunes, "—she feeds me, it's your dang fault," Dad sniped. "As for the restoration, I'm not worried about it. That shop comes highly recommended. Whatever crap is happening doesn't change the fact that the car is in the right hands."

"I hope so, Dad." I really did. "And how often did you make us boys sit at the table until we finished every last vegetable on our plates? Countless. So, in my estimation, this is payback." I chuckled.

Dad's tone changed immediately. "What a great idea, Max. Why don't you boys join me for dinner? I'm sure Lucy wouldn't mind making enough for all of us."

"Remember, Lucy is there as your nurse, not your chef, and I can't make it tonight. I've got a private lesson."

"I'm hoping the more I bother her, it'll make her want to leave." He grumbled before switching topics. "Am I going to meet this one this time? You know, I'm not getting any younger. I'd like some grand-children soon."

"It's not that type of private lesson." I walked right into that one. He'd been getting on all of us boys about grandkids for months. Maybe he knew something wasn't right with his health all this time, and this was his way of ensuring we stepped up our family timeline. Not that any of us were ready to start the baby-making factories.

Raquel's face immediately popped up front and center. What radiant vision would she present with her belly distended with our young? With the glow only pregnant women achieved?

My brain refused to veer from the track of visions of Raquel herding our children, love in every molecule of her being for them. For us.

That was the image of a mother who would do *anything* in her power for her family. Did Raquel learn to douse everything in love from her mother? Her father? Did the two work together to provide a loving home for their family? Unlike the woman who gave birth to me—who split the second it got too hard for her.

Instant dream killer.

"Max, you there?" Dad grumbled.

I cleared my throat. "Yeah, Dad. I'm here."

"I'll expect Rocky at the family table at the end of the month." Dad left no room for argument.

"Dad..." I realized I wasn't going to object to the thought of bringing Raquel around.

Not that Dad gave me a chance; he spoke right over me. "I'll tell your brothers to be on their best behavior when the time comes. We don't want to scare her off," Dad rattled.

The image of Raquel fitting in with my brothers and dad wasn't difficult to conjure up. The way she interacted with her staff told me handling Cole, Vic, and Paul would be a piece of cake for her.

Dad. I blew out a breath. Dad always wanted a daughter. Mom said she did too, but after the fourth boy, she had her tubes tied without Dad knowing. It was one more disappointment—or betrayal—she portrayed against Dad and us.

Meeting Raquel would be a dream come to life for Dad. She seemed like she'd be everything he'd want in a daughter, which was exactly what the doctor prescribed. No stress. A relaxing retirement filled with things that made Dad happy in order to reduce the strain on his heart and body.

But was I willing to give him this happiness for his health?

"... take care of it before the end of the month. Don't worry about giving your brothers the news; I'll handle it. Now, I see Lucy coming my way, so I'll let you go before she has a fit I'm on the phone and not eating. See you soon, Max."

Shit. Dad wasn't going to back down. I had to figure out how to slow Dad's expectations while I figured out what mine were.

Wait, how did Dad know Raquel's name?

Fucking Paul.

Damn it, Dad played me.

CHAPTER THREE

Max

I TURNED MY ATTENTION TO TOMORROW'S FLIGHT LESSONS AND hoped it would help keep Raquel off my mind. Anything to keep my focus off of how much chocolate she kept herself supplied with and, at the same time, thankful she didn't hold back consuming it because her curves were undeniably mouthwatering. Even under her overalls, her thick ass declared it was the perfect handle for a pounding.

I shifted in my seat and readjusted my thickening cock.

Raquel was driving me mad.

"Hey, handsome."

Instant dick deflator.

Brandie leaned against the door jam with her arms crossed under her breasts, plumping them to their full melon size. She was the type of woman who utilized every physical part of her body to her advantage.

She just wasn't the chocolate sex I wanted.

"Brandie, what brought you out here?" I asked, even though her display screamed her intention.

She straightened away from the door; one hand rubbed the hem of her dress ever so slowly while the other twirled her hair against her breast, highlighting her taut nipple.

"You haven't returned my calls, so I thought I'd come to see you. I've missed you." The slightest pout she used as an invitation. One I previously acted upon and regretted because while Brandie appeared the part of a sex goddess, she simply was not.

"I've been busy."

I had a rule: I didn't do second dates. It led the women to believe there was a possibility for more.

There wasn't.

My mind screamed *liar!* as Raquel's face flashed like a neon sign in my brain.

I shook my head to clear my thoughts of Raquel and focused on when I was eleven and the lesson my mother taught me about women leaving when they wanted something better. Women like Brandie who thought they could hook me.

She cat-walked her way to my desk with a teasing smile. She placed one hand on my desk, leaned over to better display her tits, and ran her finger along the v of her sweater. "Too busy for me?" she purred.

There was a reason why I hadn't called her back. Besides the fact she wasn't all that great in bed and too clingy, she wanted a sugar daddy. So, she upped her actions to land me the second she learned I owned Hudson Flight School. So, I knew it would be a colossal mistake to take her up on her offer.

She made an effort to strengthen her position and moved to stand between my legs with the desk behind her. She scooted her skinny rear onto it and placed one shiny black stiletto on my knee, and exposed her panty-free glistening pussy. She slid one hand down her body, spread her finger through her juices, and brought it toward my lips.

I grabbed her wrist while maintaining eye contact with her I-think-I-succeeded-look and said, "Yes."

"I knew you wanted me." A prize-winning smile spread across her face.

Not even close. "Yes, I'm too busy for you."

That wiped the smug expression right off her face.

I pushed my chair back, stood, and dropped her wrist. "Don't come back, Brandie."

"I can't believe you. You'll never get anyone better than me." She snarled and let her inner she-devil out.

"I'll take the chance." A little voice in my head told me I had already met that someone.

She stormed past me and made it out the door as Vic, the second oldest of us boys and my business partner, arrived.

Vic's eyebrow shot up as Brandie stomped past him. "I thought we agreed we wouldn't bring our exploits to work."

"I didn't bring her here."

"Is she gonna be a problem?"

"No. Brandie always lands on her feet—or more like on another boy toy." I sat back down and changed the subject. "I thought you weren't coming by today."

Vic sat in the guest chair across from me. "I hadn't planned on it, but I wanted to get some time in the air."

"What's going on?"

He shook his head. "Nothing. Have you visited Dad today?"

"No. I spoke with him earlier after I pulled all this out." I pointed to the papers on my desk that I hadn't touched yet because Raquel wouldn't leave my mind. However, after my phone call with Dad, I wasn't sure a visit was the wisest choice. It also meant he hadn't got a hold of Vic yet if he was asking me about Dad.

Vic glanced down at the paperwork and back to me. "I thought you got here early to take care of it?" His lips turned up the slightest, letting me know he knew something.

I tensed, knowing Paul had opened his big mouth. "I did. Something came up."

"Would that something be Miss Sterling?" Of course, his question was bullshit since Paul already blabbed.

"You guys have too much time on your hands if you're gossiping about me."

His laughter was that of a brother who'd teased his brothers mercilessly over the years. "Aww, so Maxie has a crush on the car chick."

"Raquel's not a car chick. She's..." So much more.

"Ah, so Paul was right." Vic's amusement immediately vanished to be replaced with keen interest.

"About what?" This couldn't be good.

"First, I called you Maxie, and you didn't threaten to castrate me." He carried on even as I flipped him off, "The other—nothing."

"If it's nothing, then you won't have a problem telling me."

He shook his head in brotherly wisdom. "A word of advice. Don't hold on to the past."

"What the hell does that mean?" I frowned.

"Out of all of us, Mom hurt you the most." He put his hand up to stop my objections. "Don't. I know you don't like to talk about it, but it doesn't change the fact that what she did scarred you—it changed you." Vic pointed to the empty doorway. "That..." His raised eyebrow completed his unspoken thought. "You're only picking the ones who give off the I'm-up-for-a-good-time-only vibe. You're keeping women at bay, expecting them to ditch you like Mom did."

"Mom hurt us all. I won't deny it, but Dad suffered the most. The DeVille..." I coughed to dislodge the emotion clogging my throat. "It's the least we can do for Dad, so he knows we appreciate the sacrifice he made for us. Besides, the doctor said no stress, to keep things cheery, so his heart won't have to work so hard. So I think the DeVille qualifies."

"It all qualifies." He leaned forward. "Because it's all fucking connected. Granddad's house burned down, leaving him with nothin'. He lost everything—not one single fucking thing left for him to remember Grandma by or the fifteen years he got to spend with her before she passed. Except for the Caddy. The car was the only memory he had..." He sucked in a breath as he sat back in his chair. "Granddad didn't hesitate to give Dad and Mom the car when things got tight because he wanted them, us, to have what he and Grandma had. It was a serious kick to the gut when mom left because the Caddy repre- sented what family was supposed to be, what it was meant to be. Mom flipped her middle finger at it, at us, when she left, and it killed some- thing in Dad when he had to sell it to make ends meet. So, yeah, the DeVille more than qualifies for *Dad*. The question is, what's it going to take for *you*?"

"Not a fucking thing. This is about giving Dad what he needs and deserves, so don't turn this around on me. This isn't about me. You were there. We all were." I bit out beyond mad at Vic for hitting too close to home. Mom proved when she left us all those years ago for a wealthy older man that women only sought one thing from a man—money. And not even five minutes ago, Brandie proved the same fucking point again.

So, no, I didn't want to have this conversation with Vic.

"We could go back and forth all day about this." He ran a hand through his hair and changed the subject. "Tell me about the restoration. Is it still on track for the original completion date, or will the zoning crap be a problem?"

Years of built-up anger and pain pushed at me, wanting out, but I held it back with the same years of practice and gave Vic the change he wanted—the change I needed. "I don't know if it will get in the way of the repair. So far, it has hindered any progress, even with the Vice Mayor being pretty adamant about it. Raquel did mention her attorney would be present to handle it, so I'm assuming he's on top of things."

"Hasn't Sterling Custom Auto been in the same location for years?"

I nodded. "Yeah, which makes the violations confusing."

"Do you know who filed the original complaint?" Vic paused. "Paul mentioned the Vice Mayor has a thing for Rocky. Are the two related?"

Damn it, I should have thought of that, but with Raquel constantly creeping into my thoughts, I wasn't on my game. "No clue who filed it, but I don't think the two are related. I got the impression Kevin and Raquel knew each other before this. If my gut is right, he should know she won't back down."

Vic leaned back in his chair, placing his right ankle on his left knee. "Why would he need her to back down? Wanting her and her keeping her business are two different things."

I placed my forearms on my desk, thinking about Vic's comments. Something about them struck a chord. "You might be onto something. Kevin seemed the traditional type to me. If he wants Raquel, forcing her to close her business would place her squarely in his time-honored gender roles." I shook my head. "But that can't be right. Surely, there must be some sort of clause that the Vice Mayor can't be involved in the case if he was the one to file the complaint. It doesn't make sense."

"I don't know."

"I'm heading over there next week to check on the status of everything." To further fuel the fire taking root between Raquel and me. "I set up a schedule for all of us to drop in and see the progress. I'll shoot that over to you in a bit."

"When are you going?"

"Why?"

"You're not the only one with a vested interest in ensuring the DeVille is completed on time."

"I know." But Vic was up to something. "What aren't you telling me?"

He ignored my question. "Are you going up today? Clearing your head?" The smirk on his face reminded me that sometimes being close to my brothers was a pain in my ass. He knew the skies were my way of clearing my head and

And we were all close. Growing up the way we did ensured we were. But times like now, when I didn't want to share, it sucked. Because Vic knew the empty skies were my escape. Add in his earlier commentary regarding Raquel and the smirk on his face from my reactions to his digging about her, it wasn't too hard for Vic to put two and two together. So yeah, I needed the time alone without anyone in my ear reminding me of life and all its suckage. It was heaven. It was the main reason I decided to open Hudson Flight School. Unencumbered access to the skies. To escape.

But there was no escaping my brothers. Vic wasn't going to let me go it alone and showed up or more like plowed me with the logic of having him as a business partner.

And, with that, *I* ignored his last question because no way did I want to discuss my inability to stop thinking about Raquel. I tried to assess Vic's other motive for going with me next week, but I knew I wouldn't get it out of him. "Later. I have a lesson. Anything I need to be aware of when I'm up there?"

He eased back in his seat. "Nope. You'll have clear skies, but I called Ryder over at Fish and Wildlife about a possible mountain lion I saw at Willow's Pass. Otherwise, it's quiet out there."

"All you had to do was tell the lion you would call Ryder. It would have disappeared before you finished speaking."

"No doubt." Vic's lips twitched at my wry but partially true humor.

I wondered if Raquel would like to fly and catch sight of mountain lions. Would she be in awe of the beauty of the open skies, or would she want to stay firmly planted on the ground? Fuck, maybe getting Raquel out of my system wouldn't solve anything.

I wasn't sure if going up would be what I needed. Unobliterated time without distractions? Raquel would be a lead weight in my brain.

"I see your mind is on—"

I flipped him off.

Vic's laughter followed him out the door.

Now, if only I could find a way to get Raquel in the backseat and out of my head.

Brandie

Men sucked. And I wasn't only talking about when they were going to get somethin' out of it, and maybe, *maybe* if I were lucky, I'd get something too. But even then, it was still all about them.

So, Max didn't surprise me. He was a man, after all. And not just one of those men who thinks he's a man. You know, the ones who play at being important or think they're a power, but in actuality, their title holds all the cards. Or the ones who truly overcompensate in all aspects because they have little penises, little minds, but huge egos.

Max wasn't one of them. Oh no. Max was *all* man. Power, title, and magnetism. He was the *whole* package. But once again, he proved that he was still only a man led by his dick. That was something I could work with. After all, I was the whole package too.

But I wasn't blind. The way he watched Rocky, he obviously wanted to feast on her. And he did it without caring who saw.

It was all kinds of hot.

If it was directed at me.

I didn't get what Max saw in her. Her name was so masculine, and she worked on cars wearing baggy, dirty overalls that did nothing to accentuate her feminine assets. And as much as I wanted to deny it, she did have curves. Curves she could use to twist men around her little finger with because all men thought with their dicks. But she didn't. She covered up *and* ruined perfectly good manicures by chipping them and getting grease under her nails. I shuddered at the thought. So, I didn't get what men saw in her when she resembled one of the guys.

To top it off, she got in the way of the sisterhood. She blocked another sister from getting her due rights when she worked her butt off—in more ways than one—to climb to the top. It wasn't like anyone was getting in her way of success. As a matter of fact, it sounded like she was going to be sitting on a fat ride to the top real soon. So, with all that, why couldn't she hold her hand out and give some love to another woman working her way up too?

Because of that, I had to teach her a lesson. No, she needed to learn the lesson. That's why I didn't pass up the opportunity given to me. I never did. I learned early to seize everything I could because everyone always took from me whether or not I wanted to give it to them. So, when the Wheldon Luxury dude left his card for Rocky, I snatched it. And, when the delivery guy wanted someone to sign for some *valuable* part but left it on her desk, I snatched that too.

She didn't want to help another female out?

Then fuck her.

CHAPTER FOUR

Rocky

FOR THE FIRST TIME EVER, MY WORK DAY HAD BEEN TORTUROUS.

Scratch that. Make that the last thirty-four hours.

All because my mind kept imagining the scenario where I sat at the council meeting and Kevin pounded his gavel—the sound reverberated through my soul—and announced the closure of my shop. Then I felt the weight of utter disappointment pressing down on me knowing I failed. Then I'd switch back to see the complete despair on Ash and Mom's faces at the news of how I let a minor zoning issue destroy Dad's legacy.

Not making things any better, my mind would jump from that horror to Max's fiery bourbon-colored eyes.

Above me.

As he moved *inside* me.

Good Lord, a few minutes with the man—one freaking day *ago*— and he starred in all my fantasies—waking or not.

Needless to say, I was wound tight from stress *and* sexual frustration.

So standing next to Mr. Quincy in the small conference room at

City Hall waiting for the freaking council meeting to start so they could determine if Sterling Custom Auto and the other businesses on my block were actually in violation was excruciating. The only positive thing out of this crapola was that when I filled Mr. Quincy in regarding Kevin's girlfriend shakedown, Mr. Quincy assured me he'd handle it. So I mentally crossed my fingers that with Kevin's illegal proposition and Mr. Quincy's legalese mojo, I'd go home tonight zone, traffic, parking, noise, and nuisance complaint free *and* Kevin free.

Mr. Quincy inclined his head to me and whispered, "Now, Raquel dear, as much as you are eloquent in eliminating nonsensical conversation, I'm going to recommend that this highly inapt skill of yours not present itself at this juncture. As a matter of fact, as your legal counsel, I'm advising you to allow me to do the majority of the conversing."

I leaned into Mr. Quincy and whispered, "Are you telling me to shut my pie hole? That it wouldn't be okay to punch the Vice Mayor in the throat while I tell him he's a douche canoe and that he can take his antiquated views and shove them right up his..."

"Good evening, Sherman. It's always a pleasure, old friend." Mr. Quincy extended his hand past me to the mayor.

As I turned to face Mr. Dixon, I grazed Mr. Quincy's shoulder, letting him know I had received his message.

I plastered on a professional smile and addressed the mayor. "Mr. Quincy is correct. It's always a delight, Mr. Dixon." Even if it was under bullshit pretense.

"I can say the same about you, Theodore." Mr. Dixon released Mr. Quincy's hand and pulled me in for a quick hug and kiss on the cheek. "Miss Sterling, the pleasure is all mine."

"Oh, now I know how Mrs. Dixon fell under your spell. You're quite the charmer." And he was. Mr. Dixon may have been a shrewd businessman who could politic with the best of them, but underneath it all, he was a giant teddy bear. I prayed both sides of him saw through Kevin's B.S. and lit a fire on the whole regulations bullshit. Meanwhile, I'd dance a little *nyah, nyah, nyah* dance around the bonfire—tongue sticking out and thumbs stuck in my ears, waving my fingers back and forth included.

My heart stuttered as the possibility of that not happening hit me.

No matter what Kevin thought, he couldn't just brush it under the rug if I fell in line with his Make Rocky My Girlfriend extortion plan. There were documented violations recorded with the city. Regardless of Kevin's pull, they had to go through the entire administrative process.

I sucked in a breath, did my best to calm my fears, and focused on Mr. Dixon's words.

"One day, the Mrs. and I will have you over for tea, and we'll tell you just how much of my charm I needed to win her over." Mr. Dixon's voice pitched with joy at sharing his love for his wife.

"Oh, Raquel and I would love that." Kevin's oblivious poise filled our space.

Moving only my eyeballs, I peered up at Mr. Quincy for... permission to freaking throat-punch the conniving bastard.

Mr. Quincy didn't miss a beat. "The younger generation is sandpaper against my chivalrous nature." He quickly shook his head in disbelief even as he smiled at me. "At least with Miss Sterling, I am assured she will retire with a true gentleman."

I loved Mr. Quincy.

"I couldn't agree with you more, old friend. However, it was a pleasure to encounter so many young faces this past weekend. Each of them is unique in their own regard with a future alight with many bright possibilities."

Unique—that's one way to put it. Although, I was thinking more along the lines of an ignorant Ward Cleaver when it came to Kevin.

"Mr. Dixon, the younger generation is lucky to have your insightful leadership. Without it, their shining futures may be in jeopardy under other less thoughtful views." Take that, goody-two-shoes Kevin. "And I would like to thank you once more for the lovely evening. Your birthday party was quite enchanting."

"Raquel is correct. We truly enjoyed ourselves and were grateful to share such a lovely evening with you and Mrs. Dixon." Kevin's hand briefly touched my arm.

"I..." All my thoughts shattered as my eyes locked onto Max's golden ones. The fire in them scorched me from his position at the entrance of the City Hall and left me burning for a whole other reason.

For a taste of him.

Max.

I did a body scan and discovered he was in the same worn brown leather jacket that hugged the massive width of his shoulders. His button-down flannel shirt was open just enough to whisper an invitation to caress, to savor the softness and solid strength underneath. The jeans? I was convinced Max wore his jeans intentionally to draw the female eye to a very specific and desirable area. Good Lord! The man wasn't even erect, and his pants were packed.

Someone must have turned the heat up.

"Raquel." Kevin's stern reprimand yanked me back to my group.

Meanwhile, both Mr. Quincy and Mr. Dixon shared an I-know-what-this-means visage.

"If you'll excuse me, I must address certain matters before calling the meeting to order. But, Miss Sterling, I do expect an introduction of your young man later." Mr. Dixon angled himself toward Kevin and said, "After you."

Fear crept in when I glimpsed the expression on Kevin's face as he walked away. It was the vision of a man not pleased. How he didn't get a freakin' clue, I had no idea. Or maybe he did, and that's why I was in this position—on the verge of losing everything because he was trying to use this to his advantage.

Mr. Quincy guided us to our seats with a hand on my elbow. "A word of warning, Miss Sterling. Do not engage in any communications —verbally, written, or whatever you young kids do these days—with Mr. Reynolds."

It pissed me off that Mr. Quincy had to give that message. All those years that I'd been working alongside my dad in his shop. I learned *everything* from him. From what a timing belt was, to calculating the correct ratio of aeration needed in certain paints, to forecasting profit and loss. I'd only ever had to utilize Mr. Quincy for contracts and mundane legal matters. It chapped my hide that I had to use him for unrequited adoration in a twisted, unrelated, but related business matter.

Kevin, however, was taking it too damn far. Not only was he trying to place me in his idea of a docile, subservient companion—my body uncontrollably shivered in horror—he was attempting to permanently close the shop. To dim my life.

No fucking way.

I scanned the assembled council members and noticed several of them were women. Once again, the urge to do bodily harm to Kevin overcame me. He worked side-by-side with these women daily, who made it all work. Work and family—neither sacrificed—yet he felt the need to hamper my ability to have it all.

Why I was surprised, I had no idea. Kevin wasn't the first man to pat me on the head and ask to speak to the man in charge. Or like Carson, my lying, cheating ex who tried to use me to get to the *men* in charge. It stung because I genuinely thought Carson believed in me and my ability to run a renowned custom auto shop as a *female*. To find out he was lying to gain access to my business contacts hurt.

Now, to sit here and watch Kevin make legal efforts to shut my life down while surrounded by strong, capable women made my blood boil.

I consciously returned to the room when Mr. Quincy's soft but firm hand encased my fisted one. "Miss Sterling, violence will not work in your favor. Please refrain from committing any such acts," he whispered in my ear.

My mouth twitched at his dry humor.

But I did heed his words and forced my body to release some of its tension. I uncurled my fist, one finger at a time. One deep breath and exhalation at a time.

That's when I felt it—someone watching me. I turned my attention to the left and saw Max staring at me. Contemplation grooved into his face; if I had to guess, he wondered how he could get out of his contract with me. Not that I blamed him. We *were* sitting in a city council meeting in City Hall, where the land his grandfather's car was being restored was going to be up for discussion. For all he knew, Kevin could shut my business down immediately, and the restoration they needed to be completed in a rush delayed. Which Paul made abundantly clear was not an option.

Yup, this was undoubtedly not a vote of confidence in my favor.

Fucking Kevin.

A hand waved in front of Max's face and broke our connection. I followed the length of the arm attached to the hand, and my breath caught. Goodness, the Man above was torturing me. This guy was breathtaking as well. He had sandy brown hair that had to be finger combed with dark chocolate eyes crinkling at the corners. A square jawline with white teeth shone dazzlingly at me as he smiled brightly.

I snapped my eyes back up at him and examined him and Max more thoroughly. The similar features made it clear this was Max's brother, and he was obviously enjoying something. And it wasn't the fact my business was under attack; otherwise, he would've had the same scowl plastered on his face as Max's.

A gentle nudge from Mr. Quincy and I steered my focus back to the meeting. To focus on keeping my past in the present. To focus on keeping my future.

No matter how handsome the Hudson boys were, I had to stay zeroed in on the purpose of this meeting—on the legacy my father left me.

Even if it meant listening to Kevin drone on about how the budget needed reallocation because the city didn't have the funds for the community garden program. Yes, it was an important camp for at-risk children, and I wholeheartedly supported it. It taught children the importance of growing their own food—something they could feel proud about—and provided a safe place while their parents worked, away from drugs and other less desirable elements. However, it was close to closing time, and they hadn't touched one of the issues yet. Would they extend the time, or would it be rescheduled? Could Mr. Quincy use that time to find some loophole to save Sterling Custom Auto? Or was I just prolonging my anxiety?

Even with these thoughts occupying my brain, I could feel Max's gaze. It felt... heated and full of wicked promises. Unable to help myself, I peered over at Max, and yup, he was staring.

My breasts grew heavy, and my body melted from the sexual promise in his eyes. I sucked in a deep breath to control my rioting body.

Max's eyes shot down to my expounding chest and back up.

My hands shot to the sides of my chair, and I held on tightly.

To keep myself...

Right.

Where.

I.

Was.

Because every molecule in my body wanted to jump across the room and ride Max.

"Miss Sterling?" Mr. Quincy touched my white-knuckled hand.

I forced myself to look away from Max and took on the herculean task of focusing on Mr. Quincy. "Yes?" It came out hoarse and full of need.

He scanned my face once and then studied Max before Mr. Quincy said, "They're about to discuss the zoning ordinance."

It was the splash of cold water I needed to bring me back to what was important—my livelihood.

I directed my attention to Kevin, who slid a piece of paper out, skimmed it, then glanced at the clock and said, "Unfortunately, we've run out of time to discuss the zoning and other ordinance concerns properly. Because of this, we will address it at our next council meeting." He viewed his fellow council members at his sides. "If my cohorts have nothing else, I call to adjourn..."

The white noise in my ears drowned out the rest of his sentence.

Vindictive

They were so wrapped up visually banging each other that they hadn't noticed me. Not that I blamed Max. Rocky was something to feast on. Her curves went on for days, and any hot-blooded male could spend days fantasizing about how he'd handle them. I'd spent too many of my nights jacking off doing precisely that. Not that she cared. She went about her way and expected everyone to slot into her plans. Not once did she take into consideration what others wanted.

All she had to do was give me what I needed. Without it, my days were numbered. No more fine dining, no more days out at the country club, no more access to easy pussy, no more of what I deserved.

To top it off, they didn't even touch any of the violations in tonight's meeting. At first, it pissed me off. I needed to savor the devastation on Rocky's face when they took the shop out from under her. But the more I thought about it, the more I liked that they didn't. It'd weigh on her, stewing in the back of her brain whether or not she was in danger of losing her shop. The *legacy* her dad passed on to her.

Fuck the number of times I'd heard her mention that beloved legacy of her father's. She cared more about that lousy wood and nail building than she did me and what I wanted.

If only she listened to me, she wouldn't be in this predicament. But she'd learn.

I'd make sure of it.

CHAPTER FIVE

Rocky

NOT ENOUGH TIME? THOSE LITTLE WORDS BOUNCED AROUND IN MY head as oxygen failed to reach my lungs.

How much time did he need to say no? To stamp a big fat veto over the ridiculous idea that Sterling Custom Auto and the other businesses were not adequately zoned in their current locations? Locations we'd all been at for at least fifty years doing the same or similar type of work.

The room got fuzzy as the blood rushed from my head. If Kevin needed more time to discuss it, then that meant there *was* a hint of legitimacy in the complaints. The thought of genuinely losing Sterling Custom Auto, of having to close it down, settled like a rock in the pit of my stomach as nausea overwhelmed me.

"Raquel, please take a few breaths for me." Mr. Quincy whispered in my ear. "And do not give Mr. Reynolds the satisfaction of demonstrating how much this affects you." Mr. Quincy pulled back and hesitated before continuing—an unusual action for him. "I've known your family for quite some time—since before you were born. While I never had the opportunity to tell your father, I considered him a friend. He was an incredible human being whose integrity surpassed most of the world. The lessons and morals he instilled in you and your brother, Ashton, while passed onto you both in a short amount of time, were a gift I'm happy you both cherished and embraced."

My eyes misted at Mr. Quincy's words.

"Now, I don't want to discount your mother in all of this. Martha's a gem beyond compare, and your father was well aware of the treasure he held."

Damn it, I was crying.

"So, I hope you don't think I'm overstepping when I tell you this." Mr. Quincy's character went from gentle to unyielding in a second. "No way will I allow Mr. Reynolds or anyone ever to remove the legacy your father built. And most importantly, you deserve a love that speaks to your every wish. Do not settle." Mr. Quincy handed me his handkerchief as he watched a tear glide down my cheek.

I tried to pull myself together as I patted the tears away with Mr. Quincy's hankie.

"Since we're discussing your family, I must state I am surprised Martha or Ashton are not here for these proceedings." Mr. Quincy's kind eyes never left mine as he changed the subject so I could pull myself together.

"I didn't tell them because there is nothing to tell." I fired out before he could utter a rebuttal. "You're terrifyingly legally adept, Mr. Quincy, so I know you'll have all this B.S. handled without unnecessarily worrying Mom or Ash."

And, because he was the shit, he gave me a small smile and let it go. "Here."

The gruff voice shoved a giant chocolate car wrapped in pink cellophane with various car designs imprinted on it in my face.

I blinked through the remaining tears and studied the chocolate, wondering what the heck.

A deep belly laugh surrounded me as I followed the hand attached to the chocolate to find Max and his brother standing before me and Mr. Quincy. His brother's head was back as booming laughter poured from him, and Max's perpetual scowl remained fixated on me.

"You're crying." He jiggled the chocolate, indicating I should seize it. "Chocolate makes you happy."

I stared at Max as I reached up slowly to take the chocolate. "Thank you." And how did he know chocolate was my cure-all? There could be no way he knew the link between it and the times I spent with my father working on cars, and eventually, it transitioned into a soothing balm for whatever drama I faced.

"Excuse me. I don't think we've had the pleasure. I'm Mr. Quincy, Miss Sterling's legal counsel." He extended his hand to Max.

He shook Mr. Quincy's hand. "Max Hudson." He jabbed a finger at his brother. "And this riot is my brother, Paul."

Paul quieted enough to exchange pleasantries with Mr. Quincy before Paul turned to me, hand out, and asked, "Rocky?"

Giving myself a mental slap, I stood up to finally meet Paul. I reached out and started to reply when I realized I'd shoved the chocolate into Paul's hand.

A snort escaped him.

"Sorry!" I moved the chocolate to my other hand and tried once more to shake his hand. "Yes. It's nice to finally meet you, Paul."

"The pleasure is all mine."

Paul's head flew forward as Max slapped the back of Paul's head.

"Hey!" Paul growled at Max.

"Gentlemen, such behavior is not allowed in City Hall." Kevin's pretentious voice broke into their brotherly interaction.

Both brothers pivoted their attention to Kevin. "Our apologies. However, an older brother's responsibilities never cease." Max deftly excused their behavior.

Paul quickly sobered as he addressed Kevin. "I noticed you had quite a turnout. Are your council meetings generally this well attended?"

"Feldspar's citizens care deeply for their town; therefore, the council meetings are appropriately frequented." Kevin's chest puffed up with his self-importance.

Baloney.

Part of tonight's meeting was to discuss the zoning ordinance that was under review for lawful change by the city council, which would severely impact not just Sterling Custom Auto but several other businesses. Not to mention the new violations that popped up today. *Therefore,* this evening's congregation represented the need to kick *someone's* ass for even suggesting it.

As I swung my head to let Kevin know his response was total crap, Mr. Quincy rushed to the rescue and said, "Mr. Reynolds, it's quite disappointing the council did not discuss the outstanding legislation concerns tonight. Do these types of time oversights usually occur?"

"Of course not. As you heard, there were other more pressing matters to discuss, and they required further investigation than the allotted time." Kevin's tone openly indicated his affront to Mr. Quincy's suggestion that Kevin or the institution he served would function in such a deplorable manner.

My eyes bugged out, and my ears burned from the steam threatening to blow. *Other more pressing issues?* As if people losing their businesses, their livelihoods weren't important enough. The self-righteous prick had some nerve.

Kevin reached out and held my elbow. "Raquel, are you feeling well? You're flushed once more." The sad thing about his statement was that he was genuinely concerned *and* clueless.

So, I strangled my need to throttle him, pulled my elbow out of his hand, albeit a little more roughly than needed, and bit out, "I'm fine."

Not in the least.

He glanced down at my elbow and back at me. "It appears the recent events have caused you some distress." A reprimanding shake of his head. "I don't understand your insistence on continuing with this charade. I'll give Ashton a call explaining how this is causing you strain, and it's best if he handles this business for you."

The poised smile on Kevin's face made it clear he thought he was doing me a favor. Not even close. I was so sick and tired of men downgrading my ability to run an auto shop, much less a business. Not to mention, less than five minutes ago, he sat right next to women on the council, and not once did he insist they step aside so their husbands could play with the big boys.

As for speaking with Ash? He had no clue who he was dealing with. The second my brother learned Kevin was trying to hijack our father's legacy away, he'd kill him. I did not need that added horror to this already frightening experience.

"Mr. Reynolds, I'm going to require a sit down regarding the current situation surrounding Sterling Custom Auto." Mr. Quincy handed Kevin his business card.

Kevin examined the little rectangular paper as if he didn't quite understand why Mr. Quincy would request such a meeting. He quickly pulled himself together and continued in his dutiful role. "I haven't noticed you gentlemen at prior meetings. Are you new to town?"

"Max lives in Granite Creek, and I've lived in Feldspar for a few years. I've just never made it to a town meeting before," Paul answered.

"So, what brought you in tonight?" Kevin showed again he was ignorant of his surroundings.

"Since Rocky is restoring our grandfather's vehicle, and there seems to be a few regulation issues regarding her business, we wanted to understand where everything stands." Paul's concern was an annoying itch under my skin for the mere fact there was *any* concern related to my shop. "And not to mention, I wanted more insight into the city council's plans for the after-school garden program. I'm one of the program directors for the program."

"I'm so sorry you both had to change your evening to come here for this. I assure you Sterling Custom Auto will provide superior quality no matter the circumstances." I wanted to shrivel up and hide at the humiliation of having to say those words to a customer.

"I have faith that you will. I just want to ensure other factors don't get in your way." Paul's sincerity touched me.

"Will the various violations be on the next docket?" Max asked Kevin.

"Considering I learned about the other concerns late this afternoon, I'd have to review the items scheduled for the next agenda before stating. If you'll excuse me, I have some more town business to attend to," Kevin stated.

What did Kevin mean by saying he had to review the list? He couldn't put off the discussion regarding the complaints indefinitely, could he? I eyed Mr. Quincy and hoped he would shed some light, but he gave me a subtle negative head shake.

"Of course." Paul turned to Mr. Quincy. "It was a pleasure to meet you."

As Paul and Mr. Quincy exchanged farewells, Max addressed me, "How are you doing, Raquel?"

"I'm fine." For the umpteenth time. "I'm sorry you came out here. I can assure you none of this will get in the way of the quality Sterling Custom Auto will provide you."

Max studied me but didn't answer me.

"Rocky, it was without a doubt a pleasure to meet you." Paul's mischievous grin was back in full force. "Hey, I know." A picture of innocence he wasn't. "Why don't you join us for a drink?"

Max's focus didn't waiver.

"I'm sorry, but I can't." But with Max's eyes on me, I wanted to... to remember he was my client and not just someone I was attracted to. A client changed all the rules when it came to attraction, dating, and sex. So, no, I couldn't enjoy a drink with Max. No matter how much I wanted to drown myself in him. I also had to remember the other men who taught me valuable lessons. Kevin, who very much wanted to box me up inside his home and never let me leave.

And Carson, who very much wanted to glide through my Rolodex to make his way further up the ladder. Six months of him using me so he could piggyback off of my hard work and reputation and when he wouldn't take no for an answer, he threw a toddler-size fit.

Clients started to avoid me or pulled me aside to let me know Carson's unprofessional behavior was casting a negative shadow on me. That was enough to shout *stop!* The icing on the cake was finding him screwing the sales rep on my desk because she also had connections.

Enough was enough.

So even though I wanted to sip away at Max, my libido and heart had to be on the back burner to my business, to my dad's legacy.

Even if all it took was Max's attention to make my soul ache for his touch.

"Next time. I'll make sure to have Maxie set it up."

"It's like you want me to hit you," Max semi-joked.

CHAPTER SIX

Rocky

"Woman, get your ass over here!"

Luckily, Coop's was visited mainly by the locals, so Bella's bellow didn't draw too many ugly side eyes. Okay, it was only me giving her the stink eye.

"Keep your panties on. I'm coming."

I made my way to the bar with many brief greetings to friends and customers. I spotted Mom and her book club in the back corner and gave them all a wave. I immediately knew with Mom's stink eye I was going to get a talking-to. There was no way Mom would let Bella and I yelling across a crowded room to each other go.

Luckily, by the time I reached Bella, Brooke had placed my much-needed beer before me.

I didn't hesitate. I grabbed it, sucked back a huge gulp, and plopped it on the bar top. "Thanks, Brooke. I needed that."

"Looks like." She knocked on the bar top once. "Let me know if you need anything else." She moseyed down the length of the bar, checking in on other customers.

"Oh no. Did the meeting go bad?" Bella incorrectly guessed my sour mood as she settled on her barstool beside me.

"It went. Just not anywhere near the zoning or other ordinances." I sipped my beer and tried to keep my worry locked down.

"I thought this meeting was to discuss all of that?" Frown lines creased Bella's normally smooth skin.

"Supposedly. However, the council discussed," I mimed quotation marks, "more pressing issues."

"What's more significant than people's livelihoods?"

"Great question." I squeezed the bottle and hoped the tremble in my hand would subside.

She frowned. "What do you mean? Weren't you there?"

"Yeah, I was." I took another sip and surveyed the room to avoid Bella.

"Uh-huh." She leaned toward me and demanded, "Spill."

I rescanned Coop's before I reached down to pull Max's gift out of my purse. "I don't think they're here, so it's safe to show you." I dropped it on the bar top in front of us.

Bella looked around before she turned back to me and asked, "First off, who were you looking for? And why is it safe to show me?" She eyed the treat on the counter and continued, "I know you have a chocolate addiction, but if you tell me you missed the meeting because you went to get a chocolate car, I will be forced to throw it in Brooke's trash compactor."

I snatched the chocolate back. "Take it back, or I won't share it with you."

Bella's gaze centered on the chocolate I treasured next to my heart. "Who gave you the chocolate?"

"What makes you think someone gave it to me?" I tossed it back between us as if it was nothing special and ignored her last question.

"You forget who you're talking to. No way you sat at a council meeting regarding your shop, your *dad's* shop, and didn't hear a thing. And you just scanned the bar and said, *"I don't think they're here, so it's safe to show you."*" She sat back, sipped her beer, and waited for me to answer.

I heard it all, and none of it was what I wanted to hear. "Fine.

Remember I told you about the DeVille that recently came in?" At Bella's nod, I continued, "Well, I met the owner yesterday, and it didn't go well."

"What does that mean?"

"It means he sought Rocky and found me instead." I shrugged and tried to lessen the sting of how I felt getting that reaction from Max.

"One or two?"

"One—the usual, you're joking, right?!" I aimed for nonchalance, but it stung. "Like a twenty-six-year-old female is unable to work under a hood."

Bella scrunched her nose. "Ouch." She nodded toward the chocolate. "Is that his apology?"

"I'm not sure." I leaned into her and said, "Get this. Max, the owner of the vehicle, actually apologized when he realized he was being a butthole. I was so stunned that I didn't know what to say."

"Wow. That's huge and shows all kinds of manliness. A man who isn't afraid to admit he is wrong and apologize for it." She fanned herself. "That's just hot. But, then, what's up with the sweetness?"

"I don't know. I had a moment with Mr. Quincy during the meeting, which led to tears. The next thing I know, that," I pointed to the chocolate, "was in my face. Max said, *Chocolate makes you happy.*" I resisted the urge to reach out to stroke it and instead wrapped my hands around my bottle and took another sip.

"Oh, Rocky, do tell." Bella hooked her foot around the bar stool rung.

"Tell what?"

She wagged her finger back and forth at me. "Uh-huh. First tears, then Max."

"Tears were Mr. Quincy proving, once more, what a rock-solid man he is. As for Max..." I shrugged. "I'm not sure. Maybe he's just trying to butter me up to finish his vehicle sooner than the agreed-upon timeline?"

After all, he gave it to me at the council meeting where the closure of my shop was supposed to be under discussion. Or maybe he's just a nice guy who saw all the chocolate goodies throughout the shop and gifted me one. There was nothing wrong with that. Customers and vendors gave me all kinds of chocolatey goodness. I tried to tell myself Max's generosity wasn't anything different.

Unfortunately, my hormones were all for naked chocolate gratitude with Max. I gave myself a mental slap and pictured Carson bent over bimbo who-knows-how-many on my desk and reminded myself to run in the opposite direction of the feelings Max stirred in me.

"I can't believe you think I'll let such a vague answer fly." Bella smiled the smile of a friend who had experience calling me on my bullshit.

I stuck my tongue out at her. "Okay, okay, okay. Mr. Quincy, in his quiet manner, wasn't thrilled about the postponement and, in so many words, let Kevin know. Kevin, slow to the draw as always, didn't understand what the problem was and then proceeded to tell me he would contact Ash to handle this business since I show every sign of being unable to deal with stress physically or emotionally."

"I don't get Kevin. How can he be so smart and so dense at the same time?"

"I don't know. I wish he'd find somebody else to harass." I sucked in a breath at the memory of his indecent proposal, leaned into Bella, and said, "I haven't had a chance to tell you, but Kevin also came by my office yesterday and said he could make all this go away if only I'd meet with him to discuss it."

Bella almost spit her beer out. "*What?!* What did he mean by discussing it? Like the horizontal tango type of conversation? Or the till death do us part type of conversation?"

"Oh my God! I didn't even think of the first option." I shuddered. "Shit. I need to call Mr. Quincy and let him know I might be wrong about Kevin extorting me for marriage." I rubbed my forehead. "Maybe I'm wrong about all of it, and that's not what Kevin means altogether."

"Or maybe you're right about all of it. I mean, how well do we really know Kevin? Or anyone, for that matter?" She shrugged.

I was sure Bella was thinking of Leonard. Someone she considered a close friend for a decade, only to find out recently he wasn't all he presented himself to be.

"This is too confusing, which is why I need another word with Mr.

Quincy. Who, by the way, is the shiznit. He made it clear he wouldn't let anything happen to the shop or with Kevin and that he thinks I'm the cat's cream." I beamed at Bella. "I love him."

"Yeah, he's the best. Now, onto Chocolate Max." Mischievousness twinkled in Bella's eyes.

I choked on my sip. "Chocolate Max?" I coughed to clear my throat. "You have such a way with words." And the imagery—Max covered in silky chocolatey goodness. I fanned myself because, Good Lord, it was suddenly hot in here.

"I'll assume that means my imagination meets reality." She winked.

"Not even close."

She lowered her beer, horror slowly replaced her humor, and whispered, "Please tell me you mean he exceeds it and not the other way around."

I picked up the chocolate and started, "The packaging is beautiful. A little rough around the edges from handling, but still gorgeous." I removed the pink wrapper and traced the outline of the sleek car with my finger. "But the definition is what draws your attention. The hard angles are solid beneath your touch but smooth and creamy. And, you know if you take a bite, you'll know once will never be enough." I closed my eyes and bit into the velvety candy. "Mmm."

"I had no idea chocolate was sooo... enticing." My eyes flew open at the gruff masculine voice, and I froze mid-chew.

I didn't blush easily, but I felt the blood rush to my cheeks again as I turned to see I was Max and Paul's focal point, both smiling.

Only Max's grin hinted at so much more.

"Wow." Bella remained riveted on them.

"Rocky wasn't joking. You two *are* walking orgasms." Brooke decided to join us and demonstrated her ears were bat-like.

I slowly closed my eyes as my cheeks burned hotter.

"Sweetheart, have you seen yourself in the mirror?" Paul eyed Brooke up and down.

"Aren't you a charmer? But not charming enough." She winked at him to lessen the rejection. "Can I get you boys anything?"

"Two Guinnesses," he ordered, taking her rejection with ease.

"Hi, I'm Bella. I'm Rocky's embarrassment shield." Her smile threatened to split her face.

I opened my eyes and saw Max and Bella shake hands.

"Nice to meet you, Bella. I'm Max."

Bella's mouth dropped open, and I clenched my thighs together to lessen the impact of his voice because his voice was orgasmic.

"You're drooling." Not that I blamed her. He was drool-worthy.

She snapped her mouth shut and glared at me. "You didn't tell me Max sounded like *that*."

I did tell her, but it was one of those things that she couldn't comprehend without experiencing it for herself.

His voice *was* a sensual priming tool.

"You suck as an embarrassment shield."

A short, deep chuckle escaped Max and caused us to gawk at him.

I told no lies.

After listening to Max speak and then feeling the vibration from his laughter float through me?

My ovaries quivered in anticipation.

"Here you guys go." Brooke slid the drinks toward the guys.

Before either guy could offer their gratitude, Bella pointed at Paul and said, "I know you."

"I don't think so because I never forget a pretty woman." He demonstrated Brooke's earlier rejection didn't bother him.

Bella snapped her fingers. "The hospital. You're the hunkalicious I saw at the hospital flirting with Nurse Booby."

"Nurse Booby?" His confusion was adorable.

Bella leaned against the bar.

"No, I'm right. It was about a month ago. You asked for a room number and..."

Recognition filtered through Paul's face. "Ah yeah. I remember you now. How's the guy you were there for?"

"He's doing better. What about you? How's the person you went to visit?" Bella asked.

"Glad to hear. Dad is doing better. He had a heart attack, and it's forced him to take things slower. Change his diet. Cut back on work, stress." Paul shrugged. "So, in other words, he's driving everyone nuts because that's not his usual MO."

I'd do anything to have my dad back, griping at everyone because he had to cut back on work or chocolate. A jolt of pain hit my chest, and the image of my dad lying in the hospital bed, tubes and wires crisscrossed on and around him, flashed through my mind. His last words to me were, *"Take care of our girl,"* and here I was on the verge of messing it up.

So, I understood the fear they'd lived with when their father had been hospitalized, and it made sense to me why the DeVille restoration was important to them.

"I'm glad to hear he's giving you guys shit. Something tells me you boys need corralling." I eyed Paul and Max up and down.

"Dad's not usually the one trying to... handle us." Max focused on me.

"Wait, before you two start flirting," Max's scowl didn't deter Paul, "I thought it was just the hospital where I recognized you, but it's not. You were on the news about a month ago. Wasn't it you and your brother—a police detective?"

"Yeah, that'd be us, unfortunately," Bella mumbled.

"Damn. Sorry to hear." Max voiced a clear understatement.

"Thanks. We're all good." Then, she added, "Now."

"She sure is. That's how she landed her hot guy." They were so stinkin' cute together it made my teeth ache.

"Excuse me." My mom's you're-in-trouble tone rounded out our small huddle.

I twisted in my seat and peered between Max and Paul, who graciously stepped to the side to give my mother full access to me.

"Hi, Mom. Are you done with your book club meeting?" I tried to evade the lecture I knew was coming by her tone.

"Yes, I am, but that's not why I'm here. I want to know why my daughters are yelling across a public venue at each other? I know I taught you both better than that."

How freaking embarrassing. My mother scolded me in front of two hot strangers who were also business clients, on top of one of them being a man I wanted to gorge on—naked.

"I'm sorry, Mrs. Sterling." Bella immediately kissed up to my mother.

Mom gave her the patented you're excused look because Bella always got away with everything—the suck-up.

On the other hand, like every kid, no matter their age, I tried to get out of my punishment. "Mom..."

She raised her hand. "Don't even start, young lady. I know all your tricks."

She totally knew I was going to blow smoke, so instead, I got up from my seat, walked the three steps it took me to get to her, and kissed her cheek. "I'm sorry, Mom. I promise to be on my best behavior."

"Good. I'm glad that's done. Now, don't stay out too late. You have work tomorrow, and don't forget you're meeting me bright and early for coffee at Margie's." She fluffed my hair and patted my cheek like only a mother could do, no matter your age. "Beautiful as always."

And just like that, she proved once again she was the best mother ever. "I won't forget, and if you get there before me, grab me one of Margie's chocolate sponge cake thingies. No, make it two. I'll have the other one with lunch."

She gave me the motherly head shake all moms do. "You undeniably inherited your father's sweet tooth; if he were still alive, you'd never get within an inch of Margie's desserts. I still don't know how he never got a cavity with all the sweets he ate. Have you been to the dentist lately? Are you brushing and flossing? What about exercising? You know you must feed your whole body and not only with confectionaries." She stared at me and patiently waited for my answer.

Luckily, Bella snorted in her attempt to keep her laughter in and saved me from answering my mother.

"Bella, what about you? When was the last time you saw the dentist? Are you still running? Please tell me Dean is going with you now. Being out on those trails alone is unsafe for a young woman. And don't even try to tell me about women's rights and how we women can take care of ourselves. Men are bigger, stronger, and appear scarier. They make great deterrents."

It was my turn to snort as my mother mothered Bella.

"Wow. Your house must have a collection of Mother of the Year awards. Do you want a son? Want to adopt?" Paul's hopeful eyes beseeched Mom to say yes.

She graced him with her aren't you adorable smile. "Ah, aren't you just a charmer?" She gasped. "How rude of me! I interrupted your conversation and didn't even introduce myself. I'm Martha Sterling, Raquel's mother by blood and Bella's by extension and honor."

Paul extended his hand past me. "Paul Hudson." He pointed to Max. "This here is my brother, Max. We're clients of your daughter and stopped by to say hello."

Mom shook both their hands. "Well, it was lovely to meet you both. I'll let you in on a secret—if it's not chocolate, it's cars for my girl. You couldn't be in better hands." The pride in her voice choked me up.

"You're going to make me cry, so you need to stop being gushy," I joked with her. Secretly, I hoped she never stopped. I hoped I never stopped making her proud. And I hoped I never stopped feeling like crying from the love she showered on me.

"Well, we wouldn't want that now, would we?" She hiked her purse up on her shoulder. "I better be going anyway. Our book club ran later than expected, and I'm plum tuckered out."

"All right, Mom. Do you need a lift? I can take you," I offered.

"No, baby. I got it." She leaned in and kissed me on the cheek. "See you in the morning."

"Love you, Mom."

Bella got up and gave my mom hugs and kisses too. "Good night, Ms. Sterling."

"Don't stay out too late. Be safe." Mom then smothered Paul and Max with her maternal gifts. "Boys, it was lovely to meet you. But, remember, the morning comes early, and you need to stay safe too." She didn't know how *not* to mother—even strangers.

"It was our pleasure, Ms. Sterling." Paul's charm knew no limits.

Max, on the other hand, was more reserved in his farewell. "Good night."

As a matter of fact, he seemed quieter than his usual scowly muted way. But before I could question if he was okay, Bella dropped a bomb. "You guys wanna join us?"

I bugged my eyes out at her. What was she thinking? Ever since she started having sex regularly with Dean—more like being head over heels in love—she couldn't help but want the same for me.

Her huge smirk didn't hide the fact she was enjoying herself at my expense.

The traitor.

I plopped back down on the bar stool. "Bella, they can't be on the prowl if they're sitting with us. We'd be a hindrance to their pickup game." I snatched my beer back up on the sour thought and barely remembered to take a decent public sip. Meanwhile, the chocolate sat on the bar top and glared at me the whole time, calling me a big fat liar.

"I know earlier I invited you to join us, and while I'd normally jump at the opportunity to be around pretty women, unfortunately, I need to bend my brother's ear." Paul smiled to lessen the rejection.

"Next time." My best friend betrayed me.

I turned to look at them. "Hey, how'd I beat you guys to Coop's?" Because I would have never pulled out the chocolate if I had known Max would show up any minute.

"We stopped at Paul's house." Max stared at me. "I'll see you next week." The fire in Max's eyes held so much sensual promise that I was afraid I'd jump him in the middle of Coop's and really earn a talking-to from my mother.

We watched them walk away, and I forced myself not to follow him. Instead, I sipped on my drink to keep my hands busy.

Too bad my mind kept thinking, *Why wait?*

Bella whistled. "Rocky, please tell me you're going to ride him."

I sputtered, and beer dribbled down my chin. I reached for the napkins and dabbed at my face. "Ever since you've been riding Dean, that's all you ever have on your brain." Not that I wasn't too far behind since I had met Max.

"Oh yeah." A dreamy sigh escaped Bella.

I was so happy for her. She'd been in love with Dean her whole life with no hope of him reciprocating the affection. I mostly ignored what brought them together and focused on them being together, on true love winning.

"So, while you and Dean are meant to be, you must remember Max is my client. I don't mix business and pleasure."

She still feasted on Max and Paul when she murmured, "You should, without a doubt, break that rule." She turned back to me. "Wait, since when have you had such a rule?"

"Two words: Kevin. Carson."

Bella's face softened. "Carson and Kevin are jackasses. You shouldn't make them the rule. Besides, if you can't tell at first glance that Max is nothing like them, we must check your eyesight."

I peered over at Max; our eyes connected for an electrifying second before I returned my attention to Bella. "They work just fine." It was my heart that was the problem. "It doesn't change the fact he's my client or that I have Kevin crawling up my ass. And as much as I'd love to hit the backseat with Max, it's not a smart idea right now."

Bella smiled a slow cat-got-the-cream smile and asked, "So later's open?"

CHAPTER SEVEN

Rocky

WALKING INTO *CAFEÍNA DOCE* AND HAVING THE INTOXICATING scent of coffee seep into my pores was almost as good as eating chocolate. Although, expecting anything less of Margie's coffee would be blasphemy.

Whenever I asked her what the secret was, she'd give me the same answer. "It's a Portuguese thing."

As long as she kept making me coffee, I didn't care what it was.

"Are you having another Margie coffee orgasm?" Bella teased me from her spot next to my mother at the counter.

"Ssh. I'm not done yet." I closed my eyes and mimicked the sounds of climaxing. "Mmm. Aaahhh. Oooh."

"Oww!" My eyes flew open, and I rubbed my arm where my mother pinched me. "What was that for?"

"Behave. There are kids present."

Bella snorted at my mom's admonishment.

I browsed the room and took in the river rock walls with blue tiles scattered throughout themed in various java beans and pastries. The high archways designated the back room, which showcased different Portuguese artwork celebrating Margie's heritage. But, more importantly, I sized up the proud, prominently red and black Portuguese rooster front and center on the archway, which Margie strategically adorned with coffee beans and goodies to complement her love of all things coffee, confections, Portuguese, and big... cocks.

I turned back to my mom, raised my eyebrows, and commented, "I'd be more worried if we were in a traditional coffee shop, but this is Margie we're talking about."

She threw her hands up in the air. "I can't take you anywhere." Then, just as quickly, she turned to me, stern motherly face squarely in place, and scolded, "But, I did teach you better. Twice now, in less than twenty-four hours, I've had to remind you of that. Really, Raquel, what's gotten into you?"

I didn't want to tell her the zoning and other bullshit complaints— and I was shocked she hadn't heard about it yet—were hammering my nervous system into chaos, nor was I ever going to tell my mother I was in serious need of an orgasm not brought on by BOB. So, I fell back on the tried-and-true response of every kid in trouble. "Sorry, Mom. I'll behave."

Bella giggled at my lie.

"*Garotas*, please, none of that behavior. We are a respectable *cafeteria*." Margie scolded us as she handed Bella and me our drinks. "Ms. Sterling, your mocha is almost ready."

"Pot, kettle, black," I replied dryly.

Margie opened her mouth to say something I'm sure would be inappropriate when she snapped it shut and mumbled under her breath, *"Merda."*

We turned to see what or who she was muttering about.

Delilah Sampson was tall, thin, and dressed to the nines in clothes I bet cost more than my entire wardrobe. Her hair was perfectly styled —not a single hair out of place. Manicured nails and expertly applied makeup. No doubt about it—she was rich and beautiful. And she had no problem spending her husband's money. After all, he owned Sampson's Gas and Mini Mart, which he quickly expanded across multiple counties. But, unfortunately, she was also a spiteful uppity cow.

"Good morning, Delilah." I didn't know why I bothered; she always ignored me.

She peered down at me from her lofty height and didn't bother with a greeting or a smile. Not that I thought her over-botoxed mouth could move to perform the function. "Margie, I want the *carioca* with unsweetened almond milk, a quarter teaspoon of monk fruit sweetener, lots of blended ice, and hold the whipped cream."

"Coming right up."

She always ordered the same thing, and she always destroyed the delicious flavors by diluting the heck out of it. Why she bothered, I had no idea.

"I can make it if you want to finish the order for Ms. Sterling," Willow, Margie's new barista, offered.

Everyone deserved a chance. So, when Willow came into Margie's shop a month ago and applied for the barista position, Margie hired her, insisting everyone needed someone to believe in them. According to Margie, Willow had messed up at least ninety percent of everything she'd touched. So, I knew there was no way Margie would let her anywhere near Delilah's Rubik's cube coffee order.

"Thanks, but I got this. Why don't you finish Ms. Sterling's and then refill the display case?"

"Margie, dear, do you have more of the *Salame de Chocolate*? The ones with port wine? Rocky ate my last one, and I won't mention her ludicrous conversation about the name. I know it's rolled like a salami, but if you called it something else, you'd sell a million of them. They're categorically delicious."

"Thanks, Ms. Sterling. Willow will bring you one after she finishes your *café*. And, unfortunately, I didn't name it—" Bella and I snorted because we had discussed what to name them before, and it wasn't anywhere near salami. "—but I'll make sure to put some samples out for people."

"Wonderful. Delilah, why don't you purchase some for your grandchildren? It'd be a tasty afternoon treat." Mom tried, again, to get Delilah to move beyond her no-flavor-I'm-afraid-they-will-gain-a-pound grandkid excruciating bland menu.

"Their meals are carefully prepared to ensure proper nutrition.

Unfortunately, chocolate salami" —said as if it was poop Delilah accidentally stepped on— "does not yield any nutritional value." Delilah peered down her very, I'm sure, surgically enhanced but narrow nose at my mother. "I can provide you with the name of my *cuisinier* to assist you."

That was a perfect example of her unseemingly behavior. She wasn't nice, nor was she flat-out mean. She was—catty. Even still, Mom didn't let Delilah phase her.

"Heavens, no! I..."

"Here you go, Ms. Sterling." Willow interrupted as she handed Mom her coffee cup, which slipped right out of Willow's trembling hand.

And right onto Delilah's winter white slacks.

"Merda!" Margie rushed around to Delilah and bent to wipe the coffee from her pants.

She stepped back and hissed, "Don't touch me."

"I'm so sorry. I..." Margie straightened back up.

"Don't bother. It's clear you need to clean your own house," Delilah snapped before she stomped out the door.

Hopefully, that didn't mean Delilah Sampson was about to go all too good for us plebeians' vengeance on Margie.

"I'm so sorry, Margie. I didn't mean to drop it," Willow said in her too-soft voice, fear etched on her face and worry stamped on her hands as she wrung her fingers together.

"Don't worry, Willow. Why don't you get the mop and take care of this?" She turned to Mom. "I'm sorry about your drink. If you have more time, I'll make another—on the house."

Mom touched her arm. "Not a problem, Margie, and don't be silly. I'll pay for the goods I'm acquiring." She then tugged the towel out of Margie's hand, gave her a gentle shove to the back, and promptly began wiping the coffee off the display glass.

Of course, my mom *did* teach me better, so I grabbed the cloth out of her hand and took over.

"Now, you're the momma every girl needs," one of Margie's regulars told my mom.

"Mmm hmmm, you got that right," her friend agreed.

"Ah, aren't you girls just the sweetest." My mother aimed her sugary, motherly smile at them.

"Just saying it how it is. But the other one?" The lady didn't wait for our response. "Let's hope her grandbabies parents take after the husband," Margie's customer muttered.

"He might not be any better if he's sleeping with her," the friend countered.

"*If* he's sleeping with her." She eyed her friend like that explained it all.

And it probably did.

"Hmm, mmm," her friend agreed.

Bella gave Margie and me big eyes at their commentary.

"Girls!" Mom scolded all of us. "If I've learned one thing in life, it's that we do not know what anyone is going through. A little kindness can unknowingly alter someone's life profoundly. And we can all agree Delilah Sampson needs a little goodwill." And then, my mother shocked the shit out of us. "And some salami and not just Margie's chocolate one."

There was a moment of stunned silence right before cackles of laughter rang through the coffee shop. Mom blushed from the hysterical attention she received and did her best to get everyone focused on something besides her.

Willow brought Mom her coffee, and she quickly made excuses about having to run some errands for her book club—anything to remove herself from further consideration.

Bella and I settled onto a couch when I said, "I called Mr. Quincy's office this morning to find out who filed the complaints, but they said he was out of the office for the next few days. Mr. Lewis was with another client, so they'll get back to me later. So, I'm going to head over to Town Hall after this, before I go to work, and see if I can get that information from them. Do you want to go with me?"

"Sure, but did you check online? It might save you a trip." She sipped her coffee.

"I did. The system is down for maintenance or something like that." Because that would have been too easy.

"Sure. I have some time before I have to get to the clinic."

Being a vet was definitely Bella's calling. Her heart knew no bounds regarding the animals in her care, which meant that they were well cared for and spoiled.

I bit into the *Salame de Chocolate* and moaned at the flavor explosion inside my mouth. I followed it with a sip of my own *galão* and thanked the Man above for bringing Margie and her Portuguese heritage to Feldspar.

"I thought you said Kevin filed the complaint as a part of his Make Rocky My Wife plan?" Bella tilted her head to the side in question.

"Yeah, that's what I thought too. But... something you said last night won't leave me. Kevin isn't stupid, no matter how clueless he behaved at the moment. So it doesn't make sense he'd do this knowing how it would devastate me to lose my father's shop. And, with both Kevin and I knowing he was the person behind it, he would or should know it automatically makes him ineligible for any romantic position in my life. So because he is intelligent, I can't believe his brilliance didn't scream *danger!* as a warning to him if he attempted such a thing."

"I agree. I couldn't wrap my brain around it either." She leaned toward me. "Shit. Then who filed it?" Surprise and concern colored her words.

"No clue. That's why I'm heading over to City Hall."

She rubbed her hands together. "I love a good puzzle."

"Me too. I just wished this one didn't involve me." I drank the last of my coffee.

"Yeah, that part sucks," Bella agreed.

"What put that expression on both of your faces?" Paul ventured up to us.

"Are you guys stalking me?" I evaded, not wanting to bring up any negativity regarding my shop, the place they hired to restore their vehicle.

"Maxie def..."

Max turned to his brother. "It's like you want me to hit you."

"No hitting. I already told these two" —Margie pointed at Bella and me— "my coffee shop is a respectable business. Please behave yourselves."

Paul eyed Margie. "What happens if I don't? If I'm bad?" His voice dropped into a seductive bass, and he stepped closer to Margie.

"Bad boys don't get dessert." She smiled, slow and wicked. "And all my desserts are breathtaking."

Paul watched in stunned silence as Margie walked away with her very effective and potent parting words.

"You might wanna pick your jaw up." I couldn't help it. I was used to giving Ash crap, and Paul gave me the same brotherly feelings.

"I'm gonna be a very bad good boy," he mumbled as he moved toward Margie.

Bella threw subtlety out the door when she gave me big eyes and tipped her head toward Max. She wanted me with him and didn't care how it came about as long as it just did.

And even though I wanted to saddle right up to him and wrap my arms around his very wide and solid chest while I shoved my nose in his neck and inhaled his very essence, I could not.

"Are you okay? Do we need to call a doctor?" Max laced his words with concern for Bella.

"No!" Bella stopped Max from pulling out his phone. "I'm fine. Just fine." She gave me a murderous glare.

"Are you sure? I can drive you to the hospital," he jokingly insisted.

I saw the teasing glint in Max's eyes and burst into laughter.

"You guys suck," Bella declared with no real heat behind her words.

"That's what you get." I stuck my tongue out at her.

Bella's face went from faux outrage to smug in a second as she looked up at Max.

I turned my attention to him and sucked in a breath at the smoldering promise stamped on his face. My body immediately joined the fire arcing between us as my breasts swelled and juices drenched my panties in preparation for what I wanted. No, what I needed from Max.

"*Oh meu Deus.*" Margie broke our silent but steamy exchange. "Get a room. Preferably one not here," she razzed us.

Max's stare didn't waiver.

Bella laughed, and my body unconsciously leaned toward him, all in for the sexy promise defined by his mere presence.

"This is where I say I told you so, Maxie." Paul held out a cup of coffee to him.

"Keep it up, and I'll add a charley horse to the smackdown." Max grabbed one of the to-go cups from Paul.

I had to get out of there. It was too much sensual stimulation for my sex-deprived soul. Besides, I had a mystery to solve and a business to save.

"Well, I have things I need to take care of, so I'm gonna head out." I stood up and accidentally placed myself squarely in Max's personal space.

Shit.

He smelled like motor oil and fresh air.

Divine.

And way too close for my peace of mind.

My body, on the other hand, was all for it.

Bella finally took mercy on me and grabbed my hand as she pulled us away. "It was nice seeing you two again." She smiled hugely at Max and Paul. "Margie, we'll catch you later," she yelled over her shoulder.

Paul and Margie's laughter followed us out the door.

But Max's unspoken promise stayed with me the rest of the day.

CHAPTER EIGHT

Max

I STOPPED WHEN THE MAN RUSHING PAST ME BUMPED INTO ME.

"Sorry." He stopped and apologized. "Oh, aren't you the guy from outside Sterling Custom Auto?"

I considered him again and realized he was the upset customer outside Raquel's shop. "Yeah." Feldspar sure was a small town.

"I thought I recognized you. I see you're enjoying one of Margie's coffees."

"Yeah." Something about the man caused my instincts to flare as I saluted him with my coffee cup.

Next to me, Paul's usually jovial self remained quiet and alert.

"I'm Carson Humphreys." He extended his hand. "I'm..." He hesitated. "Rocky's banking associate." He plastered an extremely fake apologetic grin on his face. "I'm glad I ran into you again. I wanted to apologize for my behavior at Rocky's shop the other day. She was upset over a lost deal and lashed out at me. I reacted poorly to her unprofessional behavior and took it out on you. Please accept my apologies."

I shook his hand and replied, "Understandable." Not really for a business cohort. "I'm Max Hudson." I nodded to my left. "This is my brother, Paul."

"I'm assuming Rocky's doing some work for you. What's she working on?"

My instincts screamed at me not to answer, but I had no valid reason not to. "A '67 Cadillac DeVille."

Carson whistled. "That's a beauty. Is it a partial or total restore?"

"Total."

"Wow, that's a big job. I'm sure Rocky will do her best to deliver it on time, even with her recent troubles."

"What troubles?" Paul entered our conversation.

Carson tried to come across as contrite as he fumbled with his response. "I can't really say." His shrug was as phony as him. "Rocky is a customer; I know she means well. So please forget I said anything."

"We appreciate the position you must be in, but if you have any insights on what might hinder the delivery schedule, we'd be grateful," Paul persisted.

Carson blanked his facial expression as if he didn't want to speak poorly of Raquel. What a joke. "Please don't take this the wrong way. It's just that everything at the shop has been less than stellar ever since Rocky took over after Ashton."

There was that name again. Kevin mentioned it last night at City Hall, and now Carson. Who was he to Raquel, and why did everyone keep referring back to him?

"Ashton would be?" Paul asked.

"He's her brother. After their dad passed away a few years ago, her brother and mother ran the company until Rocky completed her business degree. Once she did, she jumped in the driver seat. Ever since Rocky's been at the helm, customers have voiced their concern with her ability to handle such a huge responsibility. Including the numerous poor online reviews about her business practices." Carson held his hands out as if he wasn't one of those people. "Not that I'm saying she can't. It's just she's had some difficulties keeping to her word with clients, and I wouldn't want you to face any backlash from the stress Rocky's been under."

Observing Carson, I tried to figure out what about him didn't sit right with me. It didn't matter whether I could or not. If the information he gave us was accurate, then it didn't bode well for the tight timeline we'd given Raquel for the DeVille.

"We appreciate your willingness to share this information. We'll keep it in mind, but we need to head out now." I walked toward my truck as I addressed Carson.

"Of course, please forgive me. I'll let you gentlemen get on your way." He headed in the opposite direction.

Once in my truck, Paul asked, "Do you think that Carson fellow was full of shit, or do you think Rocky will have difficulty completing the DeVille on time?"

I waited to answer until I backed out of the parking spot and commenced driving. "I don't know. There's something about him that rubs me the wrong way." It hadn't escaped my mind that it was probably related to the fact that I wanted to know if Carson had possibly bedded Raquel or not. "But we have weekly check-ins with Raquel. We can catch anything at that time."

Paul nodded. "I'm with you. Rocky doesn't strike me as someone who would pull a fast one, but that doesn't mean we should ignore Carson's advisory. The sooner the DeVille gets completed, the better."

My body tensed at Paul's words. "Have you talked to Dad? Did something come up?"

I saw Paul shake his head out of the corner of my eye. "Not for a couple of days, but with Lucy on him twenty-four-seven, I know he'll be running circles around us before we know it." He ran his hand through his hair. "I'm just hoping the DeVille will go a long way in helping to mend Dad's heart."

Dad had been through the wringer. After he married the love of his life at eighteen, gave her four boys, and bent over backward to provide her with the world, she left him for the high life. She effectively tore his heart out and shredded it to pieces. He raised my brothers and me the best he could, and now, after a massive heart attack, he was forced to downgrade his activities or face the consequences.

"I bet Grandpa would have loved to see the Cadillac restored. After all the stories he told us about it." I chuckled, remembering some of the racier stories, and sobered just as quickly. "Dad's going to get better, and he's going to drive the DeVille around town, showing it off before we know it."

"Yeah. You know what else Dad is going to love to show off?" Paul's tone told me I should've braced.

"No. What else is there?"

"Rooocckkyyy." Paul drawled her name out as my breath left me.

"What are you talking about?" I glanced over at him even though I knew what he meant.

"Seriously? There's so much wicked combustion between the two of you. I'm surprised anyone in the vicinity hasn't had their hair singed by it." His cheeks creased with the force of his smile.

But was that all it was for Raquel? For me? Just chemistry? Whatever it was, I knew I wanted to explore it.

"You know Dad invited her to the upcoming family dinner." I waited to see what Paul would say.

"Yup, and you know what else?" He chuckled. "You said it yourself: I am a genius."

"You're never going to let me live that down are you?"

"Nope." His smile disappeared just as quickly as it came. "But you should think really hard about what you want from her before you bring her home to Dad. She's not like the others."

"Have you been talking with Vic?" I partially joked, knowing Paul only spoke the truth.

I chanced a quick glance at him and saw his jaw clenched.

"Hey, what's going on?" Paul was all about laughter. He was only serious when dealing with work and kept things light even then.

"Mom leaving us fucked us all up, and each of us handled it differently. You made it your mission to only have stringless encounters." I saw him shake his head out of the corner of my eye. "I get it. Don't let anyone in, and you can't get hurt. The thing is is that there have been some nice ones along the way, but you're too... scared, stubborn, hurt, or whatever other adjective you want to use to let one of them in."

"Are you sure you haven't been talking to Vic?" I teased because I didn't like seeing Paul upset or the fact that he was hitting the nail on the head.

"I'm not joking, Max." His stern tone hit me like a gust of wind from a newly opened window in a speeding car.

"Sorry, I'm not used to you laying the truth on me."

"I don't want you to end up alone because of what Mom did. We all deserve more. She shouldn't be the reason we settle for less."

"Hey, you okay?" I didn't like the sadness I heard from Paul.

He cleared his throat. "Yeah. Yeah, I'm fine."

"Did something happen?" Paul never gave up on Mom. Out of all of us, he was the only one who made countless attempts at connecting with her, including her in his life, at just about everything. And she'd shoot him down with one excuse or another every single time, leaving him devastated. "Did Mom do something?"

"Nothing happened." He turned to face me as I pulled up outside his home. "Don't let Rocky slip through your fingers because you have some stupid hang-up about women derived from Mom. We both know she's the last woman we should ever use as a standard for feminine worth."

"I hear you, and I'll think long and hard about what I want from Raquel before I introduce her to Dad." I patted Paul's shoulder and continued, "I'm here if you need me. Anytime." Did he finally decide to give up Mom, and this was the outcome?

"I know." He opened the truck door. "See you later."

I pulled away and made my way to work, but his words continued to bounce around my head.

Why was Rocky putting me through the wringer from a few conversations?

Enough.

It was time for me to find out.

Rocky

"Wow. That form is really long." Bella mumbled over my shoulder as she watched me fill it out.

"Uh-huh." I didn't care for paperwork. The less I could do, the better. "But this is the government we're discussing, so..."

"True," she agreed with me. "You'd think they'd have more comfortable seating though—something with padding. I mean, it is the city planning office. You'll be sitting all day planning stuff out; you should at least be comfortable doing it," Bella continued with her griping. "They should take a page out of Ava's book or, better yet, let her design the offices. As an event coordinator, she knows how to make things comfortable and fun."

I looked at her and said, "Do I need to remind you that you agreed to come with me?"

"No. I just thought we'd get here, ask for a name, and *voila!*"

I thought the same thing. "I just hope it'll be a quick turnaround with the information after I fill all this out." Because if it was Kevin, I wanted to nail his ass to the council podium after Mr. Quincy did his judicial magic. Plus, I wanted a copy of the original survey for Sterling Custom Auto since I couldn't find it in the stacks of paper Dad left me. Unless there had been a change in the ordinances, I hoped the first record would be all the proof I'd need to shut down at least one, if not all, of the complaints. I knew Mr. Quincy was on top of all this, but I couldn't stand by and just wait. This was too important.

"Umm," Bella mumbled.

I stopped writing, looked up at her, and asked, "What?"

"I hate to be the bearer of bad news, but you said, and they just did too, that their system is down."

"Yes?"

"So, whoever filed the complaints, I'm sure must have done it online. And since the city's files are digital..." She shrugged. "It might be a few days before anyone can access anything."

"Shit." I looked at the lady sitting behind the counter reading a novel. "Do you think they have paper backups somewhere?"

Bella looked at the woman and back at me. "Nope."

I closed my eyes and dropped my head.

"Sorry, Rocky." Bella gave me a side hug. "But, at least you're one step closer to finding out who is behind this, even if it'll take you a few more days to get your answer."

I straightened in my seat and said, "Yeah. One step toward catching the asshole behind all this." And one step toward keeping my shop as is.

"Raquel, Bella. What are you two doing here?" We looked up and saw Kevin approaching us.

"Just doing some paperwork," I answered.

"Is there anything I can help you with?"

Oh boy. "As a matter of fact, there is. I'm trying to determine who filed the complaints against Sterling Custom Auto. Would you be able to give me that information?" Are you willing to rat yourself out? "And at the last city council meeting, you stated you weren't sure if these issues would be on the agenda for the next meeting. Have you confirmed if they will be?"

"I'm sorry, Raquel. They were filed anonymously. I'm not able to provide you with that." He actually looked apologetic. "But I did confirm we will discuss all of the grievances at the next town meeting."

"Is that possible? To file anonymously? Isn't there something in the law about being able to face your accuser?" Bella piped up.

I mentally crossed my fingers and hoped she was right. Since her brother, Alex was a police detective, I prayed that some of his law talk rubbed off on her.

"It is true that an individual can remain unidentified on these types of allegations. It is also true that a person has the right to face their accuser. It would take an appeal, which I'm sure Mr. Quincy has already filed, to release the identity." He was full of contradictions. Helpful and not all at the same time.

"So, does that mean there is a form for the appeal?" Just in case Mr. Quincy hadn't already filed it. "Can I get it?" I looked at the woman still reading and thought she would hate me for dumping all this paper-work on her.

"Of course." He walked over to the counter and exchanged words with the woman, who then shot me a dirty look, plopped her book down, and harrumphed her way to the back of the office.

Bella and I gave each other big eyes.

"Um, I think she was getting to the good part of her story," Bella mumbled.

"She must be reading a romance book."

We giggled.

I went back to completing the ridiculously long form while Bella got up and paced the small room.

"Raquel, here is the form you'll need for an appeal to release the complainant's name." I looked up and saw Kevin holding out the paper to me.

I grabbed it from him. "Thanks." If he filed the violations, then why was he being so helpful?

"I honestly wished you would have sat down with me before it was placed on the city docket for discussion. I think we could have come up with a reasonable solution." He looked down at me.

I stared at him. He was a walking contradiction. One minute, he was helpful. The next, he wasn't. One minute, I believed he wasn't behind all this. The next, I was convinced he was. One minute, I thought he was trying to blackmail me into dating him. The next, I thought it was all just my imagination.

I was so confused by Kevin.

"I don't know how that would have been useful. These are legal claims that a conversation could not make go away." *Nor would seeing you in any romantic fashion.*

"Sorry to interrupt, but I just received a text. One of my patients is having a hard time. I gotta go check on them," Bella cut in before Kevin could reply.

"Go. Take care of the lovable pet." I shooed Bella away with my hand.

She was already speed-walking out the door when she yelled, "You're the best!"

"Kevin, Mr. Dixon is asking that you attend the upcoming meeting." The front desk lady delivered the message with a bogus smile and fabricated professionalism.

She really must have been at the steamy part.

"Thank you, Harriet." Kevin looked back at me. "I'm sorry we're unable to finish our discussion, Raquel, but I must go."

"Sure." I understood work came first.

He stared at me for another minute, and I wondered what he was thinking.

"Please take care, Raquel."

A chill went down my spine at his words.

Now, what did he mean by that?

CHAPTER NINE

Rocky

I PARKED IN FRONT OF MY SHOP, LOOKED IN MY REARVIEW MIRROR, and rolled my eyes at myself.

Even though I spent most of my day in, under, or out of a car I always readied myself for the day. I never knew where I would be needed, and I had to be prepared to step into my businesswoman role quickly.

So, I may have added extra hold gel to my hair routine this morning and a round with the curling iron for more volume. And my color-correcting foundation that stayed on no matter the situation I was in. I couldn't stop once I did that, so I added blush, eyeshadow, eyeliner, and mascara.

I had aimed for a summery glowing vibe, but after looking at my reflection, I looked like I was on the prowl for men, not for a day at the beach.

But the lipstick was overkill.

Because it would show how much I was excited to see Max. It'd been a week since I last saw him, and today was the scheduled check-in with the Hudsons. I was eager to show them the progress we'd made on the DeVille. The salvageable engine parts were cleaned to look brand new, the new braking system mounted, the remaining dents in the bumper fixed, the original radio repaired, and the steering wheel restored to its original glory. It had been a long week of hard work, but she was coming along.

So I took a napkin and wiped the lipstick off my lips. I grabbed another and rubbed my cheeks to take some of the blush off, and then I did the same with my eyes. And now I looked like I was mad and crying all at the same time.

Great.

I sucked in a breath, told myself to stop being self-conscious, got out of my car, and headed to the front door. I also reminded myself that Max was coming to see the DeVille, not me.

I opened the front door and froze, staring unseeingly at the mess. My brain couldn't wrap itself around what it saw.

I sucked in a breath, told myself to stop being self-conscious, got out of my car, and headed to the front door. I also reminded myself that Max was coming to see the DeVille, not me.

I opened the front door and froze, staring unseeingly at the mess. My brain couldn't wrap itself around what it saw.

Files littered the entire office. Planters were broken and dirt mingled in with the papers. Chairs were broken and upturned. One was embedded *in* the wall. My chocolate stash was fused with assorted bits of debris, and my desk was on its side, drawers opened or gone altogether. Where? I couldn't tell in the devastation in front of me.

My heart stuttered, and my eyes shot toward the shelf behind my desk. The mantle was splintered down the middle; jagged pieces of wood glared from its ends and pointed toward the enormous hole between its jaws. There was no picture of my dad laying a hot and heavy one on my mom over the hood of the Thunderbird—the day my dad officially opened shop—sitting in the middle of that spic-and-span prized shelf.

Just one massive opening.

Saliva filled my mouth. Acid lined my throat. My stomach whirled. My lungs burned. And my heart hurt like a son-of-a-bitch.

Oh, God.

I was going to be sick.

My feet shot forward to the side garage door, and I prayed all my babies were untouched and unharmed—my torso swung back.

It was a one-two punch.

Tools were scattered throughout the entire shop. Car windows were smashed. Dents, gouges, and scratches scored *every* vehicle in the shop. Seats were shredded. The rest of my chocolate was smeared *everywhere*. And the DeVille—oh no. It seemed worse than when it originally came in.

I bent over, hands on my knees, and sucked in huge breaths of air. Immediately, pinpricks of white spotted my vision, my knees gave way, and I landed on all fours.

"What the fuck?" Clay barked.

"Rocky, you okay, girl?" Bruno's warm hand squeezed my neck as he squatted next to me.

I lifted my head and looked into Bruno's warm brown eyes. "I think I'm gonna be sick." It was a barely there admission behind so many warring emotions.

"All right, baby girl. Take some deep breaths. In through your nose and out through your mouth." Bruno coaxed me through several of them before my despair slowly eked out to be replaced with bone-deep anger.

I peered around Bruno's shoulder and ordered Clay, "Don't touch anything. We need to call the police. Better yet, we need to call Alex and Trent. What's the purpose of having a best friend with a police detective brother if I can't use him to fry these bastards."

Bruno leaned down and extended his hand to help me up. "Never doubted it, but why didn't the alarm go off?" Bruno scanned the shop.

I froze. "It wasn't set?"

"Bullshit. I was the last one out last night, and I set it before I left," Clay fired back.

Chills slithered down my spine, and goosebumps erupted on my arms. "What the hell is going on?"

Clay and Bruno exchanged wary expressions.

I slid my phone out of my pocket and dialed Alex. I didn't wait for his usual greeting and launched right in. "I need you to get down to the shop. Someone broke in, and... damn it. They messed it up." I cleared my throat and forced my tears back.

"What? Are you still there? Anyone there with you?" Alex's cop voice was in full effect.

"Yeah, Bruno and Clay..." My words died as Max and Paul rushed through the door. They scanned the room before their gazes landed on the DeVille. Their expressions soured instantly. Devastation and anger warred on Max's face, and his eyes shot to me.

I sucked in a breath at the fury shooting from them.

Max rushed over to me and asked, "How are you doing, Raquel?" His question shattered the wall I placed up between us. He asked about me. Not the DeVille.

"Rocky! Answer me, damn it!" Alex barked in my ear.

"I'm..." I cleared my throat. "I'm here. Two of my customers just walked in the door." I continued to stare at Max.

"Get them out, but don't let them leave, and don't let anyone else in. I'll be there in ten." Alex disconnected before he acknowledged my agreement.

"Alex, Bella's brother and police detective," I clarified for Max and Paul, "wants us all to wait for him outside." No one said a word as we exited the shop, but Max's hand on my lower back screamed concern for me. Not that anything needed to be said. Anger, frustration, questions—all their emotions pressed down on me, compounding the tumultuous feelings already whirling inside me.

"I know I locked up last night. There's no fucking way I didn't," Clay reiterated as he paced back and forth outside in worry.

His frustration was evident in the rigid line of his body, the clenched jaw, and the hand he kept rubbing over his head and neck.

"Hey, don't blame yourself. This sucky incident wasn't your fault. You didn't thrash the shop. Someone... is seriously not right." I don't care if Clay left the front door wide open. Someone took some time to inflict severe damage to the shop. "The most important thing is that no one got hurt."

"How are you doing?" Max reiterated his earlier question.

"I'm feeling pretty shitty right now. Mostly pissed." There was no use lying or hiding the fact.

"That's understandable." Max's hand remained on my lower back, and goosebumps erupted on my skin from his innate heat.

Clay kicked the ground in his frustration.

"Rocky's right, Clay. She's got insurance so that we can replace everything."

I sucked in a breath at Bruno's words. But, sadly, I wouldn't be able to replace the photo. Pain sliced through me once more at the thought.

"What? What is it?" Bruno immediately stepped toward me.

"The picture."

Understanding filtered through Bruno and Clay at the same time. "Shit." Their sentiment echoed mine.

"You sure it's not in that mess?" Clay asked.

"I don't know." I shrugged. "But where it should be?" He nodded. "There's one freaking big hole, and the shelf is pretty thrashed." It's like someone saw it, and it set them off.

I chanced another peek at Max, who was looking over at his brother.

"Excuse me." Max left me and walked over to his brother, who was staring at the building.

"Don't worry about them. We'll kick ass to hit our projected target date even with this mess." Bruno didn't miss where my focus was centered.

"I know that, but put yourself in their shoes. How would you feel?" It's terrible enough to have a customer concerned about the screwed-up city regulations surrounding the shop. Now, add this into the mix— I wasn't exactly hitting a hundred in the I've-got-this side of the column with him.

"You sure you're worried about this or the fact that boy lights a different kind of fire in you?" Bruno pitched his voice low—for my ears only—and completely got my attention.

I swung my head to him, a rejection at the ready, but Bruno cut me off before I could utter it. "Don't. I've known you a long time, Rocky, so don't try your bullshit on me."

"I... It's not like that." I made a feeble attempt to evade Bruno's accurate assumption.

His finely sculpted eyebrows shot up at my lie. "Bullshit. But, I'll let that obvious lie lie for now."

"I feel like shit, Rocky. I was on the phone with Casey, but I know I locked up." Clay was devastated at his possible oversight.

I reached out and grabbed his hand. "Stop. I believe you. I'll call the alarm company and get the log pulled. I want to know who unarmed it. Plus, I'll access the online security video, and hopefully, it caught the dickhead in the act. And, you know, Alex and Trent will fingerprint the crap out of the shop, and I'm sure they'll also ask the neighboring businesses for the security footage. But, more importantly, you didn't do this, so let it go."

"I'm gonna walk the perimeter of the building and see if I can't find anything." Clay squeezed my hand once and let go.

"Okay, but don't touch anything. I want whatever possible evidence you find untainted, so Alex and Trent can fry this jerk hole." I'd prefer to connect a live battery to their genitals, but rotting in jail would suffice.

"Excuse me, Rocky, but has this ever happened before?" Paul's serious tone seemed foreign to me. All of our prior interactions were based on fun and humor.

"No." And I hoped it never happened again. "I..." My words died when Alex and Trent pulled into the parking lot hot and heavy.

Alex was out in a flash and had me wrapped in a brotherly hug that I didn't know I needed. "You okay, Rocky?" he mumbled into the side of my head.

I sucked in a deep breath, and semi-nodded slash shook my head against his chest.

"Anyone inside?"

"No. Clay is checking things around the shop," Bruno answered Trent.

I stepped back from Alex's embrace. "I want the asshole who did this," I ordered.

"Okay, we're going to do a preliminary once-over. When we're done, we'll need to get information from all of you," Alex said as he and Trent headed toward the front door.

"Are you that friendly with all police officers?" Max watched me.

What the hell did he mean? "He's pretty much a brother to me."

My eyes shot to Bruno, and a slow smile crossed his face.

I pointed my finger at him. "Don't you say a word."

He raised his hands in surrender. "I didn't say anything."

"Crapola. I'm going to have to tell Ash." I rubbed my forehead, feeling the headache fast approaching. "My brother is going to burn down Feldspar finding out who did this."

"Why does it matter if Ash knows?" Paul pointed toward the building. "You've got two police detectives inside."

"My brother is a little... protective." Shit. I would have to jump into overdrive to fix all this before Ash decided to mount a hunting party.

Bruno snorted.

Paul sized the shop up. "Looks like you need it."

And just like that, my sour mood returned. "Fortunately, I'm more than capable." Because the second I got my hand on the dick who did this, I was going to nail them to the wall.

Paul returned his attention to me. "I don't doubt it, but wouldn't more help work in your favor?"

I sucked in a huge breath.

I'd had enough. My shop was destroyed, the melt-your-heart-swoon-worthy picture that represented it all gone, and I had to call my brother. "I appreciate your concern, and I assure you once I learn more about the circumstances, I will pull the appropriate individuals in to handle it. I also pledge that Sterling Custom Auto will do its best to deliver on its promise regarding your vehicle's restoration. This inconvenience will not deter us from our mission nor the quality Sterling Custom Auto was built on."

I closed my eyes and rubbed my forehead again—the headache sitting squarely front and center now.

"I'm sorry. I don't mean to come off as a dick. I just know if I need a hand, I call on my brothers." He eyed the building once more. "And, the damage inside screams help."

I opened my eyes and mouth to let Paul know what I thought of his lovable logical concern, but Alex and Trent walked out of the front door at the same time Clay came around the corner.

"You were the first here, Rocky?" Trent asked.

"Yeah, and not long after, Bruno and Clay showed up, followed by Max and Paul." I tilted my head to them. "The DeVille in there belongs to them."

"We're going to need some information from you both before you can take off." Trent pulled out his little black cop notebook.

Alex directed his attention at me and asked, "Who was the last one to leave last night?" as Trent talked to Max and Paul.

"That'd be me." Clay rubbed the back of his neck. "I was on the phone with my girl, but I know I set the alarm. Lockdown procedures are so second nature. I know I didn't fuck it up."

I reached out and squeezed his arm. "This isn't on you."

"I'm going to need the information from the alarm company. I want to know how it was disabled." Alex backed my confidence in Clay. "You still got the video monitoring system?" At my nod, Alex continued, "Tape or digital?"

"Digital. Ash wouldn't let me go any other route." Hopefully, his paranoia paid off, and we caught the S.O.B. on camera.

"You gonna tell him? Or do you want me to call him?" See? Alex was just like another brother.

"I'll do it." So what if I sounded resigned to torture? My brother would come here, guns blazing, which meant I would get pushed to the side. There was no way Ash's very protective-big-brother-alpha-DNA would let him sit on the sidelines and let me figure this out. That meant I had to double-time my investigation and solve everything before Ash stepped foot in Feldspar.

My eyes shot to Bruno at his quickly cut-off strangled noise.

"What?" Trent asked as he, Max, and Paul joined our huddle.

"I think you're forgetting who you need to be worried about, and it's not Ash." Bruno shifted his six-foot solid frame from one foot to the other.

"Shit," both Trent and Alex mumbled.

I tilted my head in confusion as I noticed Bruno, Alex, and Trent all gave the impression that they wanted to be anywhere else but here. "Who could be worse than my brother?"

"Martha," they said in unison.

"Rocky's mom?" Paul's sweet confusion bounced away as I finally sat on the ground.

I stared unseeing at the blacktop and wondered where I'd gone wrong. First, I was considered incompetent because of my genitalia by so many ignorant men. Not to mention my youth being a so-called factor for inexperience. Second, someone had a burr up their butt regarding the ordinances surrounding my shop. Third, someone laid waste to my business *and* took the one thing that meant just as much to me as my dad's shop.

The one photo that represented it all.

My dad gave my mom a scorching hot kiss over the hood of the T-Bird that started it all. He used to joke that that kiss set him and the shop up for success. Without it, without my mom's approval, it wouldn't be what have been what it was then or now. Of course, Mom, being the sugar she was, would say their love coming together made it all.

Darn it, this was going to devastate her.

Max squatted next to me, circling me between his outstretched legs, and blocked me from the guys' view. He gently squeezed my neck. "Hey, you okay?"

I gazed up into his whiskey eyes and thought "who are you? Are you indeed one of those jerks, or are you something else?"

"Yeah." I cleared my throat and repeated much stronger, "Yeah." Because no way was I going to let anyone take everything my dad gave me, my brother, or my mom away.

Fuck that, and fuck them.

He scanned my face and landed back at my eyes. "Yeah," he whispered.

Whoa.

The certainty and the absolute faith behind his one word rocked me.

Maybe Max was something else.

Vindictive

No. No. No. No.

They weren't supposed to be having a moment.

Max was supposed to stay devastated at the damage to his precious DeVille and be pissed at Rocky.

Not comforting her and certainly not drawing her out of her misery.

No! No! No!

I wanted her to wallow in it. To be so mired down with it, she couldn't see straight. I wanted her every breath to be wrecked. So, I took the one thing I knew would guarantee everything.

That fucking picture.

Everyone knew what it meant to her and her family. Everyone knew they believed Sterling Custom Auto wouldn't be what it was without it. Everyone knew, without the photo, Rocky was just some chick trying to be something she undeniably wasn't. But, more importantly, *she knew* she wasn't anything without it.

So, why wasn't she crumbling? And why was her face set in determination?

No fucking way I was letting her think she could move on from this. She was determined to move on?

I'd make sure she couldn't.

CHAPTER TEN

Rocky

IN THE HOURS THAT PASSED, I VACILLATED BETWEEN WANTING TO kick someone's ass and doing everything I could not to fall apart. So I stood outside my shop and hugged myself against the predawn chill as police officers and crime scene technicians swarmed inside. Alex and Trent warned me it would be a few hours before they would be done with the scene.

The scene.

My shop was now a scene. A full-body shudder wracked through me as I watched police personnel move from spot to spot.

My beloved shop, my creative haven–ravaged. Violated. I wanted to scream, to sob, but could only stand numbly, watching the investigation unfold.

"Raquel?"

I turned to see Max hurrying up the sidewalk towards me, concern etched on his face as Paul pulled away from the curb. The closer Max got to me, the harder it was to keep the tears at bay.

Once at my side, Max pulled me into his embrace, looked down into my eyes, and said, "Hey. It's going to be okay. You're going to be okay."

I nodded, close to tears. "I just can't believe it. Who would do this?" My voice cracked as emotion swamped me.

He ran his hand down my arm, grabbed my hand, and said, "Let's go for a walk and get you away from this for a bit. Help clear your head."

With my hand in his warm one, I gratefully let him steer me down the block away from the swirling police lights and activity. We strolled in silence for a few minutes. I let downtown Feldspar's peaceful early morning hours seep into me. I breathed deeply and tried to calm my racing mind.

"Thanks for getting me out of there." I scanned the other businesses opening up for the day. "Do you mind if we stop at some of these so I can ask about their surveillance videos?"

"Not a problem." He turned to me with a wicked smile on his face. "It's not a hardship walking with a pretty woman and holding her hand."

A small chuckle escaped me.

"Ah, so there's an alternative motive." I swung our hands up. "You just wanted to hold my hand." The electricity from his touch zipped through me and helped eradicate the nausea from this morning's horrible event.

"You found me out. I'm taking advantage of your distress in order to get close enough to touch you." Max winked at me. "I say it's working." He gently squeezed my hand as evidence.

If only he knew I'd been trying to find excuses *not* to get close to him. All of them were nonsense, and it was getting more and more difficult to come up with them.

"Yeah, well, consider it your lucky day." I'd say mine too, but the state of my shop called me a liar.

"I am." His tone indicated he wasn't joking.

I looked up at him as we continued on our walk and saw the seriousness stamped on Max's face.

"You're my customer." Denying the connection between us would be ridiculous.

"That I am." He shrugged. "Is it a problem?"

I opened and closed my mouth. I looked back to the sidewalk. Was I going to let my pitiful dating history stop my future? Was I going to let Carson's asshole behavior color every man's image for me? Was I going to stay scared in my shell in order to protect myself from what-ifs?

I looked back up at Max. He had demonstrated he was outside of Carson's douche sphere. Max's apology regarding the misconception of my name and automotive capability screamed he was worth a chance.

"I don't know. Will it be?" I held my breath, waiting for his response.

"No. It won't." He let my hand go and draped his arm across my shoulder. "We'll start slow. How about dinner this Friday, once things settle down?"

My belly dipped at the thought. "That depends. Where are you taking me?" We were making our way back around the block toward Sterling Custom Auto. Our stops along the way didn't prove fruitful. Some of the businesses that were opened didn't have functional cameras. They took a risk and hoped the physical item would be deterrent enough.

"Where would the fun be in me telling you that?" He gently squeezed me closer as we neared the shop.

"Oh. A mystery. I like puzzles."

"Are you afraid of heights?" He looked down at me as we stopped in the parking lot.

"Um, no. Not normally."

His smile was triumphant as if my answer pleased him.

"But, I gotta say, your smile has me worried."

"Don't be. I'd never hurt you." All joking fled Max to be replaced with a quiet but firm sincerity. He stared at me, and his eyes begged me to believe he was one hundred percent serious about his intentions.

My heart stuttered when I saw the conviction on Max's face. He truly believed he was never going to cause me pain. Hope fluttered inside me, and I leaned closer to him.

He turned me to face him and wrapped his arms around me.

"This isn't the right time, but I'm going to kiss you. I can't avoid it anymore."

Max's head slowly descended, and he watched me closely, looking for the slightest sign I'd say no.

Not that I would. Horrible timing and all; I wanted Max's kiss.

The moment his lips touched mine, warm and soft, it was like the whole world slipped away, and it was just the two of us. All of my senses flooded with Max. He moved his hand to my cheek, and the rough calluses on his palm against my face sent tingles down my spine. He smelled of soap, leather, and open air, and the solid strength of his shoulders under my palms melted me and made me feel safe. The world around us faded away, and all I knew was the thrill of his mouth on mine.

When we finally parted, my eyes blinked open, and the fire in his gaze set everything inside me ablaze. I wanted to wrap myself in Max and live forever suspended in this perfect moment. No violations. No break-ins. He cradled my flushed cheek with such tenderness that my heart squeezed as I told it to slow down.

But words weren't needed. We came together again and learned the contours of each other's lips. Max's expert kissing and the wandering course of his fingers tracing down my arm sent shivers through me. Our body's responses represented this magnetic and irresistible language.

I luxuriated in the kisses Max gave me. I savored the thrill of this undiscovered relationship, yet to be mapped but so full of promise. My heart jumped ahead of my brain and danced in contentment, not wanting out.

"Ahem."

Reluctantly, I pulled my mouth away from Max's. As we stared into each other's eyes, our breaths intermingled, my soul irrevocably changed.

The fire in Max's eyes seared me, and I sucked in a deep breath to control my runaway heart and hormones. My nipples brushed Max's chest, and his nostrils flared at the touch.

"Ahem."

Woodenly, I turned to the right to see Alex standing next to us.

"Sorry to bother you." Alex's smile called him a liar.

"Ye..." I cleared my throat. "Yes?"

"I wanted to remind you it's going to be a few more hours, so if you want to take off..." Alex trailed off as he gave me and Max a knowing look. "I can lock up for you when we're done."

"You'll call me when you're done?" I wanted to touch base and see if they found anything in their preliminary search.

"Of course."

I stepped back out of Max's embrace and immediately felt alone. "Have you found anything?" I pushed for answers.

"Nothing yet."

"What's your instinct telling you?" My spidey senses vibrated.

Alex hesitated. "I'm not going to speculate until I have more evidence." He held his hand up to stop my objection. "I know you want answers, but if I give you inaccurate information and we go down the wrong path, then that's just a clusterfuck I don't want to participate in. Nor do I want to give you any false hope."

I did my best not to roll my eyes at Alex. "Fine." Not really. "By the way, we stopped at a few open stores, and none had working cameras." They took a risk and hoped the physical item would be deterrent enough."

"Okay, I'll double-check them anyway."

"Is Raquel safe?" Max asked.

"I don't believe she's not, but it goes without saying, Rocky, you need to be careful," Alex warned me.

"Yup. I know the drill." Having an overprotective brother who taught me about safety as a teenage girl was annoying. Now, as an adult, I was extremely thankful for all of his irritating lessons.

"Okay, I'm heading back in to take another look." Alex briefly touched my arm. "I'll reach out later. Until then, stay safe, Rocky."

I watched him walk away and wondered what he wasn't telling me.

"Alex and his partner, Trent, seem more than capable. I have no doubt they'll figure it out. Until then, try not to worry too much until they have more information." Max gave my shoulder a reassuring squeeze.

"Yeah, they are." I sighed and looked up at him. "But will something else happen until then? I mean, whoever did this, will they come back for round two?" I had an itch between my shoulder blades that warned me whoever was responsible for this horrendous act wasn't done with me.

"Hey. I'm not going to lie and say everything will be okay. I don't have that crystal ball power. But, I can say your friends are doing everything they can to quickly catch whoever is behind this to keep you safe. You have top-of-the-line security, even with the hiccup, which is another added protection. Not to mention your employees who, from my minimal interactions, seem like they would stand in front of a train for you. This will make it more difficult for anyone to get to you and should be a huge deterrent for their future nefarious plots." Max did his best to console me.

"Uh-huh." Why didn't it stop them now?

Beep. Beep.

Max and I turned to see Paul sitting in his truck at the curb.

"That's my ride." Max turned back to me. "I want to help you however I can. I know you have a ton of people behind you, but I'd be honored if you included me in that lineup."

"Thanks, Max. I appreciate it." He was knocking down all of my walls. If I wasn't careful, he would take off with my heart before I knew what hit me.

"I don't want to leave you here. Are you going to head out now?" he asked.

"Yeah. There's nothing I can do here until they're finished. I might as well go home and get some work done there."

Max grabbed my hand and walked me to my car. Everything was different now. I had crossed a line with Max. Those kisses unwrapped a new world for me—frightening and exhilarating all at the same time.

We stopped at the driver's side door, and a wave of shyness overtook me. I didn't know if I should get up on my tiptoes and give him a kiss or a hug. Or none of the above.

Max chuckled.

I looked up at him. "What's funny?"

"The few times I've been around you, you've been a take-charge kind of woman. Now, you look lost. It's cute." He tapped my nose.

"Ha ha ha." It was kind of scary how easily he could read me.

He bent down, gave me a too-quick peck on the lips, stayed in his bent position, and said, "I'm not going to deepen that even though I want to. We would need a bedroom if I did that."

My legs trembled, and I grabbed onto the side of his t-shirt to hold myself up.

"Dammit." He slid his thumb across my bottom lip.

It was instinctive to flick my tongue out and lick his thumb. His taste quickly became a drug I couldn't go without.

Max's nostrils flared as he pressed his thumb down on my lip. "Be a good girl, or I won't bring you more chocolate."

For the first time in my life, I contemplated the loss of my addiction in order to get more of Max's goodness.

He dropped his hand and stepped away from me. "Shit. You make it hard to walk away."

My eyes automatically dropped down to his crotch, and I saw the bulge straining against his pants.

He tipped my chin up and said, "Save it for Friday."

Something to look forward to after the shitty beginning of this day.

"Try to take it easy the rest of the day. Call me if you want to talk or need anything," Max continued.

"Thanks. I'll do my best." But without Max as a distraction, I knew today's events would play over and over in my brain.

He stepped around me and opened my car door as a silent command to get in. Not in the mood to argue, I got in and started my vehicle. He shut the door, and I watched him walk toward Paul.

There was no turning back now.

I was definitely taking Max for a spin.

CHAPTER ELEVEN

Rocky

FOR THE FIRST TIME EVER, THE CHOCOLATE IN MY STOMACH FELT like a car jack inching its way back up slowly but surely. Of course, it wasn't a surprise with the constant hammering of Kevin's relentless girlfriend assault, the numerous violations debacle, and the destruction of the shop that my chocolate cure-all wasn't working as effectively anymore. But what I was about to do pushed me closer to vomit territory than I'd been in in years. No matter what my mom said about my college years.

"I wondered how long it'd be before you called me." Ash's gravelly voice greeted me.

"I know I shouldn't be surprised you already know, but I am." He knew everything and anything—it didn't matter that he was probably hundreds of miles away. "Does Mom know?"

"No. Do you want me to tell her?"

He was the best big brother ever, even if I didn't always want him fixing everything for me. Always willing to step in and do anything to make life easier for me. Including telling Mom about all the crap swirling around me.

"No. She's my next call. Then I'll hit Mr. Quincy or Mr. Lewis if Mr. Quincy's not back yet, who'll handle everything else on top of all the other infraction crap."

"You got this."

Besides my mom, dad, and Bella, Ash was the only person who never doubted my abilities. An image of Max popped up in my brain, and I eyed the blurry image of his name next to my family's. "Yeah, I know. But I need you to let me lead this." I babbled before he could object. "I know you have more experience and skills in this area than I ever will, but this is..." My voice cracked. "I have to do this."

"Okay, Rocky." Ash's gravelly voice softened.

He acquiesced way too easily. "You're not really going to leave it to me, are you?"

"No, but you won't know I'm investigating either. Unfortunately, I can't dig into it like I want to until I finish my current job. A week, two —maybe."

"Fine." I wasn't mad. I wanted whoever had a burr up their ass to stop.

"Rocky?"

"Yeah?"

"Me investigating this isn't about whether or not you can handle it. I don't need to tell you; you're one seriously kickass woman. It's just no one fucks with my family." The steel in his words melted my heart.

"I love you, Ash." My chocolate stash wavered before me as I blinked back the tears.

"I love you too, Rockstar."

A short chuckle burst out of me. "Don't even start with that nickname." And, for good measure, I changed the subject. "So, tell me how your call went with Kevin."

My brother gave me my play and said, "It went as expected. A bunch of nothing. Did you find out who lodged the complaints?"

"Honestly, I'm surprised you don't know." As I said, Ash knew everything. "But I'd guess Kevin, since his wooing isn't working, I thought he changed tactics."

"I've been preoccupied, and I expected you to have whoever filed them hung up by his balls by now."

"Well, I'm getting closer to that outcome, but I've encountered some roadblocks. First, I called Mr. Quincy's office last week for that information, and he was out of the office for a few days. I plan on following up with his office today. So, then I went down to City Hall to find out. That was a mess. Their online system is down, so they can't access their digital files or forms. Let's just say that after filling out the hundred-page–" slight exaggeration– "documents, I'll be surprised if I receive that answer this year. To top it all off, Kevin informed me it was an anonymous filing. And guess what?"

"What?"

"That was another hundred-page form I needed to complete to unseal that information." So, I was a little irritable about the manual process. It did cause my hand to cramp.

"It seems like you have that under control," Ash's words were laced with humor at my expense.

"Hahaha." I hoped I did. "Do you know where the original zoning survey records are for the shop? I can't find it in all the papers Dad had crammed in the filing cabinet. I want to review them and compare them to the new survey I will have completed."

"Last time I saw them, they were in that stack shoved in the back of the metal death trap." Ash despised anything administrative, so I wouldn't be surprised if he were the one who shoved it there.

"Great. Hopefully, I can find it when I'm allowed back in to clean up." And I mentally crossed my fingers that they weren't destroyed in the vandalism. "What are your thoughts on this? Because I don't see Kevin tearing the shop apart. That'd be beneath his civilized demeanor. So, two perpetrators? Kevin for the legalese stuff and another jerkwad for the break-in?" I wanted to know what Ash's train of thought was.

"Maybe."

He didn't sound convinced.

"What I don't get is why take the picture? They left everything else in one huge mess, but it was still there. So why gouge the wall out and remove the photo?"

"Are you sure they took it? That it's not just somewhere in the mess?"

His tone sent warning signals down my spine. "I don't know. I haven't received the green light to touch anything yet."

"Shit. I don't like this, Rocky."

"I don't either, but I feel like we're talking about two different things. What aren't you saying?"

"If the picture is missing, then that hole is very personal. Meaning this wasn't a random act. *You* were targeted."

Goosebumps erupted on my arms.

"By who? I didn't do anything to anyone, much less more than one person."

"I don't know."

I was hoping he wasn't sure because he was distracted and not because I made someone angry enough to attack me on multiple fronts.

"Well, after I call Mom, I'm going to log into the security system and see what the code logs and videos show. Then I'll send it over to Alex and Trent." Maybe, just maybe, the jerk smiled nice and pretty for the camera.

I heard someone in the background getting his attention.

"That sounds like a great plan, but I gotta go, Rocky. I'll reach out later. Until then, stay safe."

One down, one to go.

And, as easy as Ash's call was, Mom's was going to be a whole heck of a lot harder.

Each tap into the phone felt like a hammer pounding in my gut. I blew out a breath and waited for Mom to pick up.

"Hello, dear." Mom's sweet voice soothed some of my hurt.

"Hi, Mom. How are you doing?"

"What's wrong? Are you okay?" A few simple words and Mom already knew something was amiss.

I choked back my tears as emotion weighed me down. "I've had better days, and unfortunately, I gotta share it with you." I never wanted to share it with her, especially regarding Dad's shop.

"All right, Rocky, give it to me." Mom didn't waiver. She never did.

I didn't know how to tell her, so I vomited it all out. From Kevin's possible wifey assault to coming clean about the zoning and other complaints to today's shop disaster. Every last bit of it. I didn't leave one tiny detail out—even the missing photo. And then I waited for Mom's response.

"Well, my goodness, Raquel. You've had quite a bit going on. No wonder you've been Rock*ier* lately." Mom so downplayed my edginess. "But, let me get some things straight for you. You will never be satisfied donning socks while catering to your husband's every need, so needless to say, Kevin was never in the running. He'll figure it out soon enough and move on because a man like Kevin—who's been behaving like an imbecile but isn't—will figure that out soon enough. As for this nuisance with the complaints—which I already knew about because nothing is secret in this small town—one, I know you're handling it. Two, it's in Teddy's capable hands. Between the two of you, I know neither one of you would let anything happen to Sterling Custom Auto, much less the other citizens whose livelihoods are also dependent on the outcome of these grievances to remain as is. So, let that uneasiness go as well. As for this break-in, it's also in Alex and Trent's qualified hands, and *you know* they will not stop until they find who is responsible."

Mom saved the best for last. "All of this is a pain in your derrière and just plain ol' bothersome, but what it is is not the end of Sterling Custom Auto. Even with the picture missing." Her voice lowered, and she dropped more knowledge on me. "The hole in the wall where the picture was, and the missing picture is troublesome. It seems rather personal, but it also shows me that whoever did this does not know you. While the photo is sentimental, the one thing it is not is Sterling Custom Auto. Your father was, and now you are. So now, I want you to do what you always do: dust your bottom off, roll your sleeves up, and attack all this one step at a time because that's who your father and I raised. A woman who is more than competent to handle anything she sets her mind to."

"Have I told you lately you're the bomb, Mom?"

The parental sass went right out of Mom to be replaced by her motherly sweetness. "Not lately, dear, but you could tell me over dinner when Ash gets in town. We'll make it a family affair."

"Thanks, Mom."

"Anytime, sweetheart. Is there anything else you need?"

"Yeah, I can't find the original survey for Sterling Custom Auto. Do you have it or know where it is?" Mom used to help Dad around the office before he passed. She kept on when Ash took over and then me but eventually cut her hours back. She was always willing to help with whatever we needed, but her true calling was helping at the library and the reading programs for young kids.

"Oh goodness. It's been so long since I've seen it. Did you check the filing cabinet?"

"Sort of. I skimmed it before the break-in. Now, I gotta wait to recheck it." And I prayed it was still there.

"I'll look around the house just in case and let you know either way. Now, I have to let you go. I need to go to the grocery store. I love you, Rocky."

"I love you too, Mom."

My family rocked.

Now, all I had to do was what my parents raised me to be and find the prick who thought he could fuck with me.

My next call was to City Hall to find out the status of the forms I submitted last week, with no luck. Their computer system was still down due to some nasty virus, and a water pipe broke in the basement and flooded it. Of course, that made accessing the old paper files impossible. So until they cleared that all up, I was in a holding position.

I tried Mr. Quincy's office and learned he wasn't back in town yet. So, I updated his partner, Mr. Lewis, on the break-in, and he said he'd call Alex and Trent. Then he stated they also filed the same petitions as I did, along with the other businesses who were also under attack-my take on it-and that they were waiting as patiently as me. Well, maybe they were a little more patient than me. I also asked Mr. Lewis if he would let Mr. Quincy know that I finally told Mom and Ash about all the shit happening with Sterling Custom Auto, so he didn't have to worry about keeping that from them. Mr. Lewis, a professional down to his marrow, stated a notation would be entered in my file. Ha! A notation in my file.

Then, I had to follow up on my possible misreading of Kevin's intentions with Mr. Lewis. It was like conversing with your grandfather about the birds and the bees. Not comfortable. He stated this would also be a notation for future follow-up.

I snorted.

I'd love to be a fly on the wall during *that* conversation.

Then, to wrap it all up, I let him know I would have a new survey performed. He thought it was a brilliant idea and provided some recommendations for surveyors.

I quickly hired one for next week since I didn't know what the timeline would look like with cleanup, and then I prayed I was one step closer to solving all these annoying problems.

Then I pulled out my laptop to review the security footage when my doorbell rang, and my phone chimed with a text at the same time. I wasn't expecting anyone and figured Alex and Trent would call me to tell me when I could start repairing the shop. Sure enough, Alex's text stated the shop was clear for me to access.

I made my way to the front of the house, texting a thanks to Alex when I reached the door. I looked through the peephole to see Bella standing outside. I opened it and said, "Hey! What are you doing here?"

She pushed past me and said, "It's good to see you too."

I closed the door behind her and followed her into my kitchen. "You know I love to see you anytime, but I wasn't expecting you. What's up?"

"Did you think you'd have someone vandalize your shop and I wouldn't hear about it? Much less not show up to be here for you?" She stopped at my kitchen counter, grabbed some of my chocolate, and waited for me to answer.

I plopped down on my barstool, grabbed my own piece of chocolate, and said, "Sorry, I've got a lot on my mind and forgot the best friend code of having each other's back in everything."

"Now, tell me all about it." She sat next to me.

So I did. Even the part about getting ready because I was excited to see Max. I even sucked it up and admitted to Bella that she just might be right about him—kiss, date, all of it.

"First, in regards to Max, I'm just going to say I told you so." Bella's smug smile represented years of being my best friend and participating in all my romantic escapades. "Secondly, hot damn!" Bella shouted. "Finally!"

Even with all the shit flying around me, there was a glimmer of hope lit inside me with Max's name written on it. The slight smile on my face was a by-product of that hope and something I couldn't stop from appearing.

Bella pointed her finger at my mouth. "Ha!" She jumped up and did a little happy dance. "I told you so!" She sat down next to me.

"Whatever." Giving Bella any more ammunition to gloat wasn't in the best-friend code.

"We have to go shopping for a new dress. Something that will make Max's jaw drop." Bella plotted. "And hopefully, your undies too."

"Bella!" Even though I wasn't totally against the idea.

"Don't fight me. I only have your best interest in mind." She feigned innocence.

"Uh-huh."

"Moving on to the shitty part of the day." Bella steamrolled my meager objections. "I knew your prices would send someone to the dark side." Bella's attempt to lighten the ugliness of my morning events fell short. "Sorry, Rocky, that sounded better in my head."

"Don't worry about it. And, if I'm being honest, right about now, the idea of joining the dark side seems pretty darn appealing." I'd love to get my hands on the dickhead who did this.

"What did Alex and Trent say? Any clues?" Bella mumbled, "Although I'm sure they gave you their usual cop excuse. In other words, they didn't tell you crap."

"Well, to be fair, they've only been on the case for a few hours, so I don't think they've had time to get much." No matter how much I wanted answers now.

"Well, I'm getting Dean on it. Unlike my brother and Trent, he'll get answers quicker because he can blur the lines." She rushed before I could object. "I won't take no. And please don't make me stand by and watch you go through this alone. I couldn't handle it."

I figured she'd pull Dean in on it. Bella's huge heart had no boundaries regarding the people she loved.

"Well, I wouldn't want to make you suffer," I acquiesced.

"Huh, that was easy. I expected more of a fight."

"Nope. I want the jackhole who did this. The sooner, the better." I slid my laptop closer to me. "Which reminds me. You got here just in time for the good stuff."

"Oooh. Do tell." Bella scooted closer to me.

"I'm about to pull up the footage from the security cameras. I hope it caught their ugly ass." With a few clicks, I scrolled through the files for the correct date and approximate time.

She rubbed her hands together in glee. "This is exciting. I never get to be a part of the investigation."

"Here we go. I'm going to start with closing time so I can confirm with my insurance company that Clay did indeed follow lock-up procedures."

After thirty minutes of watching my shop being lifeless, my first thought was, *how did Alex, Trent, and Dean do this every day?* It was slow and boring. My second thought was that Clay did as he said—lock up.

The shop was dark and quiet. It was even a little eerie and made me rethink working at night ever again.

Since it was lethargic, I invited Bella to stay for dinner. We propped my laptop on the counter and prepped our meal, occasionally checking on the video. But in those four hours, we hadn't encountered anyone.

Three hours later, Bella hugged me goodbye. She was eager to get home to Dean. I didn't blame her. I wanted to curl up to my own hot guy.

Max immediately popped up front and center in my brain. I shook my head and told myself to focus on catching the bad guy and not catching the handsome guy.

I got ready for bed, grabbed a glass of wine and my laptop, and settled into bed for a round of boring video surveillance. I hit the fast-forward button and sped through the video, and looked for any hint of the dickhead.

And then I saw him. It was two thirty-four in the morning when he showed up. He dressed in all black from head to toe. I mean head to toe—gloves, hat, shoes, pants, shirt. He even had on one of those ski masks that cover everything but your eyes. I couldn't tell his eye color even with that little bit exposed. Nothing looked familiar.

A few things sent chills down my spine. The first? He disarmed my alarm system with a code. A valid code. The second? He went straight for the photo. So very much personal. The third? He knew every one of my chocolate stashes. He didn't leave one behind. Again, very much personal. Fourth? He tried desperately to open the filing cabinet. That was puzzling.

Then I watched him attack everything in my shop for twenty minutes. He was angry and used my place of business to throw his tantrum.

I watched it another two times before giving up on figuring out who he was.

Then I opened up my alarm account, scrolled through the logins for the douche's time of entry, and froze because staring at me was my alarm code.

My passcode.

How could that be? I never gave it to anyone.

I was one big goosebump of fear.

What the hell was going on?

I immediately reset everyone's passwords. Then I shot over the video and login history to Alex and Trent, letting them know what I saw—ending the email asking them to use their keen detective eyes to figure something out–fast.

Needless to say, I didn't sleep a single wink.

Because this was very much personal.

And I was fucking scared.

CHAPTER TWELVE

Rocky

NO MATTER YOUR AGE, THERE WAS NOTHING LIKE GETTING A talkin' to by your parent. And every time, it made you feel exactly like you did when you were a kid.

Guilty.

"I want to know why I heard about this from Betsy and not my daughter." Mom's sharp tone whipped through the phone.

"Moommm..."

Yup, that was me whining like a kid. To my mother.

"Don't mom me, Raquel Marie. Do you know how annoyed I was that *that* woman knew something about my children before me? You'd think she won the lottery with the way she shared the information. I had to *fib* the truth, and you know how I feel about lying, Raquel." Mom rightfully chewed me out. "Now, I expect Max over for dinner this weekend. What's his favorite meal? Is he allergic to anything?"

I cringed at the fact mom heard about anything from Betsy–her childhood frenemy–but there was no way I was having Max over for a meet-the-family meal. With Mom on the warpath for grandkids, some-thing I had no clue if Max wanted. Whoa. I slammed a huge red stop sign up in my brain. I did not need to be thinking about Max and babies. At least not before I learned if he was what I thought he might be—someone who could handle Rocky *and* Raquel. "Betsy misread the situation outside the shop." She did not. "Max is my customer, and we were only discussing his vehicle. Nothing else." Lie. Lie. Lie.

"Raquel Marie. Are you saying I'm blind? That I did not see how you two looked at each other at Coop's? That the chemistry between you two did not carry over?" Mom chastised me.

"I am not saying any of that." I valued my life too much to call my mother a liar *ever* and she just proved that mothers really did have keen observation skills.

"Are you also saying that while you were making googly eyes with Max at Margie's, Betsy was also mistaken in what she saw?" Mom was not deterred. "Or while you two were holding hands *and* kissing outside the shop, Betsy was also mistaken?"

Darn it. "Our attraction," and there definitely was, "does not equate to…"

"You didn't answer me. What is his favorite meal? Allergies?" She moved on past my objections.

"I don't know."

But it was like she didn't hear me. "You should probably invite Max's brother, Paul, as well. Does he have any other siblings? Never mind, invite them all. We'll make it a family affair, and I'll check in with your brother about coming home for the weekend."

Changing mom's mind on anything was akin to moving a mountain alone, unaided without modern technology—impossible. I mean, she was where I got my stubbornness from, but having Max or his family over this weekend was *not* going to happen. At least not until I had one date with him. "Mom, Ash won't be here for another week or two. So, dinner won't happen this weekend."

"Well, then…" She was not going to be deterred. "We'll plan it for the end of the month. Now, update me on the happenings surrounding the shop so I can begin all the preparations." Mom steamrolled over my objections.

I sucked in a deep breath. I'd have to fight mom's family making plans later after I handled all the other more craptastic details—my disheveled front office glared at me—events flying around me. Because the shop didn't look any better the next day and I needed to focus on one thing at a time.

So, I laid everything out as best as I could, ending with, "I'm meeting the insurance adjustor this morning, so we'll get this part moving soon. Alex, Trent, and Dean are on it. Mr. Quincy and Mr. Lewis are on it." Hopefully they put the fear of the law in Kevin. "I'm on it. They're not worried about it, so neither am I." Maybe a little. "Also, I reset your access to the shop. We'll get you a new login when you come in next time."

"Of course they are, and we know if Teddy takes care of it, then it's all but handled. It's like your dad used to say, *'Once in Teddy's hands, it's as good as done.'* And I figured you'd have to do that after the break-in. I'm in no hurry, so we'll take care of it whenever you have free time."

Mom downplayed the whole predicament. I wish I could be as confident as she was, but Kevin was a dog with a bone. Unfortunately, this bone didn't want to be gnawed.

At least not by him.

"You're right." The bell above my office door jingled, and a well-groomed man with a sleek, fashionably distressed satchel strode through. "I gotta go. Someone just walked through the door."

"All right, Raquel. I'll let you get back to work. I love you, baby girl."

"Love you too, Mom."

I barely clicked the off button on my cell phone before I got up out of my seat and headed to greet the man. "Sorry about that, but you know, moms. Work or not, you gotta answer their calls." I swiftly made my way to the front door and prevented the suave-looking guy from stepping further into the disaster of the reception area.

"My mom calls me weekly to remind me to get groceries and do my laundry." He smiled in commiseration.

He was in a swanky, fitted two-piece charcoal gray very-much-tailored suit with shiny bronze derby shoes. All of it hid from what I could perceive as a trim, fit body. And none of it stated momma needed to worry.

So, my chuckle was positively wry when I said, "I'm sure you didn't come here to talk about our moms—not that I don't love talking about my mom—but what can I do for you?"

His smile was that of a son who loved his mother and wasn't afraid to show it. "I was hoping to speak with Raquel Sterling."

"Well, you found her."

"Fantastic. I'm Patrick Rocklin, Avery Wheldon's executive assistant." He took one small step in and extended his hand.

I accepted it but couldn't help my eyebrows shooting up in surprise at the name of his employer.

"As in *the* Wheldon Luxury?" I asked for confirmation.

He released my hand. "The one and only. If you have a moment," he scanned the disarray surrounding us, "I'd like to set up a time for Mr. Wheldon and you to meet."

Like I'd say no to a meeting with the owner of *the* premier luxury automaker around even standing in the center of a tornado.

Yeah, the scattered files, broken planters, ground in soil, and upturned chairs—to name a few—were not a great indicator of my business acumen, but I wasn't going to pass this opportunity up.

"I think I can spare a moment." I smiled through my blatant lie. I had a million moments for Wheldon. "And I apologize for the state we're standing in. It seems someone didn't like my style of decor."

"Well, I'm glad to know the reason you didn't get back to me was because of poor design etiquette and not because you weren't interested in a discussion with Mr. Wheldon."

My stomach dropped at his little bomb.

"I apologize for not getting back to you, but I can't say I recall meeting you." There was no way I would pass up the opportunity to work with Wheldon Luxury Automotive.

"We actually haven't met. I came by about two weeks ago and dropped my card off with another member of your staff. I was getting ready to head out of town and thought I'd drop by again."

He wasn't upset or bothered by the Sterling Custom Auto chaos. No, he rolled with the punches. I, on the other hand, was. Who on my staff didn't give me his contact information? Was it in the mess behind me? Or were there some other nefarious goings on? It didn't make sense. "Well, thank goodness you did. You wouldn't know, by chance, what Mr. Wheldon wants to discuss?"

"I'll leave the honor to him."

To say I was intrigued was putting it mildly, and because Patrick stated it would be an honor, my curiosity spiked even further.

We set a meeting for next week, said our goodbyes, and I watched Patrick get into his vehicle, then back down at the card in my hand and knew I would frame the precious little thing. My gut told me this little beauty was the bringer of something monumental.

I crossed my fingers and hoped this surprise visit was a precursor for fabulous news from my insurance adjuster, who showed up an hour later, took one step into the reception area, whistled, and then said, "Angry customer?"

It was the first time I laughed about this whole freaking predicament.

And while he was friendly and made the whole encounter seem less nerve-wracking, he was still an agent for the insurance company. So, while it wasn't the most fantastic news, it was expected. They needed the major items accounted for and a rough estimate for the smaller items. They also wanted Alex and Trent's official police report to confirm it wasn't negligence on my part. Inventorying the shop would be time-consuming and something in my control, but Alex and Trent's part was not. I knew whatever they found would be in my favor because my crew was *not* careless. It was the fact that their investigation would take longer than my itemization. And my itemization was already going to put us behind schedule on *all* my contracts.

Just great.

More phone calls and explanations.

THE ONLY THING I had left to take care of in the reception area was the mangled filing cabinet. It took some effort, but I finally opened it to find the elusive original zoning survey for Sterling Custom Auto. And, yes, I gave a little shout of triumph when I pulled it out.

A quick scan of the document confirmed my thoughts–my shop *was* in compliance.

The last twenty-four hours taught me one thing: I needed backups of my backups. So I set out to scan everything and upload it to my digital filing cabinet, starting with the survey, which I immediately sent to Mr. Quincy and Mr. Lewis's office, and a quick text to Mom and Ash to let them know I found it.

I was almost done with the scanning when I watched Max and— another brother? —step through the door.

The usual scowl on his face wasn't present. It was more of a displeased, but I'm trying not to be an ass about it, guise. Was he upset because he realized our kisses were a mistake and he didn't know how to back out without possible repercussions to the restoration of his vehicle? The other man presented as being unbothered by it all, and he was just as attractive. It's like Max had a collection of hot brothers to pull from.

I sighed.

Today was all about one step forward and two steps back for me.

"Hi, Max. What can I do for you?" I tried to be pleasant, but I wasn't sure I pulled it off at the rate I was going. I extended my hand to the newcomer and said, "Raquel Sterling, but everyone calls me Rocky."

He grasped my hand and said, "Vic. I'm Max's older brother." He shoulder-bumped Max.

"Nice to meet you, Vic."

"We stopped by to see how you were doing. To see how things were going." Max's concern and the fact he was there for me shifted something inside me, opening the barricade I had begun to erect between him and me.

We scanned the room, and I saw the progress I had made in a few short hours. "Well, as you can see, I'm almost done here. The guys are in the shop sorting it out." I sucked in a deep breath, preparing to rip the band-aid off. "I'm glad you came by. You saved me a phone call."

"Oh yeah?"

I had Max's full attention. No way to mistake it with the full effect of his bourbon eyes focused on me.

"Yup. Unfortunately, with the state of..." I lamely eyed my surroundings. "We're going to have to push back the completion date. I don't know how much more until we get the complete itemization. I really do apologize for the inconvenience, but I guarantee the quality you receive will remain the same—superb."

I braced for unpleasantness. I knew the deadline was important to him and his family. So, I knew the delay would be a problem.

"I figured as much. How long before you get things situated here?"

My mouth dropped open. I did not expect Max to accept the delay so easily.

"You okay?" His thick eyebrows lowered in confusion.

A short bark of laughter escaped Vic.

"I was gonna ask you the same thing."

"Why?" His forehead squished further.

And, good Lord, his adorableness was off the charts.

I shrugged. "Well, your usual disposition is grumpy, so I figured you'd be more sour when I told you about the delay. I wasn't expecting indifference. So, yeah, are you okay?"

He smiled.

Holy crap.

I creamed my undies.

"I'm not a total dick, no matter what my brothers say."

Vic fake coughed, and Max's smile slowly disappeared as he approached me and grabbed my hand. "You never answered me. How are you really doing?"

I stood in stunned silence. It was one thing for my friends and family to check on me, but Max? Oh yeah, that blockade was collapsing in a pile of dust.

"Well, I've had better days." Complete understatement, but with my hand in his and gazing up into his soulful eyes, my day perked back up. Wow, I never noticed the tips of his eyelashes slightly curled, giving them a cute flare. Oh, and the flecks of gold hidden in the brown of his eyes. My nerves made me blurt out, "I need more chocolate." With all the little things popping up, my intake was reaching a personal high, and I needed something to nibble on that *wasn't* Max.

And give my poor sex-deprived body a break from his nearness.

"Well then, it's your lucky day." In his other hand, he held an antique toy milk truck filled with chunks of assorted chocolates.

I stared down at it, my brain muddled with everything.

He gave it a slight shake at the same time Vic softly chuckled.

I pulled my hand out of Max's, grabbed the chocolate truck, *and* stepped away from him. "Thanks." Twice now, he has given me a vehicle-related chocolate confection. My eyes flew to his brother, but I knew I couldn't question Max about his sugary motivation. It was difficult to ignore the beauty of the two men. Three out of three Hudson brothers were biteable. "So, I gotta know. How many more Hudson boys are there?"

"One more. Cole's the oldest," Max answered.

"No girls?"

Vic shook his head. "Nope, all boys."

"I'm not sure if that's a good thing or not. Four of you..." I gave them a thorough once-over. "How'd your poor mother handle four of you?"

Wrong thing to say. Neither Max nor Vic visibly changed, but the discontentment in the air pressed heavily down on me. I considered them both. "Sorry, I didn't mean anything by it. It's just that I have an older brother, like I told you—" I tilted my head toward Max, "—who my mother claimed gave him every gray hair she has. The three of you remind me of him." Max's silence around my mother the night at Coop's niggled at me. Was there more to his mom? Or was I trying to make something out of nothing?

"Nothing to apologize for." Max brushed it off.

"How is your dad? Any improvement?" It was a lame transition, but I had some valid reasons for being off my game this morning.

"More of the same," Vic answered.

Their apprehension filled the air. "I'm sorry. I know it's difficult when a parent is down. I'll keep your dad in my thoughts for a speedy recovery."

"Thanks." Vic's one word held a hint of sorrow.

"As for speedy recoveries, I can see you've made a sizable dent here, but do you need any help? I've got time." Max continued to chisel away at my self-imposed wall.

"Umm."

The chocolate dug into my hand as I stared up at Max. It'd be so easy to gorge myself on him. Pain shot out from my hand as I squeezed the hard metal toy truck, and it was a welcome reminder to keep things professional. To remember he was a customer *while* I was at work. A little voice in the back of my head told me this weekend's date was going to be a lot of fun.

So I tried really hard to ignore his very kissable face.

Vic chuckled and broke the spell Max cast on me.

I took a step back and said, "Thanks, but the guys," I pointed to the back with Patrick's card, "and I got it."

"Wait. Is that *the* Wheldon's luxury automaker business card?" Vic didn't hide his curiosity as he focused on my hand.

"Yes, it is." I couldn't hold my smile back.

"Do you do a lot of business with them? Other luxury automakers?" Max's pride engulfed me in warm fuzzies.

"We've had the pleasure of working with various quality auto professionals. As for Wheldon, I can't say we've had the satisfaction." But hopefully, that was going to change soon.

"That's great news. Congratulations." Vic smiled.

"Well, nothing is set yet. It's just a discussion." I didn't want to jump too far ahead of myself. To jinx my recently crappy luck.

"It's formalities." Max's confidence staggered me.

The wall was such fine dust I was going to need an industrial shop vac to suck it all up.

"Do either of you have any other questions regarding the DeVille? Sorry, but I can't take you back there to see her until we clear things up."

"Nope."

I nodded at Vic and mentally braced before facing Max.

"None for me either." Max stepped closer, and the rich timbre of his voice flowed through me.

I didn't back down from the determination in his bourbon eyes and held onto my resolve not to fall prey to his charms—at work. Who was I kidding? His charms had melted my panties days ago.

He took another step closer and ran his knuckle down my cheek.

I locked my body in place, fought against the shudder Max's touch caused, and yelled at my body to stop responding uncontrollably to him.

Vic cleared his throat and snapped me out of Max's trance. I purposely stepped back and away from his magnetic pull.

I cleared my throat, which I hated the fact I had to do, and stated, "If there's nothing else, I do have work to get to." Anything to escape before I jumped Max in my reception area in front of his brother.

Not bothered by his brother's interruption, Max smiled like a man on a mission. A sexual mission. "How about lunch? Care to join us?"

Yes. No. Yes.

"Thank you, but I can't." The rest of the shop wouldn't straighten itself out by itself.

"Another time." He clearly was not bothered by the rejection.

With the smorgasbord of everything manly in front of me, I wished I didn't have a pain-in-my-ass cleanup to do because I genuinely wanted to have him for lunch.

"Come on, Maxie. We gotta head back."

Max's trademark scowl appeared as he muttered, "It's like you guys want me to kick your asses."

Vic chuckled deep and knowing.

Whoa. Good Lord.

These Hudson boys were hard on a woman's vow of celibacy.

Max

"A word of warning, brother." The somber tone in Vic's voice caught my attention.

"What?" We shot the shit most of the drive home from Sterling Custom Auto, but his solemn tone caught my regard.

"Don't sleep with her."

I snapped my head toward him. "What the fuck?" I bit out.

"Pay attention to the road."

I forced my eyes back to the road and semi-repeated my question, "What are you talking about?"

"Rocky. Don't bed her."

Every molecule in my body tensed. "Vic..."

"Don't," he interrupted me. "She's not your usual. She's not one you shrug off when you're through with her."

I breathed deeply to control the need to pull the fucking truck over to throttle my brother and waited for some of the tension to leave me before I spoke. "I know Raquel is not the kind of woman to hit it and leave it." It was more evident with each interaction I had with her.

"You're the guy who crooks his finger, and women drop their panties right then and there." Vic didn't back down.

"And you're not?"

I registered the shake of his head out of the corner of my eye.

"You're not listening."

"The fuck I'm not. You just stated I'm an uncontrollable horny dawg and demanded I stay out of Raquel's pants."

"Rocky is the girl you bring home to Dad." Vic ignored my anger.

"I know." And the idea wasn't something I was opposed to.

"He's expecting her at the family dinner at the end of the month." In other words, do whatever it takes to make Dad happy and bring her home.

"I know." I sounded like a broken record, but my brothers were harping on something I clearly knew.

I heard Vic shift in his seat before he said, "You do? Does that mean you're bringing her home to Dad?"

"How about I take her out on a date before the lot of you marry me off to her?" Because I had to know how far this feeling ran before I committed to anything but a date.

Silence.

I chanced a quick glance at Vic before looking back at the road. "Why are you staring at me?"

"I hope you do, and I hope you see what we all see." I heard him shift again. "You need to stop punishing yourself for what mom did. You deserve happiness, a good woman, and love."

But was Raquel that woman?

CHAPTER THIRTEEN

Rocky

IT'D BEEN FORTY MINUTES SINCE MAX AND VIC LEFT. FORTY minutes of catching whiffs of Max's smell in the air. Forty minutes of catching myself touching my cheek as if I could feel him. Forty minutes of catching myself daydreaming about him.

So I grabbed my purse, hollered at the guys that I was leaving, and made my way to the police station. I needed an update, even if it was just them saying they didn't know anything yet—something else to think about besides Max.

It was a short walk, which didn't help, but it was one step closer to finding answers in all this garbage surrounding me.

"Hi, Ms. Folgers. How are you today?" She once told me she took this job to escape her family. According to Ms. Folgers, her children thought of her as free daycare, and while she loved grandchildren, she was done raising babies.

"Just wonderful, Rocky. How are you today?"

"Not so bad. I was hoping I could speak with Alex and Trent?" I tilted my head toward the bullpen.

"Let me check to see if they're available, and I have to say it's just terrible that happened to your business. What is wrong with people?"

"Yeah, it's a pain, and I have no clue what would make someone want to do that." I just wished I knew what burr was up this particular person's butt so I could remove it.

She clicked away on her phone, murmured into her headset, and said, "Go on in, Rocky. They're expecting you."

"Thanks, Ms. Folgers."

After Bella and Alex's parents passed away, Bella and I spent a lot of time hanging out at the police station while Alex worked. They both needed to be with each other after such a devastating loss. To know they were together and safe. It was the one place where she didn't get continually hounded about that night in a gossipy manner.

So, I was familiar with the layout and the officers and said my hellos until I reached Alex, Trent, and Dean.

"Hey, guys. How are you all doing?" I looked at the three of them.

"All good here," Dean, the love-bitten man, said.

"Not too bad," Alex answered. "What about you?"

"Well, I've been better, but I'm not bad. And you, Trent?"

"I can't complain." As he yawned.

"I hope you're tired because you were doing something fun with Dusty—how is he, by the way?—or because you had a breakthrough in my case?" I lifted my eyebrows in question.

"So far, we don't have anything. Sorry, Rocky, I know that's not what you want to hear." Trent's face softened when he replied, "Dusty's doing great. He's the usual teenage boy."

"Good to hear about Dusty." I figured they wouldn't have anything on my case, but it still sucked to hear it. "Were you guys able to figure anything out on the video I sent you? Any ideas on how someone got my code?"

"We're still reviewing it, but we did give it to our tech guy to do his magic. We're waiting to hear back from him." Alex pulled out his note-book from the mess of papers on his desk and continued, "How often do you change your alarm code? What about your employees? How frequently do they change theirs? Do you have a cleaning crew that comes after hours? Who has access to the codes, and have you ever given them to anyone?" I'd never really been on the receiving end of Alex's cop side before. I knew he had it in him, but to experience it firsthand was kind of intimidating.

"First, you're kind of scary when you get into cop mode. Two, I change it every three or four months. Everyone does. Ash wanted us to do it more frequently, but I kept setting the alarm off because I couldn't remember the code. Three, I have a cleaning service that comes in twice a week at night, and they are under the same code change schedule as everyone else. Four, besides the alarm company, me, Mom, and Ash are the only ones with access to the master codes. And last but not least, I have never given my code to anyone. Ever." I did my best to answer every one of Alex's questions.

"When you arm or disarm your system, are you by yourself? Is anyone ever with you? Staff or not? You said you had trouble remembering it. Does that mean you write it down somewhere? Keep it on your phone?" Trent continued Alex's line of questioning.

"No, I've never written it down. Again, Ash drilled me about security, so I know not to do that. Sometimes, I get to the shop before everyone else. Other times, the guys are there before me." I studied Trent. "Do you think someone watched me put my code in? That it might be someone on my staff?" My brain wouldn't let that thought be possible. They weren't just staff. They were family. I couldn't, wouldn't believe it.

"I'm saying the suspect list is short," he somewhat evaded.

"What about prints?" There had to be something they could use.

"I had the tech guys come out and dust for fingerprints, but you have a lot of traffic in and out of there to have too much hope. Besides, the guy had on gloves the whole time. As soon as that's complete, I'll get the report to you so you can file a claim with the insurance company," Alex answered.

"Shit. I forgot about his hands being covered." He wasn't taking any chances. The dickhead couldn't get away. He had to have left something behind.

"We're going to need a list of people who were there when you disarmed the alarm since the last time you reset the codes." Alex pushed me to think of someone who could have betrayed me.

"I can't..." I sucked in a deep breath. "The thought of someone I work with daily being responsible for this." I blew out a breath. "I'm going to need some time to think about it." This was going to hurt more than it already did.

"I know this sucks, Rocky, but we'll figure this out." Dean tried to temper some of my discomfort.

"Thanks, I appreciate your guys' help." I hesitated, unsure if I should bring up the missing business card.

"What?" Alex and Trent barked at me while Dean lifted one finely sculpted eyebrow.

I broke down my conversation with Patrick from that morning regarding his absent calling card and how I spoke with everyone on employment with Sterling Custom Auto, and that they all stated they have yet to talk to him. "So, that means Patrick gave his card to someone who represented themself as an employee of mine because he doesn't strike me as someone who lies. I was also going to say my staff wouldn't either, but you two are making me doubt that."

"Have you found it in the mess?" Dean asked.

"Nope. I cleaned the reception area before I came here. Nothing," I answered. "But I will go back into the security system and review the day Patrick stated he came in. I want to see if I can recognize whoever he spoke to."

"You did the right thing by telling us. I will need his contact information to talk to him about who he left the card with. I'll make sure to relate it as a part of this ongoing investigation," Alex said.

Trent picked up where Alex stopped. "Is there anything else you can think of that we should know? Anything small that you would normally blow off? Regardless of whether you think it's related, we need to know." Trent pushed me for more answers.

"Besides the zoning, traffic and parking, noise, and nuisance complaints? Nothing." And now they had me questioning all my interactions.

"Hmm. Bella told me about that." Dean murmured.

"I'll speak with Kevin about it and verify it's unrelated," Alex said.

"I don't think they are related. I think it's Kevin's way of getting me to be his baby momma." He wasn't a get-down, dirty type of guy. "And the complaints were filed anonymously. I've filed an appeal to have it released, but the computer systems are down at City Hall, so it might be a few days." I leaned into Alex and Trent; hope took flight inside me. "Hey, can you guys get that information released sooner?"

"No, sorry. We'd need to obtain a warrant, and we don't have probable cause for it at this time." Alex shot down my expectant butterflies.

"You're just a party pooper." I stuck my tongue out at Alex.

"Wait. What do you mean? Do you think this is Kevin's attempt at extortion?" Trent's eyebrows shot up in disbelief.

"I don't know. I thought so, and then I didn't." I shrugged. "Kevin's confusing me. I told Mr. Quincy about it, and he said since Kevin wasn't blatant about his proposal, there wasn't much Mr. Quincy could do but that he'd look into it anyway." I held up my hand to stop their objections. "If Kevin is using his position to do something as outrageous as this, then I will run down here and do whatever I need to do to get him arrested. But I don't want to come after Kevin erroneously until Mr. Quincy confirms my suspicions and there aren't any uncertainties regarding this horrendous possibility." But the second it was verified, all bets were off.

"We hear you, but we'll speak with Mr. Quincy anyway," Alex, the cop, not my friend, told me.

"Well, he's out of the office, but Mr. Lewis handles things while Mr. Quincy is gone," I warned them.

"Noted," Trent replied.

"Anyone or anything else you can think of?" Dean asked.

I shook my head, uncertain if I should throw Carson or Desk Bimbo in the mix.

"Don't hold back. Let us figure out if it's relevant or not," Trent advised me.

"I don't want to speak any more ill of Carson or the woman I found him with than warranted," and it *was* warranted, "but do you think they had something to do with this? I mean, Carson is a creep, not a thief." I never thought I'd vouch for him, but there I was. "And from what I heard, she's more of a corporate bedroom marauder." I shrugged. "Neither were happy when I broke it off with him."

Alex scratched his chin. "Dean did mention something along the lines that Carson said you would regret not taking him back. This might be his way of getting back at you. And what about the woman? Do you know her name?" Alex was in full investigative mode.

"Like I told you, Carson is a cheating, lying bastard, but he's not a thief. Even if he is a successful banker or maybe because he is." I shrugged. "As for getting back at me, he'll take his car somewhere else and have his buddies do the same. That's how I had an opening in my schedule to take on the DeVille. He'll go the financial route, not the physical route. Anything else is beneath him." While I agreed with Bella's assessment of Carson on many things, I couldn't grasp this one. "As for his *liaison*? I can give you the company she worked for but not her name. We didn't get to introductions."

"That'll work too," Alex said.

"What exactly was this threat? When did it occur?" Trent questioned me like the police detective he was and kept at the Carson angle.

"Suit yourself, but I'm telling you, I can't see Carson doing do this. It was last week. He's mad because I won't take him back." I shook my head. "No, that's not true. His ego was bruised because I thwarted his avenue toward a prospective client. Anyways, he came by the shop attempting to coax his way back. When I refused, he said I would regret it." I shrugged. "Carson's all chest puffing and no action. He's harmless." I hoped so.

"How long ago did you and Carson separate? Did anybody else hear him?" Trent didn't let it go.

"About a month and a half ago." When I caught him screwing the auto representative on my desk. "No. No one heard him, but Kevin might have seen Carson when he stomped out of the shop."

Both Trent and Alex jotted notes on their little notepads. "We know you're having issues with Kevin and Carson, but we will need to talk to them. We'll ensure it doesn't add to your stress load," Trent promised me.

"I'd appreciate that. I don't need Kevin or Carson upping their douche factor." Neutral was more than enough. "Anything else you guys need from me before I take off?"

They all shook their heads. "No, but we'll keep you updated if we find anything out," Alex said.

"Thanks. See you guys later."

CHAPTER FOURTEEN

Rocky

I MADE MY WAY OUT OF THE POLICE STATION AND WANDERED TO Central Park. My mind was flipping through the horrible possibility that someone I cared for was behind all this ugliness. My soul vehemently rejected the idea. No matter what the appalling evidence tried to tell us, we were a family.

It was my third time around the green when I decided to call Bella and ask her out for lunch. I needed to center myself before putting pen to paper in what I felt was a betrayal against my family.

And like any great best friend, Bella met me at Harper's Corner. It was the best mom-and-pop diner in Feldspar. Although with Emma leading the helm, it was turning more into Sunday dinner bests at mom and dads without the dressy attire with all the scrumptious food.

It was also Bella's and my go-to whenever we ate out, and the reason why I focused on my delicious meal and not Bella because if I had been, I would have seen the sparkle in her eye, letting me know she was up to something.

"Soooo, have you received any more delectables from Max? Or, you know, tasted more of Max?" Bella asked right before she bit into her hamburger.

I choked on my salad. Figures Bella would ask me something ridiculous while I had food in my mouth. I reached for my water and sipped to soothe my throat. "What kind of question is that?"

"Well, you two steamed up the coffee shop last week, and you told me about the sizzling stroll around the block. Not to mention the soul-melting kisses you two shared." She shrugged and feigned innocence.

"He did give me a toy truck filled with chocolate." I took another bite before Bella could grill me for more information.

Bella's smug smile almost made me want to smash the rest of my lunch in her face. Almost. It was a delicious salad.

"I bet he did." She pointed her finger at me. "Don't think I haven't noticed that you haven't made time to go dress shopping for your date this weekend."

"A, I'm going casual because he said something about heights, which doesn't constitute a dress. B. Don't get your hopes up, Bella." Because I needed someone to keep my feet firmly planted on the ground since I was doing a terrible job by myself. "He's just being nice because I'm working on his vehicle." Liar, liar, pants on fire. Because I knew a quick spin in the backseat wouldn't be amiss. Okay, with Max, I was confident a quickie wouldn't suffice.

Her smile disappeared. "Do you think so? Or is he financially conservative?"

I sighed. "No, I'm just using it as an excuse to keep some barrier between him and me." There was only so much lying to myself I could stomach. "And, you do *know* how much I charge, right?"

"That means I don't have to entice you ladies into ordering dessert because Rocky is loaded." Emma teased us.

Like we'd need enticement for Emma's baked deliciousness. Harper's yummy factor ratcheted to unbelievable since she took over after her family's debacle.

"Heck yeah. I want your chocolate cream pie."

Bella nodded enthusiastically. "Me too."

"Let me guess. Chocolate cream pie?" Dean stopped by Bella's side and bent down to kiss her quickly.

"Oh yeah." Bella's smile insinuated so much more than dessert.

Imitating throwing up, I demanded, "You two are souring my appetite for sugar. Knock it off." In truth, I hoped they never did.

"How many times do I have to tell you not to do that with my sister in front of me?" Alex agreed, but for a whole other reason.

Trent laughed the laugh of a longtime friend who'd watched his friend's discomfort at his sister's hormonal antics for years. "Would you rather some other guy do that with Bella?"

"Fuck no." Dean's growl permeated the air.

Both Dean and Alex glared at Trent.

Emma chuckled. "Will you guys be joining the ladies?"

"Not today. We're only stopping to grab something to go." Trent shook his head.

"Everything okay?" Bella's voice pitched with worry as she leaned toward them.

"Yeah, it's just work." Alex pulled out his big brother expression.

Bella sat back and threw her balled-up napkin at Alex, who deftly caught it before it ever reached his face.

"I'll be right back with the pie." Emma walked away smiling.

"Do you have to be such a pain as my big brother?" Bella eyed her utensils as alternative missiles.

"Yup," Alex smirked.

At Bella's aggravated growl, Dean grabbed her hands before she lobbed her utensils.

Trent and Alex smiled, and the women sitting in the booth beside us stopped mid-conversation.

I leaned forward and warned the women. "Let me help you ladies out. They're both twenty-eight and single. Chocolate goodness right here," I pointed to Trent, "co-parents his nine-year-old with his not-so-pleasant ex-wife. Peanut butter blossom here," this time I pointed to Alex, "doesn't have any kids or psycho exes. They're both police detectives but total pigs. I mean, being a cop doesn't mean they have to imitate the whole persona of being a swine." I shook my head in grave mockness. "But I saw it with my own eyes, a total pigsty." Yes, I may have left out it was a dump because it was ransacked after Alex was kidnapped. Technically, I'd never been inside Trent's house, but he did have a young son, so it wasn't too far-fetched of an assumption.

They slowly blinked and eyed both Trent and Alex. I was sure pondering if they wanted to attempt to handle all that for the hotness before them.

Alex and Trent's scowls confirmed they didn't find my statements funny, even as Bella snorted through her laughter.

"Excuse me, guys. I've got some goodness here I must deliver safely." Emma's cheerful voice stopped me from harpening further on Trent and Alex's bachelorhood and my case. Who was I kidding? She had chocolate.

The guys stepped back to allow Emma through with the plates of pie and I did a little happy clap once the goodness was in front of me.

"That's our cue." Alex stepped forward and gave Bella and me a peck on our cheeks. "Ladies, enjoy your pie."

I loved how Alex treated me as another sister. It comforted me when Ashton wasn't around.

Trent's sendoff was sedate compared to Dean's farewell kiss he planted on Bella.

"I know Dean's yours, Bella, but those three guys could make a girl give up chocolate." Emma placed our pies in front of us.

She wasn't joking. They were mouthwatering, but Max was the only man my body consciously considered giving chocolate up for. It was like he'd become my new addiction.

"True. Unfortunately, they're all like brothers to me." I shoved a piece of pie in my mouth.

"I don't think Rocky has a problem with chocolate being a replacement," Bella deadpanned.

"Yeah, sweets are great for a lot of things," Emma concurred. "If you need anything else, just holler." She hurried away just as quickly as she came.

"Now that they've left, tell me if you finished watching the video? Did you see anyone?" She sipped her water before she continued, "I was going to ask Alex and Trent if they had any updates on your case, but I know how stingy they are about discussing anything related to their cases."

"I spoke with Alex, Trent, and Dean before I called you. I also stayed up and watched more. The jerk entered the shop around two-thirty in the morning, disarmed my alarm system with *my* code, and then went to town wreaking havoc inside." Chills shot down my spine at the reminder someone close to me was out to get me.

Bella stopped with her fork midway to her mouth. "Your code? As in your personal code? Not a long-forgotten code?" She watched me in puzzlement.

I swallowed my bite of pie. "Yup. My code. He was also covered from head to toe in black. Nothing was visible except for his eyes, which I couldn't identify because he kept his head averted. Needless to say, I reset all the codes." I wasn't going to give the asshole another chance at causing more chaos.

"How many people have access to your code?" Bella put her fork down as the severity of the situation hit her.

"Nobody. Everyone has their own codes. I told Alex and Trent the same thing. They think someone watched me input it and used it. Now they want me to come up with a list of people from the last three months—since the last time I changed it—that could have seen me enter it." I sucked in breath at the pain of the thought. "I just can't believe someone I know, someone I would let that close to me, could be responsible for all of this." I couldn't wrap my head around it.

"Shit," Bella whispered. "I'm so sorry, Rocky."

"Thanks." I drank some of my water. "I forgot to tell you, but I spoke with Ash yesterday before you came over, and he thinks this is personal. At first, I didn't agree with him, but after I watched the security footage, I couldn't come up with an argument against it. The creep's first move after disarming the system was to take the photo and destroy the shelf it was on. Kind of hard to argue after that."

"Double shit. But everyone knows what the picture signifies, so maybe it's not about you but the shop itself. Have you had any bad experiences with customers lately? I mean, someone who was pissed more than usual about their car? The invoice? Anything?" Bella did her best to get me out of the madman's limelight.

"Hmm. I hadn't thought about it like that. I will have to think about it and talk to the guys at the shop. Maybe they had an encounter with someone." It was another avenue to explore that didn't point the finger at my chosen family.

"Anyways, I gave the video and logs to Alex and Trent. Their tech guy is doing his magic, so hopefully they find something I didn't." Anything would be great. "And they haven't had any luck with the prints because, again, the dick wore gloves."

"Well, if anyone can find something, it'll be Petey. He's a genius behind the computer." Bella did her best to give me hope.

"I hope so."

"Now, tell me about the Wheldon rep who came by earlier. What did he want?" Bella demanded before taking a bite of her pie.

"He wasn't just any Wheldon rep. He was Mr. Wheldon's executive assistant, and he scheduled a meeting with me and Mr. Wheldon." I barely contained my excitement.

Bella's mouth dropped open. "Holy shit! That's fantastic news!"

"I know, right?! But nothing is a done deal yet. It's only a discussion."

"Discussion, baloney. Sterling Custom Auto is landing a contract with *the* most desired luxury automaker." Bella leaned toward me. "And they sought *you*."

Bella's words bounced around in my skull. She was right. They approached me.

My father built Sterling Custom Auto and its reputation on hard work and integrity. When he passed away, Ash and my mother ran the business the same way until I took over several years ago. I didn't alter the foundational principles my dad utilized, but Bella was right. *I* was running Sterling Custom Auto, not my father. My daily decisions repeatedly brought customers back, and now, *the* luxury automaker in the nation came to my doorstep.

I pumped my fist and shouted, "Hot damn!"

Bella's only response was to shake her head at me.

Screw Kevin and his antiquated views. I was Raquel "Rocky" Marie Sterling. Businesswoman, possible future wife to some hot guy I planned on meeting in the hopefully not too distant future, and mother to our mini beautiful kids we copiously enjoyed making. Max's face popped up, telling me I had already met the scrumptious mancake who would be thrilled to enthusiastically procreate and make gorgeous babies with me.

I couldn't get upset at Bella's smug smile, but I did point my fork at her and said, "Don't get too cocky. It doesn't change the fact men will continue to question and doubt me."

She shrugged. "Yeah, that sucks, but it doesn't matter. They're still coming to you." She dug into her pie and casually stated, "You know, something you could be doing with Max."

"What?"

She stopped with her fork midway to her mouth and answered, "Coming."

I almost choked on my pie.

"Damn it, Bella! Would you stop that?!"

She wriggled her eyebrows up and down.

"I'll admit Max makes me want to take a bite out of him. A tiny nibble." Lots and lots of nibbles. "But he is my customer, which worries me a little." I raised my hand and stopped Bella before she could rebuke my no hanky panky with the customer rule. My upcoming date with Max called me a hypocrite as I tried to justify that I wouldn't be sleeping with him, so it didn't count.

"If you're adamant about keeping that stupid rule, then I suggest you finish that car. Fast." Bella shoved a bite of pie in her mouth.

"You can't rush something like that." I scrunched my nose at the thought.

"Besides, no one said you had to sleep with him on the first date." Bella's eyes twinkled. "And if you're going to be a stickler for the rules, there are other preliminary pleasurable activities available."

I choked on my pie.

"Sorry, Rocky, you're going down." Her palm met the front of my nose. "Before you object, you didn't see what I saw. The man ogles you like he wants to devour you. One reciprocal tiny little nibble at a time." She fanned her face. "And don't think I haven't noticed all the chocolate delights he's been bewitching you with. He may not know the true significance of the gifts, but the man is unquestionably hitting very close to home."

It sucked having a best friend sometimes because it made it hard to ignore the chocolate spells Max was casting on me. He unintentionally batted at all my spots—my dad, cars, and plain mouthwatering delectation.

"Okay, fine. There's chemistry, but that doesn't mean anything." Liar. "If I allow myself, I could have chemistry with a sack of potatoes or worse, Kevin."

We both shuddered.

"I know Carson was a major dick, and you've suffered some hits to your business acumen lately, but I'm worried about you. I know you promised to keep the door ajar on any prospects, but your guard is high. I know it's justified, but how will you spot a good one if you can't even peek around the corner?"

I loved my best friend.

"If he's a good one, I won't need to peer around the corner. He'll be right there in front of me." I winked at Bella.

"Or in you."

CHAPTER FIFTEEN

Max

"Do me a favor?" I tried my best not to let my smile slip through, to give Paul a false sense of seriousness.

"Anything. You know that." Paul, not missing the solemnity, immediately gave me his full attention.

I opened the door to Margie's coffee shop and carried on with my somber tone and as straight of a face as I could muster, which was difficult, and said, "It's been a week since we've been here, and I'm hoping you've pulled yourself together in that time. So, when we get up there, don't embarrass me."

Paul didn't bother with a verbal response. No, his middle finger said it all.

"Man, don't be like that. You're not the one standing here watching you rip your man card to shreds," I teased him.

"That's not what they say." Paul didn't miss a beat.

I couldn't hold back my bark of laughter as I turned to him in disbelief. "Really?"

The jolt on my shoulder forced me to straighten forward. "Sorry."

My mouth snapped shut at the vision of Carson, and I clenched my jaw as unexpected annoyance filled me.

"Oh, no. My apologies. I was distracted by my phone." He lifted his phone as confirmation, and I watched recognition spread across his pompous mug. "Oh, wait. Max, right?" He looked over at Paul next to me. "And Paul?"

"Yup." And, how convenient was it that we ran into him again? What the hell was it with this guy? Was he staking out the coffee shop for our return days later?

"Back for more of Margie's savory coffee?" His smile was as fake as he was.

"Yeah." My tone stated that no further conversation was welcome.

Something the jackhole didn't heed. "The scenery isn't bad either." His eyes roamed over Margie's ass as his tone verbalized he imagined a whole lot more.

Paul walked past him to the dessert counter and intentionally blocked Carson's view of Margie.

Carson tried to mask his irritation with a sip from his cup. "I'm taking it with the coffee stop that you're going to Rocky's? Shit. How's the DeVille? Did it sustain any damage during the break-in?" His fabricated sincerity annoyed me.

His acting was a joke–like him.

"Unfortunately, it didn't escape harm." The itch between my shoulder blades blazed with his innocent enough question. Something in me knew not to tell him anything. Something in me also told me he was full of shit in his fabricated concern. Something unknown and potent in me knew I had to defend Raquel from him. "But I'm not worried. Raquel's demonstrated she is more than capable of delivering on her word."

"Hmm." Carson viewed the dessert case, doing his damnedest to act thoughtful.

Too bad the asshole had sleazy dickhead written all over him. I couldn't imagine what banking intellect Raquel saw in this guy.

"I'm sorry about the road bump you've encountered with the DeVille's deadline, but it's good to know Rocky is keeping to the standards her father built the company on." Carson's pause was deliberate and all for show. "Most customers wouldn't be as forgiving as you." He put his hands up in a placating gesture in an attempt to state he wasn't one of them. "As her banking associate, I must ensure her less-than-stellar management doesn't impact the business. So, it's good to hear her customer speak highly of the work she's putting out."

Every word out of his slick mouth felt like sandpaper against my skin, and the desire to rip his tongue out with an aviation snip was difficult to restrain.

"Well then, as her *banking associate,* I'm sure you're happy about the Wheldon Automotive contract." Of course, I had no idea whether or not it was definite. Still, as someone who claimed to be her financial advisor, an advocate for said client, he insinuated a lot of doubt regarding her business acumen.

Carson froze for a split second. Hmm, this was new news to Mister Banking Associate.

"Well, I can't discuss client business." Bullshit. He dropped dubious comments every time we met. "But, of course, any possible contracts with Wheldon Automotive is a boon for any business." Most people would believe Carson's good ole boy persona if they weren't paying attention. Too bad I'd had years of dealing with pompous asses to know better.

"Of course. Either way, the possibility in itself speaks volumes." I stepped forward and made it clear any further conversation was not welcome and ended with, "Good thing for me Raquel has such high-quality standards in her business dealings."

Carson's scowl made it clear he didn't like being dismissed, nor did he like someone disagreeing with him. All of my spidey senses flared bright red, and it took a lot more control to not turn around and demand the shithead stay away from Raquel.

Paul gave me a side-eye. "Is the dick gone?"

I turned back around, and through the front window, I saw Carson walking away.

"Yup." Something told me Carson's presence wouldn't be easy to get rid of. Now, I had to figure out if it bothered me because of what it would mean to Raquel or the DeVille.

"What did His Doucheness have to say this time?" Paul glanced over his shoulder and back.

"Just for that, your coffee is on the house," Margie interrupted before I could answer.

"Just the coffee?"

She patted his cheek and purred, "I'm worth more than the mutual distaste for His Doucheness, and that's saying something because my *café*..." She trailed off, her body undulated from the memory of the taste.

Paul leaned forward and pulled out his panty-dropping smile. "Woman, your nectar could bring a grown man to his knees." He ogled her up and down. "Not that I'd mind being on my knees in front of you."

"Girl, he's hot, a smooth talker, and confident enough to let you know he wants you." Margie's female customer slowly eyed Paul up and down. "Mmm hmmm, I say let the man kneel before you."

"She ain't lying," her friend agreed.

"Like anything worth eating, you must first appreciate the taste of each delicious ingredient—a subtle foreplay with your food. What you don't do is shove the whole thing in your mouth all at once. Instead, you savor each delectable tiny bite at a time." Margie winked at Paul. "And there's a lot to love about me."

"Have mercy on me." He placed his hand over his heart.

I shoved Paul's shoulder and demanded, "Man, have some dignity. You're embarrassing yourself and ruining the Hudson name."

He flipped me off and then leaned toward Margie. "You heard the man. You're damaging my fragile ego." He leaned closer to Margie and whispered, "How about a kiss to make up for it?"

She leaned closer, leaving a bare inch between them, and outlined his bottom lip with her finger. "I think you're—big enough to handle it."

"Excuse me, Margie. The brewer is stuck. I tried to unstick it, but the filter started leaking, so I put towels down to soak it up. But it wouldn't stop, so I shut off the water line connected to it. I'm so sorry, but I don't know how to fix it." Margie's meek employee quietly rambled her explanation and wrung her hands together, waiting for Margie's reaction.

"No worries, Willow. Remember I told you it gets stuck, and all you have to do is jiggle the green line behind it? So why don't you try it before I come back?" Margie encouraged her.

"Umm... okay," Willow said with all the confidence of a church mouse as she glanced at Paul and then back at Margie before she headed back to the machine.

"Anything else I can do for you boys before I rescue Willow?"

I shoved Paul to the side and answered, "Yes. Two of all your chocolate desserts."

"Trying to butter Rocky up?" Margie's question implied so much more.

"I wouldn't say that." Butter wasn't exactly what I wanted to spread on Raquel.

"Chocolate, maybe," Paul mumbled under his breath.

"Keep it up, and you can walk your ass home."

"Margie'd give me a ride."

"Dreams, baby, dreams." Placing a container full of chocolates on the counter, Margie turned to me. "I gave you everything Rocky likes."

"I appreciate it." I paid for the bag of goodness and told Paul, "All right, if you two are done flirting, I wanna head out."

"Man, you have got to loosen up." Paul pointed to the chocolate. "Hopefully, this helps you with that."

I hoped the same thing. Another taste of Raquel and I prayed everything would settle.

I opened my mouth to thank Margie when I heard, "Max. Paul." And everything inside me soured at *her* voice.

My muscles locked, my jaw clenched, and my brain spiked with disgust as I turned to face the one woman who destroyed our family and ruined my view of all things female.

My mother.

Delilah Sampson.

"Mom."

A silence descended over the shop at Paul's one word.

"How are you boys faring?"

She left us and never looked back. As kids, *her* kids, we repeatedly tried to reach out to her. To get her to come back. When it was evident it wouldn't happen, we reverted to trying to get her to attend our school events, sports, anything. Delilah rarely answered our phone calls, and messages were just as scarce. She made it clear—we were not her concern. We were no longer her family. So, the fact she stood there and asked us how we were doing? No fucking way.

"Good, and you?" Paul never gave up on her, no matter how many times we boys talked to him, and after our last conversation, I assumed he'd given up on Mom.

"I am doing well." It was both a statement and a correction. "Max?"

"Do you care?" My name in her mouth put acid in mine.

"Is that any way to speak to your mother?"

She was impeccable in appearance and taste. Luckily for us, our father taught us what really mattered was what most people didn't glimpse with the naked eye. Values, integrity, honor, truthfulness, loyalty, and more. The things she didn't have nor taught us.

"If I had a mom, no."

"Max," Paul quietly reprimanded me. He never liked it when I bit into her. He was the ever-loving can't we get along guy.

I didn't blame him. He was too young to really grasp the enormity of her actions like Cole, Vic, and I did. Paul just knew Mom was there one day and gone the next.

"When are you going to let this go? I mean, it's been years. I'd think you'd move on from this silliness by now." She shook her very coiffed head in disappointment.

Her words felt like I had been struck by aircraft-grade aluminum tubing.

"Every word you speak just proves my point. You have no clue."

"That is no way to speak to a lady. I'm not surprised though, with *your* father raising you boys."

I froze. Delilah did not have the right to speak about how Dad raised us. He did everything for us. He bent over backward to make sure we had what we needed. He attended every *fucking* event, teacher conference, games, all of it. While she remained completely absent in every sense of the word.

"Do not *ever* speak of my father again. You do not have the right. You gave it up nineteen years ago." Each word out of my mouth was forced through my clenched jaw. It hurt to get them out with the fury riding me.

"Stop. Both of you." Paul gave the coffee shop a once over. "This isn't the time nor the place."

Before I could apologize to Margie, Willow tripped on her way past Delilah. The coffee cup in her hand flew forward and landed with a heavy thunk as it splintered into several pieces, and coffee spilled everywhere.

Delilah took a step away from the mess, nose up in the air, but looked down at Margie and stated with all her pretentious arrogance, "It's obvious you haven't cleaned your shop yet."

"I'm so sorry. I don't know how I tripped. I was just walking, and my foot caught on, I don't know." Willow's words were barely audible as she bent down, head lowered, avoided all eye contact, and picked up the debris.

"Why don't you throw that away and clean yourself up?" Margie helped Willow up. "I got this."

"You know you'd save yourself so much expense and headache if you just removed the incompetencies around you." Mom tried to educate Margie and failed miserably.

"Like you did us?" Two could play this spiteful game.

Mom opened her mouth to respond, but Paul beat her to it. "Mom, why don't you and I go out to breakfast? Then, we can catch up." Paul gently tugged her elbow, leading her out the door and away from me.

I bent down next to Margie and took the cloth from her hand. "Go grab a mop, and I'll take care of this." Because my father did raise us right.

Even though Margie stayed in her bent position next to me, she grabbed my attention with the steely conviction in her tone and asked, "Are you okay?"

I twisted my neck from side to side and tried to release the tension that had built up. "Yeah. Just another day with the wicked witch."

She scanned my face to ascertain if I was full of shit. "It's not my business, and I don't know you or Paul very well, but your *pai* raised two amazing human beings. You have every right to be proud of your dad and the sacrifices he made for you and your family. But, more importantly, you have every right to be happy with the lessons he provided you. So don't let that *bruxa* take everything he endured for you go to waste."

Margie unknowingly delivered the most effective blow with her parting words. All these years, everything my dad did, he did so us boys would have what we needed. Opportunities opened for us, and he never once balked at the cost or the time it took for him. And it did. We played every sport available and did almost everything else we ever asked for. He made it all happen without once bitching about the cost or time. And there I was, holding on to the wicked witch's lessons instead of the more potent, valuable teachings of the one true person I admired—my dad.

Vindictive

What the hell was their problem? A vandalized shop and car, doubts regarding the ability to deliver on something they made clear was important to them, yet they went about their business as if nothing was wrong.

It was apparent they were being led around by their dicks. Yeah, Rocky's body was worth a spin. Underneath the greasy overalls, her curves were noticeable. And, like the average Joe, I imagined Rocky more than once splayed on the hood of one of her builds. Her thick brown hair spread across it with her back arched, offering her plump tits to me. And those legs? Fuck yeah, she'd have them open wide, pussy glistening for me. Ready for the pounding I'd give her. But that didn't mean I would let her sweet cunt control my cock. No, fucking way. I'd be the one controlling her, and, in the end, she'd beg for it.

They always did.

I watched his truck pull away and knew Max wanted in Rocky's pants. Anyone not blind could see the way he watched her. I didn't have a problem with that. He could have her *after* I was finished with her.

No matter what I did, she wasn't giving in. Instead, she was sticking to her self-righteous morals and digging those hideous work boots in the ground. Finding ways to get around the mishaps, blinding people with her assets, and pulling a fast one on men who let their damn dicks lead them around.

Obviously, I had to step my game up. Because, after what she did to me?

There is no way I would allow Rocky to succeed.

CHAPTER SIXTEEN

Max

HUDSON FLIGHT SCHOOL WAS MY BABY, EVEN THOUGH VIC WAS MY partner. It was my vision, my determination, and my dream that brought it to life. I never purposefully shared it with a woman.

Except for today.

Today, I deliberately made the choice to share my dream, myself, with Raquel.

She proved at every turn that she wasn't like any other woman out there. She'd been upfront and transparent about every possible charge the DeVille might incur. She'd been forthright about any delays and adamant that Sterling Custom Auto would provide the best possible product no matter what. Even if it meant Raquel took a financial hit.

So the peace and joy I felt for flying soared as I watched her bounce up and down in excitement as she entered the hangar.

"I'm so freaking excited!" She spun toward me. "Can we do loop-the-loops? Spirals?"

"Sure, why not." Her enthusiasm was contagious.

"Right on!"

A chuckle escaped me. It was like watching a little kid in a candy store.

"Don't laugh at me. I've never been on an airplane before, and commercial airplanes don't count. This baby is a two-seater where I'm gonna be at the helm and get a bird's eye view of everything."

Being up in the air was the only thing that ever gave me any kind of reprieve from life, from the pain my mom left with me. But this last week with Raquel was coming in stronger than the skies.

And her infectious eagerness to be up there, to experience something that meant everything to me, only heightened my feelings for her.

"I've already done all the prechecks, so all we need to do is climb in."

She took off so fast her hair flew behind her as she ran to the boarding stairs.

I shook my head at her earnestness, but my soul felt the lightest it'd been in years. Her exaltation for something I cherished lifted me in more ways than I ever thought possible.

Once we were up in the air, Raquel's head pivoted from side to side, doing her best to take everything in from every angle. She was so fascinated by it all that she completely ignored the chocolate desserts I gave her. She grilled me countlessly on everything in the cockpit. What did this gadget do? What about that button? If she pulled the lever back, would the plane nosedive? How did I make the plane go faster? What was the fastest I ever flew the plane? Could I do tricks?

She reignited my love for flying with her boundless curiosity.

As we landed, she finally asked, "How did you get into flying?"

"Dad. He made sure all of us boys had something to do. He knew if we had any idle time, we'd get up to no good, so he kept us all occupied with one thing or another. I didn't care for sports, but I liked being up high. I made a fort up in the tree in our backyard. The higher, the better. Dad couldn't get me out of it." I shrugged. "So, he got me flying lessons for my birthday, and that was it."

"What about Vic? He's your partner, right?"

We hadn't moved from our spots inside the plane.

"Yeah. Dad was working and couldn't make it back in time to drive me to my lesson one day, so Vic did. While waiting for me, he struck up a conversation with another pilot, and one thing led to another, and next thing we know, he's up in the air."

"What did your mom think about you flying? Or was this after your mom left?"

"She didn't. Flying came after she left. Dad worked a ton to make ends meet, but he never prevented us from pursuing our dreams or trying new things. Mom didn't like it. She wanted him to spend any extra money on things she wanted." I shook my head. "To this day, I still don't understand how she birthed four children knowing she'd have to care for them but yet didn't."

"Not that this excuses her behavior, but did your dad spoil her before Cole was born? I mean, was she pampered before the addition of four more mouths to feed?"

I shook my head. "No, and yes. From all the stories I've heard, Dad spoiled her with love and attention. Everything a husband should indulge his wife with. But, those weren't the riches my mom wanted. She wanted material things and the money to do as she wished. How she thought she'd get all that hitching her star to a blue-collared man, I don't know." I shrugged in confusion.

"Wow, your mom sounds like a real peach. She kind of reminds me of one of Margie's customers. She's very much into her appearance, thinks everyone should be in service to her, but misses that she's just as human as the rest of us." Delilah fit his mother's image perfectly.

Max's eyebrows shot to his hairline. "Let me guess. Perfectly straight brown hair down to the middle of her back. Not a single hair was out of place, and absolutely no gray. Her perfectly put-together face does not have any visible signs of aging, and her tailored clothes accentuate and fit perfectly."

"No freaking way! It can't be!"

"Delilah Sampson—the one and only unmotherly mother," I confirmed.

Raquel's irresistible mouth dropped open.

"Shit, Max. I'm sorry. I can't even make that work." She looked flustered because she was unable to find a way to create the impression that my mother wasn't a total self-centered cow. "But it explains why you got quiet around my mom the other night at Coop's."

And, for the first time when speaking about my mother, I laughed.

Her smile was hesitant. She was unsure if she should laugh with me or cry for me.

I reached out, grabbed her hand, and held it on my lap, letting her know it was okay. "Yeah, I'm not used to seeing real moms at work. By the way, my dad wants you at the family dinner next week. It's super casual, and it's his way of checking in on us and ensuring we're all good." I gently squeezed her hand, hoping it conveyed how much I wanted her to meet my dad and family. "I'd love it if you came too, but I should warn you. Dad's been on the rampage for grandkids. I'm not trying to scare you off, but I just wanted to give you a heads-up."

Raquel sighed and plopped her head back on the seat. "Oh my God. We can't get our parents together. My mother also wants grand-babies. Between the two of them, we'll be plopping out the next gener-ation of Hudson/Sterling mini-humans by the middle of next year." She shook her head from side to side. "Besides, my mother will freak out if I have a meal with your family before she can make you dinner," she said to the roof of the cockpit before she turned to face me. "Mom's longtime frenemy, Betsy, heard or saw us together, and now Mom is insisting she makes us, your family included, a joining of the families–her hopeful meaning–banquet when Ash gets back in town, which won't be for another week, two max. Is there any way we can combine the two family meals without you totally thinking I'm trying to hitch myself to you, and you take off running for the hills?"

Raquel looked adorably unsure of herself, and it warmed me. She wanted us to work and was nervous about how I would respond.

Nope. Raquel was not like other women.

I reached out, pulled her head toward me, and gave her a quick kiss.

I pulled slightly back and said, "Would it be horrible if we gave our parents each of their numbers to coordinate the meeting of the fami-lies?" I stared into her dazed eyes as she slowly blinked.

"Uh, yeah. Horrible idea. Mom will have us married and pregnant before dessert," she mumbled.

I smiled. "So, boy, girl, twins?"

Raquel's eyes popped wide open, and I laughed before I kissed her again.

Her taste was addictive. She was earth, fire, and all woman. And she went straight to my cock.

I fisted her hair in my hand and kept her where I wanted so I could plunder her mouth. I gorged on her flavor.

She grabbed my head and kept me fused to her.

Giving and taking.

She moaned into my mouth and ramped the growing need inside me. I pulled away from her mouth and kissed down her neck. I licked and sucked the taut cord in her neck. She squirmed in her seat as I made my way down to her cleavage. Her breasts pumped up and down as her breathing grew erratic.

I wasn't about to let the opportunity pass me and, with my other hand, rubbed her nipple through her shirt. It beaded immediately and begged me for more. I twisted it once and continued a slow, methodical glide back and forth on it.

Raquel tugged my hair and demanded, "More."

"Your wish, my command." I yanked her shirt over her head and unsnapped her bra in record time.

Fuck, the site of Raquel bare from the top sitting in my airplane caused precum to spurt out.

I bent down and licked one nipple. Then the other. Unable to decide which flavor I liked best.

Raquel's squirming and moans pushed the need in me more. She grabbed my shirt to take it off, but her erratic movements from me sucking her breast made her lose traction.

"Off. I want it off," she begged.

With one last pull of her berry, I reached back and yanked my shirt off.

We stared at each other. Sitting across from each other in the cockpit, bare from the waist up. Both our faces mirrored each other's lustful cravings.

Raquel's hands flew to her jeans and quickly unzipped them. She semi-squatted to push them down her legs. She quickly glanced at me before she kicked her shoes off. "You're not undressing."

My pants were mid-thigh when Raquel climbed over the console and sat on my lap—completely naked.

My dick bounced, and precum glistened the tip.

Raquel grabbed hold of my cock and rubbed the moisture across the head.

I squeezed her thighs as pleasure jolted through me. "Behave," I warned her.

Her laughter was evil, but I knew I'd love whatever she planned. She knew she had me at her whim.

"I don't think so. I want to see you let go." She nipped my lip. "Tell me you have a condom?"

I tapped the condom sitting on the console and was thankful I had the wherewithal to think of. "I never leave home without them."

Her smile suggested all sorts of wickedness. "Okay, lover."

She didn't finish her words before she tore open the package, rolled it torturingly down my shaft, and then fitted me to her entrance, where she sank fully onto my lap.

My head dropped back as the feel of her warm, wet pussy engulfed my rod. It was the best damn torture, and I didn't ever want to leave.

She took advantage of my position and nipped, licked, and kissed my face and neck. I'm sure she left evidence of her loving.

"I gotta move, honey."

Her legs bunched under my hand as she leveraged the sides in the small cockpit to ride me. Up and down, she swallowed my member. With each movement, my penis stretched her pussy wide, and the tip hit her walls. I tilted her hips because I wanted her to feel me tomorrow. I wanted the imprint of my cock to stay permanently inside her.

Raquel's movement faltered at the additional pressure inside her, and she leaned back and tried to impale herself on my cock. I slid my finger down and circled the taut, swollen bundle protruding from her stretched feminine lips.

It was an unbelievable sight to watch our joining. Raquel's pussy opened wide and welcomed me. But it was the combination of my cock inside her and my finger on her clit that rewarded us; her juices saturated me. Our combined nectar coated my shaft and glistened on her intimate lips.

"I want to fucking eat you."

"Max," she breathed her agreement.

She was magnificent.

"Faster, Raquel," I commanded as my balls shot up, readying for release.

She obeyed, but her movements were frantic as she neared her surrender.

I leaned forward and sucked her breast into my mouth. I savored the feel of her and wanted everything in me to own her.

"Oh, God, Max." She moaned.

I tightened my suction on her breast, squeezed her ass, and applied firm pressure on her pleasure nub.

Raquel blew for me.

I didn't let up. I continued pulling from her breasts, alternating between one and the other. At the same time, I used my grip on her firm rear to keep her moving up and down. Finally, I slid my finger out from my torture, and at her whimper, I brushed her clit to remind her we weren't even close to being done.

Raquel's hands gripped my hair, and she gained her rhythm once more. She held me to her fountain and demanded, "Harder."

I fucking loved that she knew what she wanted and wasn't afraid to ask for it. So, I obeyed and bit the side of her breast.

"Mmmm." Raquel's moan was slow, long, and croaky. Her pleasure escaped in unintelligible sounds.

I switched sides, swallowed her breast, and slammed her down on my penis.

Her juices coated my lap as she flung her head side to side as she reached for her second orgasm.

I reached up, pulled her hair back, fully offering her bounty for my delight, and spanked her.

"Ahhh." She lost her rhythm.

"Don't stop," I demanded.

She stopped, looked me dead in the eye, squeezed her inner muscles, and said, "Fuck me."

Later when I had two fucking working brain cells, I would thank the Gods that Raquel met my sexual appetite. But with her legs squeezing me to her, my cock buried in her sweet pussy, and her heavy breast in my hand, I did as ordered.

I fucked her.

It was fast.

It was hard.

It was fucktacular.

"Baby," I warned her of my imminent eruption.

Her response? She squeezed her inner muscles again and milked my penis.

"Raquel," I tried once more.

"Let go." She moaned through her release.

I obeyed her once again and joined her in orgasm.

"I'm so damn glad you're flexible," I mumbled against her breast-bone as we did our best to get our breathing under control.

She giggled. "Me too."

Her hands idly rubbed up and down my back.

"Does this mean that I'm officially a member of the mile-high club?" Her tone was lazy and well-satiated.

I lifted my head and smiled. "Sorry to disappoint you, but we have to be in flight while having sex to join that particular club."

"Next time, then."

CHAPTER SEVENTEEN

Rocky

"I APPRECIATE THE OPPORTUNITY TO DESIGN A NEW LUXURY LINE for Wheldon Automotive. However, I'll need time to review the contract with my business team."

Mr. Wheldon was a handsome, elegant older man. Silver at his temples, a tan from all his outdoor activities, and the physique to match his outgoing personality. And his attire? His personal shopper deserved a raise for the sharp presentation he always sported. However, all of it was a tool he utilized to hide the keen intelligence hidden behind his eyes. Make no mistake about it—Wheldon Automotives wasn't *the* luxury automaker of the world simply because of the fine vehicles they produced. Mr. Wheldon directed that ship to success.

"Of course, Miss Sterling. I pleasantly await your answer." He walked around his desk and extended his hand to me.

I stood up and shook his hand.

"Before we adjourn, I wanted to offer my sympathy on the vandalism at your shop. I understand how difficult it can be when those with envious hearts strike." He gave me an isn't-it-a-pain smile.

"It also lines up with the fictitious rumors circulating about Sterling Custom Auto." He shook his head. "I always wondered if the people behind these machinations don't realize how their shenanigans represent themselves and not their intended victims."

My stomach clenched. What rumors?

"To say I'm surprised would be an understatement. I have not heard any unpleasant chatter about my business. Would you mind sharing it with me?" Was this related to everything else? Was it possibly a disgruntled customer or *the* dissatisfied numskull who was giving me my current headache?

"Of course. There are some perturbing reviews online regarding the quality of care they received from your facility. Nothing outrageous. Just more troublesome than anything else." He shook his head. "Sometimes today's modern world is a blessing, and sometimes it's not."

No way! That is one thing Sterling Custom Auto never, *never!* faltered in—quality of work. Our workmanship was beyond comparison, and we never sacrificed. As soon as I could, I would find out what the heck and who the hell wrote those lies.

"I appreciate you bringing this troubling information to my attention. I promise I will get to the bottom of this ugliness, and I guarantee Sterling Custom Auto will continue to provide the same high-quality standards my father set years ago."

"I never doubted it." His smile was warm, friendly, and confident. "As an heir to my own distinguished car company, I know that people with covetous souls can be... troubling."

It took considerable effort not to let my mouth pop open and not trip over my feet as I made my way to his office door.

"Again, I thank you for the opportunity to work together." I shook his extended hand.

Wheldon Luxury sought me.

Wheldon Luxury asked for me.

Wheldon Luxury wants *me*.

I barely managed to control the desire to dance to my car. I knew Wheldon had to have cameras in every corner, and I didn't need him to question me any further than the lies around me did.

My mind whirled as I drove back to work. Zoning. Traffic and Parking. Noise. Nuisance. Vandalism. Rumors. What in the freak was going on? Who had I pissed off to such an extent that they would seek this kind of vengeance? And why now?

I pushed those ugly thoughts aside and focused on ideas for the luxury line Wheldon wanted me to design. I envisioned using the same basic concept my dad used on the Thunderbird—sleek, smooth, and sharp lines.

Classic.

But when I entered my office, my mind fell back onto the crappenings. It'd been a week since the break-in, and the boys and I had put a serious dent into the cleanup and inventory. But there was more to do, and we couldn't wait to finish it. We all wanted to go back to normal.

I tossed my bag onto the desk and shouted, "Bruno!" once I reached the inner doors.

I wanted to share the exciting news. We hadn't officially signed the contract, but I couldn't contain my happiness even with the cloud of Mr. Wheldon's departing words.

"Over here, Rocky."

I semi-skipped-ran on my heels toward Max's DeVille, where I heard Bruno's voice and commenced yell-singing the excellent news.

"Wheldon wants us to exclusively design his new luxury auto line aannndddd he wants to leave room for the prospect of future auto lines. Can you believe it?"

By the time I reached Bruno, I was waving the Wheldon folder in the air in a celebratory dance and singing, *"Wheldon wants us! Wheldon wants us! Wheldon wants us!"*

"That's great news, Rocky. Of course, he'd want you," Bruno said, his white teeth shining through his smile. "What's the timeline?"

"Well, we gotta hammer out all the legal mumbo jumbo first, then we'll have some planning sessions to understand his vision. So, I'm guessing it'll be a while." My cheeks hurt from the smile on my face.

"That is fantastic news." Bruno sobered. "I don't want to cut your excitement short, Rocky, but we have a problem. The boys can't find the box that was delivered the other day with this beauty's parts." Bruno patted the DeVille's fender.

"What do you mean you can't find it?"

"I mean, it's missing. Clay signed for it, left it in your office, and now it's not there." Bruno answered in his no-nonsense manner. "There's a possibility that whoever broke in the other day took it because we haven't found it."

I grabbed a piece of chocolate from the tool rack—a supply I happily restocked—and shoved it into my mouth while I worked through how this would further impact the schedule I had set for the DeVille. Time was of the essence, but compromising on quality wasn't.

"Where did Clay put it when he signed for it? Maybe it's just in one of the piles we haven't got to yet." Acquiring a new part would be a pain.

"He put it on your desk. It was pretty packed in your office, and one of the customers bumped into the delivery guy who knocked everything off your desk. It was a little chaotic at that point, with everyone trying to help. The only other thing that stands out is the woman who was there. She turned down assistance from Clay and left right after the commotion." Bruno scratched his chin.

"Did you recognize her? What'd she do while she was here?" A chill went down my spine. "Maybe she's the person Patrick left his business card with the other day when he came by?" I really needed to sit down and recheck the footage for that day.

"No, I didn't recognize her, nor did Clay." Bruno tilted his head in contemplation. "No clue what she was doing and it's possible Patrick gave her the card."

I rubbed my forehead, the beginning of a headache was rearing it's ugly head. "Did the surveyor complete everything this morning while I was gone?"

"The assessor stated it'd take three to five days to finalize and that he'd email the finished product. He also said he'd file it with the county afterward." Bruno provided me with some good news.

"I need more chocolate." With all the little things popping up, my intake reached a personal all-time high.

"Well then, it's your lucky day." Max's voice sounded from behind me.

He extended a bag from Margie's coffee shop to me, did a slow perusal of me in my business outfit, and froze at my shoes.

It was simple, but I'd like to consider it a classy business suit. A pinstripe navy outfit with three off-centered buttons holding the blazer together, exposing minimal cleavage, thick pointed cuffed sleeves, and a deep red hanky peeking out from my left breast pocket. My pants tapered down to my ankles where my heels rocked my outfit to smokin' hot. They were pencil high fuck me, red stilettos.

He took another slow, lazy stroll back up my body and stopped minutely at my partially bared chest and up to my red lips before landing on my eyes.

And the fever I saw—scorched me.

And it caused a mini orgasm.

My body swayed, and I would have teetered over if it wasn't for Bruno grabbing my elbow and murmuring, "You might wanna eat some of that chocolate." A very deliberate pause. "Now."

Max's grin was slow and smug as he jiggled the bag.

I reached out by rote and responded, "Thanks." But I stopped short of collecting the bag because of the Wheldon folder in my hand. I quickly moved it to my left hand and reached for the bags.

"Is that the Wheldon logo?" His attention remained riveted to the file in my hand.

"Yes." And, because it wouldn't hurt to restate Sterling Custom Auto's impeccable reputation with the shitshow swirling around it, I said, "Mr. Wheldon wants to discuss a new luxury line to be developed by us." I waved the portfolio. "This is preliminary talks." So what if I was feeling a little smug. I'd like to think anyone would be in my position.

Max's eyebrows shot up to his hairline. "Really? Wow. That's huge. Congratulations."

"What is? Why are congratulations in order?" Kevin, always with impeccably horrible timing, waltzed up.

"Rocky here scored a contract with Wheldon Luxury," Bruno bragged.

Kevin's eyebrows fluttered up. "Really? That's quite impressive."

He didn't have to sound so shocked.

"Not really. Rocky's work says it all."

God, I loved Bruno.

"What can I do for you, Kevin?" The next council meeting wasn't for another two weeks, so there wasn't any other business between us we needed to address.

"Well, I was hoping to have a moment of your time." He glanced at Max and Bruno to indicate privacy was in order.

"Sure, we can talk in my office." And if he brought up anything possibly related to a personal nature between us, I would have fun sticking my fuck-me stilettos up his ass. "If you'll all excuse me." I looked between Max and Bruno.

"If I didn't say it before, I am truly sorry about the vandalism to the shop." Kevin scanned my office. "But it seems you've accomplished a great deal in the last week."

Yeah, we worked our asses off trying to get back to normal. Every single one of us itched to get back to work.

"Yeah, I have a good group of guys. But I'm sure you didn't come here to discuss my cleanup status."

He nodded. "Since the last town hall, it's come to my attention that the original violation requisites were not met by the specified date. I apologize for the miscommunication, but unfortunately, the require- ment still stands." He raised his hand before I could object. "Even with the deferral at said meeting, the deadline still stands. Therefore, until you can meet the requirements and-slash-or the matter is handled at the appropriate meetings, I will have to ask you to close the shop until the situation is rectified. I will also be speaking with the neighboring businesses to advise them of this condition as well."

"Wait, what?" I shook my head hoping that would clear it. "I thought all the work Mr. Quincy and I had done was sufficient? I mean, it wasn't that long ago when I got the additional complaints."

"Again, my apologies for the misunderstaning but I must follow policy. The shop must close until everything is rectified," Kevin said.

My surroundings faded away to fuzzy, monochromatic nothingness. My ears buzzed with the sound of my blood rushing, my lungs consciously but haltingly pumped breath for me, and my mind seized on *"close the shop."*

"Raquel!" Max snapped my name.

It wouldn't matter if he pinched me. My entire being was frozen as the words *"close the shop"* ricocheted through my soul.

"Raquel, baby, what's wrong?" He guided me to my chair, sat me down, and squatted before me. "Talk to me."

I stared at him, but I only saw an image of my dad. The I'm-so-fucking-happy grin he had when he opened the shop. The I'm-so-fucking-happy expression he gave my mom when not just the first customer but the tenth customer walked through the door on opening day. The I'm-so-fucking-happy essence emanated from him as he laid a hot and heavy kiss on my mom bent over the hood of the Thunderbird at the opening.

"What the hell did you say to her?" Max barked at Kevin.

Kevin jumped. "I..." He cleared his throat. "I told her she had to shut down until the city resolves the multiple violations. I..." He sucked in a breath. "I didn't think it would affect her like this."

"Shit." Max scowled up at Kevin. "Raquel, sweetheart, this is temporary. You are not going to lose the shop over this." Max lightly squeezed my hands. "Baby, you need to pull yourself together and get on the horn with Mr. Quincy."

Max's face slowly formed in front of me as his words penetrated. It was *temporary*. I was *not* going to lose my shop.

I lightly shook my head. "I'm good." But I was going to make sure Kevin wasn't by starting with a phone call to Mr. Quincy to end this stupid bullshit.

"You sure, baby?"

Max's words.

Max's concern.

Max's actions.

Oh shit.

I was falling for Max.

I flew past the no sleeping with the client rule and jumped right into the love lake. I pushed aside my newfound realization and sucked in a fortifying breath.

"Yes." I turned to Kevin, removed my hands from Max's, and pulled my shit together. "Thank you for relaying the message, but from now on, any communication must be through my attorney, Mr. Quincy. If you do not heed this, I will file a harassment suit and restraining order against you. Do I make myself clear?"

Kevin's already pale face blanched further.

"Yes, I... I'm so sorry." His movements were stilted as he made his way out as if he wasn't sure of himself.

I pushed Kevin out of my mind for the moment and addressed Max. "I'm gonna do it like a band-aid." Max's eyes scrunched in confusion. "We're missing parts for the DeVille. I think it happened during the break-in. The missing part and the break-in are messing up our timetable. That means I have to push back the deadline. Again. If you wanna transfer it somewhere else, I completely understand. I'll have it transported, on me, wherever you want it delivered to."

I held my breath as I waited for Max's disappointment and confirmation that he wanted to take his vehicle elsewhere.

"We figured that would happen after the break-in. Do you have any idea how much longer?"

"Right now, I can't say. I need to talk to Mr. Quincy and the guys. I should have a better idea by the beginning of next week."

"All right, Raquel. What can I do to help you now?"

I stared into his swirly amber eyes and thought I could get lost in him.

"You can..." *Give me space to process what I just realized: you are so much more.* His proximity muddied my thoughts and brought out more powerful, needy emotions. "Nothing." I stood up and rubbed them on my thighs.

Max slowly stood up, taking in the sights of my body as he did, and stopped bare inches from me.

Damn it!

That was the wrong move. I was squarely, and very much, in Max's personal space. And he smelled all kinds of heady. Masculine. Sexy. And just plain yummy.

Oh, good God.

I wanted to taste his lips again. I missed them. They were a light mauve color, plump with tiny creases. And his trim but coarse beard outlined them perfectly, almost like it highlighted the inarguable truth of the importance of his mouth. Almost like they were being offered up as the most exquisite delicatessen.

And then I was.

Tasting him.

And I was so fucking wrong.

He was so much better than the finest, most delicate, melt in your mouth, to die for eclair.

My taste buds exploded.

My entire being sparked to life.

I wanted to gorge myself on him.

I fisted my hands in his hair—and yes, it was just as thick and soft as I remembered—and held him closer to me as I devoured him.

I didn't need to worry, though. Max's right arm banded around me, and his left hand bunched in my hair and tilted my head for his continued but delectable assault on my mouth. The other firmly held me to him while his thumb erotically and oh so torturingly leisurely rubbed up and down on the side of my breast.

I had no doubt he could feel my pebbled nipples against his chest. I wasn't ashamed my body undulated against his, doing its best to get closer and create *more* of everything.

Max, the gentleman I was learning he was, pushed his thigh between my legs and gave me the outlet I needed to rub my core against. His hand slid down to my rear, grabbed a handful, and encouraged me to ride his leg. Then, he tore his mouth from mine and kissed, nibbled, and sucked down my neck.

My breaths were erratic, my chest rising and falling with the effort to breathe, and I held onto his head, making sure he didn't deviate from the pleasure he gave me.

I'd say prayers for my choice of outfit later because my suit jacket was veed, and the off-centered low three buttons allowed for, oh my God, yes! gaping access. Something Max did not hesitate to use.

He nipped, licked, and sucked his way inside my jacket—and I said a little prayer that my outfit didn't require a shirt—and where he took a huge pull from my nipple—*right over my bra!* I bucked against his leg as juices poured from me, and a low moan escaped me.

Max yanked my bra under my breast, offering it to him, and stopped.

I pressed against his head, trying to get him back to pleasuring me. But he didn't budge.

I slowly opened my eyes and saw Max's gaze fixated on my breast.

"Fuck, you are gorgeous."

My body involuntarily rippled.

Max lifted my breast and drew from me. At the same time, his hand on my butt slid down further, and his finger pressed into my seam, gliding back and forth. Getting closer to my clit, but not quite. Teasing me.

The assault on multiple fronts, my breast, my rear, and my clit overwhelmed me.

"Max." I breathed. I could feel my orgasm coming. "I'm..."

He grasped my nipple between his teeth and halted all movements.

I straightened my head and looked down at him. "Don't stop."

He slowly moved his hand out from between my legs and engulfed my breast in his mouth.

I felt the minutest orgasm slide through me.

And, ever so slowly, Max released my breast.

"Make no mistake, Raquel. I'm going to fuck you again. You're going to scream my name. And you're not going to come just once."

He righted my clothes, lingering and torturing me with gentle caresses of my rear and breast.

I stared at him in shock. I was beyond primed to explode, and he just... stopped.

He leaned into me and said, "I'm sorry I didn't respect you enough to remember we're not alone." He gave me a peck. "I'll make it up to you when we are."

Crap.

My heart melted along with my panties.

CHAPTER EIGHTEEN

Rocky

AFTER MAX'S PLEASURE-CRASHING PARTY POOPER DISPLAY OF gentlemanliness, I told Bruno and the guys about Kevin's pain-in-my-ass announcement that we had to stop all work until the even bigger pain-in-my-ass violations were resolved. They handled it as well as I did but with a lot more f-bombs.

They weren't worried about their pay. They knew I was good for it. They just wanted back at their work. Of course, I *wanted* them back at their jobs. But until Mr. Quincy squashed this bullshit, they weren't allowed to work on the cars. And maybe I used semantics to my advantage because I didn't consider cleaning, itemizing, and reorganizing the shop as our natural state of business. So, I gave the guys a minimum day to wrap up the last bit and then told them to head out but not before I asked them to make me a list for Alex and Trent about any possible customers who weren't especially enthusiastic about work, customer service, whatever from Sterling Custom Auto.

So, I used the grumbling moment to call City Hall to find out the status of my filings, only to be met with the same message, *"Our system is down for maintenance."* Ha! *"Please call back at another time. Blah. Blah. Blah."* It was just more irksome news.

The sooner I got this all resolved, the better.

I plopped down at my desk, fired up my laptop, and pulled up the video from three weeks ago to see who Patrick had spoken to when he had originally stopped by. Luckily, I didn't have to sit through hours of footage to find him, and it was just like Bruno stated. The reception was packed. Staff members conversed with customers and vendors, one of them being Clay, who signed for the missing part and placed it on the desk, and Patrick speaking with the mystery woman who dressed more like she was out on the prowl than someone who worked in an office, much less an auto shop.

While she didn't hide her face, she also didn't give me a full frontal view. This irritated me because something about her seemed familiar, but I couldn't place my finger on it.

Then chaos ensued when the distributor tripped over his own foot and caused him to bump into the desk, which then made him lose his grip on the dolly where everything came crashing down and out of the boxes, not to mention several items on my desk met the same result as the boxes. Everyone jumped into action to set everything right except for the Mystery Woman–the bitch–who pocketed Patrick's business card and shoved the missing part in her oversized purse and sashayed right out of my shop.

Well, that answered two questions–what happened to the business card and the missing part. Unfortunately, more popped up. Who was she? Why did she take those items? And what the fuck did I do to her?

I rubbed my forehead feeling a headache emerging from all this garbage, and told myself to suck it up. I had more work to do, like discovering what rumors were spread about Sterling Custom Auto.

It didn't take long to find the bad reviews written by *badhorsey*. Really? Badhorsey? Right off the bat, it sounded immature, and the comments reinforced it. This person clearly didn't know anything about cars, nor were their ramblings coherent enough to identify a possible customer. So I shot an email to everyone on staff asking if they recognized anything from the crappy words.

Since I was pounding away at my keyboard, I sent my insurance company a copy of the itemization from our inventory retake. Then I sent another email to Mr. Quincy, Alex, and Trent closing all the loops hanging off me. The first was any possible customers with burrs up their behinds. The second was the ridiculous reviews. Enough said. The third was the list of people with me when I entered my alarm code in the last four months. The fourth was Patrick's contact information, along with a copy of the video from the day he delivered it showing the woman, who I didn't know, took the card and the part Clay signed for. The fifth was Carson's desk buddy's employer's information. Last but not least was letting them all know about Kevin's surprise visit today stating Sterling Custom Auto had to close its door until the complaints were resolved and could they possibly get a move on shutting down that fucking problem.

Then, I turned everything off and searched for Bruno to see what else needed to be completed before we shut down for the day. Irritation welled inside me, knowing he was in the back taking care of some last-minute things before he left for the day. It pissed me off because it was not a regular normal workday activity. It all sucked, and watching everyone else leave irked me even more.

However, at the moment, I wasn't focused on any of that. No, I watched as Max stared at the DeVille lost in his memories. In my beginning conversations with Paul regarding the restoration, he stressed the importance of meeting the timeline for its completion and hinted at the significance of the vehicle. Adding the sore spot of their mother, which I was still stunned Delilah was his mom, it wasn't too difficult for me to put two and two together. The DeVille represented a happier time in the Hudson men's lives.

I knew any movement on my part would interrupt a private moment for Max, but I couldn't stand by and watch him suffer. The pain etched on his face bruised my heart. Something in me wanted, no needed, to ease his hurt. To alleviate some of the pain he endured because I knew what it meant to have your father hurting. I knew what it meant to fear his success of survival. And I absolutely knew what it meant to lose him.

I couldn't let Max stay in that torment.

"I promise we'll get this gal to you as soon as possible and faring a whole lot better than when they first put her on the road." As a matter of fact, I was going to talk to Bruno about reworking our production schedule and figure out if we couldn't get this baby completed sooner without compromising on our other projects.

Max started, forgetting where he was and that he wasn't alone. "I'd appreciate it." He cleared his throat, dislodging whatever emotion clogged it.

"I meant to ask earlier, but with everything going on, I forgot. How's your dad doing?"

"He's adjusting. Learning to rely on help and take things easier." He chuckled. "For a man who was constantly on the go with us four boys and never took a breath until his head hit the pillow at night, this is agony."

"He sounds like my mom after my dad passed away. Even though Ashton was twenty-two and I was nineteen and we were able to help around the house, Mom never stopped," I commiserated. "Well, to be fair, Ash was still in the military and I was in school, but we pitched in."

"He's stubborn and not used to relying on people to help him personally. To give us kids help? No hesitation reaching out for a hand, but for himself? No way in hell. So, this is kicking his butt in more than one way."

"I'm taking it this baby made him happy once upon a time?" I smoothed my hand along the hood of the DeVille.

"Yeah." Max's guard slipped as he gave me a slow nod. "It was originally my granddad's, but as my folks started expanding our family, Granddad sold it to my dad for a buck." He shrugged in an attempt to downplay their rough upbringing. "It was all my dad could afford then, and his pride wouldn't let him accept it for free. Mom... she wanted more."

"She didn't like the car?" I was curious what he meant.

He shook his head once. "No, she wanted to drive around in luxury. She didn't understand the beauty of this classic and bitched about it all the time. Among other things."

"Not everyone can appreciate the classics or even understand what a classic means. Most women aren't built that way." I wasn't sure why, but I tried to defend his mother. To love cars wasn't a guy or girl thing; take me as evidence. Most girls didn't give a crap about cars as long as it got them from point A to point B.

"My mother wasn't built for a lot of things." His intensity weighed on me. "She was built for being pampered, ordering people around, and genuinely caring only about herself. That's why she left my dad, married a wealthy older man who employed people to handle everything, including raising his kids, and never checked her rearview mirror."

Holy shitballs. Max's mom was a total bitch.

"I'm sorry, it sounds so lame, but I will say it anyway. I'm sorry." My chest ached from the hurt I heard. "How old were you when she left?"

"Eleven. Delilah left on my birthday, at my birthday party. My entire class witnessed her grand exit. Her sugar daddy parked right in front of our house in the middle of the street like he owned the damn thing. Then his chauffeur got out, walked around the limo, and opened the back door for my mother. The whole time, the guy was inside on his phone with a mini desk spread before him with papers sprawled across it, talking on his phone. Not once did he lift his head from his work. Not to see my mom make her way to him. Not to see her kids crying and begging her not to leave. And definitely not to see the devastation he left behind."

I stood there stunned and did everything I could to keep my cool. "First off, I'm going to go with I'm sorry again, even though we both know it's totally lame for everything you just told me. And I have the sudden urge to hunt your mother down and kick her ass for being such a total bitch. What mother abandons her kids for money? And on their birthday? At their birthday party? What the fuck is wrong with her? I mean, if the marriage isn't working and you've done everything you can to course correct *together*, then, by all means, bow out, *gracefully*. But you do not leave your children. And not on their damn birthday. You bend over backward to make it as seamless and painless for your kids as much as possible. You do not under any circumstance cause your children unnecessary discomfort, pain, or harm. What the hell was she thinking? It's not like she wasn't an active participant in the making of you boys. She knew what she was doing and the likely outcome of having sex with her husband. What? Did the condom break? No, screw that. She can assume responsibility for birth control too. Especially if she didn't want children. It takes two, for fucks sake, and she did it at least four fucking times!" I sucked in a much-needed breath. "Okay, I lied. I might just camp out at Margie's shop and wait for her to show up again."

It was Max's turn to be stunned silent.

Not me. I was still reeling from the blow Max's mother had landed on them years ago. "I know it was a long time ago, but it's never too late to learn a lesson. That's another one of my dad's sayings and one I believe in. Chocolate was another. Well, not really a saying. More like an edible omen. He said chocolate improves everything, helps activate your brain cells, and comes close to solving all life's problems. He wasn't wrong about that, either. So, I'll make sure to up my consumption—more—before I have a discussion with your mother." I tapped my foot impatiently.

"Dad's going to love meeting you. He's always wanted a daughter."

I blinked.

"He wants to meet you, hear about the restoration, and he wants an excuse to get under Lucy's skin. Lucy is his nurse and keeps him on the straight and narrow." He kept going like he hadn't just rocked my world. "Paul and Vic might join us because Dad likes having us all over. Not sure if Cole will join us, but I wouldn't doubt it."

"What?" All my firesome aggravation drained out of me, and sheer confusion immediately replaced it.

"I don't think I told you because I was distracted." His smile was all kinds of wicked. "But dinner will be served at six because Lucy is a stickler regarding Dad's regime, but you can come anytime before then. He'd love the company."

"Ookkaayy." Was there really another response? "But just so you know, there is no way Mom will allow your dad to make supper for everyone. We have to move it to my house so she can cook."

He chuckled. "Not a problem. I wouldn't want to get on your mom's bad side."

"Don't encourage her. I already told you if it were up to her, we'd have mom's grandbabies before she served dessert." I joked. Sort of. I wasn't so sure about mom.

"Umm, yeah, I wasn't joking either when I told you my dad was riding us boys for little rug rats. Maybe we shouldn't get your mom and my dad together then."

"Too late. Your dad and my mom will have numbers, names, and our children's college funds settled before dessert hits the table. We're screwed."

"This is gonna be fun." He winked at me. "If you have any pictures, pamphlets, or brochures about the shop, bring them. Dad will love pouring over them. But, I should warn you—he'll give you unwarranted advice." He raised his hand to stop any objections on my part. Not that I had time to voice any. "Not that he thinks you're incapable. He doesn't know how not to give out advice. It's one of his fatherly vices."

Pictures I could do. I quickly decided and moved toward the back wall where I shelved our build portfolios. Luckily, the fiasco didn't severely damage them. I pulled down the oldest, most worn leather binder and walked back to Max.

I laid the binder on the hood of the DeVille and flicked through the pages until I reached the most important one.

Dad's 1955 Ford Thunderbird stared up at me.

"This is the car my dad started Sterling Custom Auto with. He never sold it, but it's what set it all," I swirled my hands around the shop, "into motion. My mom was pissed because they were financially in a bind then, and my dad used every last penny they had saved to buy it, build it up, and then did nothing with it." I shook my head; my eyes never left the picture. "That's not true. He took pictures at every stage of its development." I flipped through more pages to show Max. "He spoke to everyone about it and showed everyone pictures. He wouldn't stop going on about the car. Then people started asking him for advice on how to fix their cars best, how he thought such and such was possible, and so on. The next thing you know, Sterling Custom Auto is born."

I flipped the page, scanning the pictures for the one I wanted to show Max.

"Mom didn't understand Dad's fascination with cars, nor did she get his dream with this shop. Still, to this day, she doesn't understand mine either." I braved facing Max and hoped for his sake that his earlier admission was wrong. "Some women aren't built that way."

His eyes softened as he skimmed his knuckles along my cheek. "The difference is your mother loved your father, loves you, and your brother."

Mom absolutely did, and after Ash's earlier text to our family chat, she was ecstatic to know that he would be in town some time next week.

I hurt for him. I didn't know anything else but my parents' love for each other. Even when Dad spent their life savings on a dilapidated car, she still loved him. To not grow up in a household with undeniable love? My soul hurt just trying to imagine it.

I wanted to alleviate his hurt from growing up with a mother who didn't love her husband unconditionally. Who didn't love her family unreservedly. Who didn't love her children boundlessly.

I didn't know how to give Max a reprieve, but as I stared into his eyes, I felt the unknown pull to him. I slowly reached up to his face to give him time to pull away, to reject the comfort I wanted to give him.

I lifted up on my tiptoes and pulled his neck down a little so I could reach his mouth. He didn't resist. He bent and allowed me to softly kiss his lips.

He held my head to him as he deepened our kiss. It wasn't hurried or rushed like our earlier engagement. Instead, he savored me this time, and I returned the favor.

Our bodies came together unconsciously, and Max's arm wrapped around my waist, holding me to him as we worshiped each other. My arm snuck around his shoulders, and my other arm held onto the back of his shirt.

I was overwhelmed with the emotion of Max's kiss and touch. He was giving everything back to me that I tried to give him.

Until I heard a throat clearing. We slowly pulled apart but never lost eye contact.

"I didn't mean to interrupt, but I was about to head out and wanted to ensure you were good." Even with my back to Bruno, I could hear the smile. "I think you're more than good."

I turned around and glared at him. "Don't be a smartass."

"Me? The smartass?" Bruno's eyebrows shot up toward his bald scalp.

"Whatever," I mumbled. "All done in the back?"

"Yeah. I also wanted to tell you that while this is a pain, it'll pass soon enough. So keep your chin up, and let me know if you need anything." Bruno touched my cheek as he made his way past me.

Max and Bruno exchanged those manly chin lifts in their silent goodbyes.

"I gotta head out too." He looked at me. "I have a lesson I need to get to."

"I understand." I was disappointed. I wanted him to stay to finish what we'd started twice.

He pulled me into his arms. "I don't want to. I, without a doubt, want to finish what we've started. The promise of you is beyond tempting, but I can't back out of work. But I really fucking want to."

I melted into him. "You don't have to explain. I understand you need to work." I pulled his head down and whispered against his lips. "I want you too, in case you didn't know."

He smiled.

Screw it. I licked him.

That was it.

The heat from Max engulfed me, and I wanted to drown in it.

Until he pulled back and held me at arm's length.

"Motherfucker."

Um, yeah.

Why did he keep stopping?

"You just had some troubling news delivered, and while I want to be the reason to help erase it for you—more than you fucking know—but our second time won't be under these circumstances."

Each word out of his mouth was deliberately forced out through clenched teeth and landed with as much ferocity in me. Melting me. It appeared Max would be more than a quick roll in the car's back seat.

"Can it be the third?" I teased.

CHAPTER NINETEEN

Rocky

"MOM, IT'S FINE. THEY'RE GOING TO LOVE IT," I SAID FOR THE millionth time.

"Did you get the beer? What about wine? Do they drink wine? Maybe we should have had this at my house. I know what I have and don't have." She stopped mid-buttering the bread. "Can Max's dad have alcohol? Did you check in with his nurse, Lucy, about his dietary restrictions? "

I watched Mom spread another vat of butter on the second loaf of bread she had made. "One, you have a key to my house and did indeed do an inventory of my refrigerator and pantry. So you know what I have more than I do. Two, I think alcohol will be the least of his problems with tonight's menu."

"What? Why?" Mom's grimace of terror was hilarious only because she held bread drenched in butter in one hand, and in the other hand, butter slowly slid off the knife. It was also so darn sweet. Max and his family were on their way over for a family dinner. Well, it was a pseudo-family meal. Ash wasn't there, but it was a definite mingling of the people we loved. And my mom was worried they wouldn't like the food, my house, whatever. She wanted it to go perfectly. She wanted Max to stay. She wanted grandbabies.

I walked up to Mom, removed the bread and butter knife from her hands, and held her hands in mine. "Mom, I love you."

Some of her worries melted away at my words. "I love you too, Rocky." She graced me with a quick mom smile.

"I love that you're worried about what they'll think. I know that you care enough to want to make this a special night for everyone. But, Mom, if they don't like the food, we don't want them at our table because your cooking is unparalleled." I wasn't going to let Emma in on that secret. "Or the soft jazz playing, then we definitely need to kick them out. Or the colors of the napkins... okay, I might give them that one." Mom chuckled. "More importantly, if they can't see past all that to the two beautiful, kind, and caring women who did all this for them, then they don't deserve us."

Mom's shoulders dropped as she gave me an I-went-overboard-didn't-I smile.

"I'm overreacting, aren't I?" Mom, who was never nervous, asked me.

I pulled her into my arms and whispered in her ear, "Never." Then, I pulled back just a bit and added to ensure I eradicated Mom's nerves, "I'm just gonna go grab the vise grips out of the garage and put them at each of their place settings. So, if any of them get out of line, I'll just attach it to their..."

Mom's hand shot up and covered my mouth. "Don't finish that sentence, young lady." She laughingly warned me.

Mission accomplished and just in time. The doorbell chimed through the house, letting us know Max and his family were there.

Now, it was time to take my advice.

It'd been four days since I last saw Max, and I was nervous. Would he treat me differently after we'd had sex? After opening up to me about his mom? Did he feel the same way about me as I felt for him?

I left Mom to finish preparing the heart attack loaves and sucked in a deep breath to calm the butterflies taking flight in my stomach. I went with casual attire for tonight's dinner. My pants were extremely loose, so they flowed around my legs and resembled a long, flowy skirt.

I loved them because they were the softest material in the world, and I felt like I was floating anytime I wore them. I paired it with a white tank and oversized denim shirt tied in a fashionable knot in the front. I topped it off with bare feet and a bun on my head that took forever to get just right. I wanted Max and his family to know this was casual and to feel at home, but I didn't want them to think I didn't care either.

Damn it, I wanted Max to know he meant something.

I sucked in a massive breath for encouragement and opened the door, only to be sucker punched by the sheer mountain of male hotness before me. The good man above did not hold back when he graced the Hudson men with undeniable lickable good looks.

The I'll tower over you as I make you come for me height. Check.

The I can't circle my arms around your solid I work hard chest while you're fucking me. Check.

But you can sink your hands in my thick, lush hair instead. Check.

And the playful wickedness twinkling in their eyes. Check.

Max leaned in, cupped my cheek, and whispered against my mouth, "You're drooling."

I focused on his laughing eyes and forgot a smorgasbord of Hudson males were in my doorway, and I didn't even try to whisper. "You're drool-worthy."

Max kissed me quickly before gently guiding me back into my home.

"Forgive me. It's not every day I have the entirety of the male hot species on my doorstep." I waved my hand inward. "Please come in."

"I like this one, Max." His dad held a massive bouquet as he stepped in, then mumbled, "Not that I met any of the others." His eyes shot to me. "Not that there were others to meet."

I chuckled. "No worries. I know Max wasn't a saint before me." Hopefully, he was with me. Well, maybe not entirely.

"That's my dad, Phil, and as you can tell, he might be a little excited to finally meet someone worth meeting." Paul stepped in, bent down, and gave me a cheek peck. Then, he shoved the most stunning turquoise plant I'd ever seen, nestled in a gorgeous clay pot with child-like designs, into my hands.

"They're beautiful." I twisted it side to side in an attempt to inspect it better.

"The kids at the after-school program painted it." Paul's pride in their work was evident in his tone.

Vic, done with flowers, stepped in, did the same welcoming combo as Paul without a bouquet, and said, "Hey, Rocky."

My mind whirled on the brotherly love from two of the four Hudson brothers when it was clear the oldest one stepped in. He had the I've wrangled them so many times, I've seen past their bullshit, and I'm tired of it visage that all big brothers had. What he didn't do was bend down and give me sisterly welcome smooches. No, he extended his hand and said, "I'm Cole. It's nice to finally meet you."

I shook his hand and said, "It's nice to meet you too." And I hoped I conveyed that I got he wasn't welcoming me with open arms because he was worried I'd trample all over his baby brother's heart. But, more importantly, I hoped he saw it by the end of the night that I was hoping I could keep it.

I did the welcome-to-my-home spiel and corralled them into the family room, where they all sat down and gazed at all the appetizers Mom had placed on the coffee table.

I bent down, placed the gorgeous plant next to the food, and said, "Please help yourself while I peel Mom away from the kitchen and grab something for you all to drink. Water? Beer? Wine? Whiskey?"

The brothers ordered beers, and Phil attempted to request a whiskey before four sets of hardened eyes aimed at him. He shot his hands up and said, "Okay. Okay. Okay. Don't get your panties in a bunch. I'll have red wine if you have it."

I knew my smile was wobbly. I missed my dad, and their interaction reminded me of how we all were before he passed. The quick banter, the laughs, the looks. All of it.

"I'll be right back." I quickly spun on my heel, hoping they didn't catch the wetness in my eyes.

I hadn't even taken a step when Max's arm snaked around my middle, and he whispered in my ear, "You all right?"

I melted into him and laid my hand on his arm. "Yeah. You all reminded me of what it was like before when my dad was here."

"I'm sorry, baby." He gave me a gentle squeeze.

"Oh, there you are!" Mom exclaimed as she walked in.

Max stepped around me and held his hand to shake Mom's hand. "It's a pleasure to see you again, Mrs. Sterling."

"It's wonderful to see you too, Max, but call me Martha." Mom leaned up, patted his cheek, and continued, "So handsome."

Mom scanned my face and then quickly glanced at the Hudson brood. Her smile briefly wavered before she winked at me and continued her trajectory toward our visitors.

All four of them stood as Mom got closer.

"Mom, you remember Paul."

"Of course I do." Again, with the motherly pat on the cheek. "Are you resting? You look a little tired, dear." Concern enveloped Mom as she stared at Paul, waiting for an answer.

The men froze, their eyes riveted on Mom and her genuine motherly tenderness. And I wanted to hunt their mother down and pound the living crap out of her.

"Yeah, I'm fine, Mrs. Sterling." Paul's usual jovialness wavered.

"Martha, Paul." She touched his cheek again and turned to the remaining members of the Hudson clan.

"I'm Vic, and this is Cole." Both leaned forward to shake her hand. "It's a pleasure to meet you, Mrs. Sterling."

Not knowing how not to be motherly, Mom did the whole cheek pat thing to both, even though she just met them.

"Please call me Martha. I think we're past formalities." She smiled at them. "That leaves you, the dad."

"It does. I'm Phil." He extended a gorgeous bouquet toward Mom. The subtle burst of red lilies softened by the peach roses, pale yellow mini carnations, and green hypericum berries topped off with blades from the lilies, all sitting in another child-painted pot—it was stunning. "Thank you for having us."

"These are unbelievably lovely. Thank you, and I'm sure you know I'm Martha by now." Mom smelled the flowers before she placed them on the table.

"Please, everyone, sit," I said. "I'm going to grab the drinks and be right back."

"I'll go with you. I have a few more things to wrap up before dinner," Mom said.

"I hope you all brought your appetite because Mom's cooking is the best, and she did not disappoint with tonight's meal," I said as I looked over my shoulder at them as I made my way to the kitchen.

"I know I can't wait for a good home-cooked meal. My diet lately has been bland," Phil stated and received four harassed expressions.

Max ignored his dad and said, "I'll give Raquel a hand with the drinks, but do you need help with anything, Martha?"

Mom's step faltered at having another male offer to help her. "That's sweet, but there isn't much left to do." Ash helped a ton after Dad died, but his business meant he spent a lot of time away from Feldspar, from home. Mom and I were used to doing things on our own.

Tonight would be different for all of us, full of emotional hits that we would need to adapt to.

Max and I quickly got the drinks together and headed back to the living room as Mom placed the bread in the oven.

The conversation was easy, and I didn't feel awkward with Max's arm spread across the back of the couch behind me.

"It'll be another twenty minutes before the bread is done," Mom said as she joined us.

"That sounds perfect," Phil said. "Since we have some time, I gotta ask. How did Sterling Custom Auto get started? I've read everything online, but I'm looking for the behind-the-scenes story of how it all started." He leaned forward, interest clear on his face.

"I can do you one better. I can show you." I stood up. "Follow me."

Everyone trailed me to the enormous red and white barn out back. I unlocked and disarmed the alarm as everyone stepped indoors.

The whistle that pierced the air was long and sweet as the lights illuminated all the beauties inside.

"Now, those are some smooth, sexy curves," Vic said.

"Rocky, you've been holding out on me," Paul scolded me as he beelined for the 1967 Ford Bronco. "Please tell me I can take this sweet girl for a ride." He shot big puppy eyes at me as he smoothed his hand down the baby blue hood.

"If you're giving out free rides, I'd love to take this bad boy right here." Vic eyed the turquoise '67 Charger.

Cole hadn't said a word, but the look he gave the gypsy red '55 Apache said it all. He wanted in on the action too.

"I don't know. I've noticed your truck, Paul, and it's a disaster." He owned a landscaping business, so his truck was constantly dirty.

"Hey! Not fair. I work around dirt. It's hard to keep it clean," he whined.

"Now that's a beauty." Phil ignored our banter and stood beside the platform where my dad's 1955 Thunderbird rested.

"Yes, and she's a complete man-eater." Mom stood next to him on that horrid announcement.

"Mom!"

"Am I wrong? She lures men to her when she's resting. She lures men to her when she's awake. Heaven help us if she purrs." Mom looked back at me. "She turns every man's head and catches every man's eye. No man can deny her in any state, and every man wants to put his hands on her. I'd say that's the definition of a man-eater."

My mouth hung open. I never knew Mom paid that much attention to the workings and feelings of the vehicles Dad and I worked on. Because we said those words so many times when we were together, he'd tell me she was the only woman who ever made my dad do a double take, even if mom was the only woman who ever held his heart.

"She's got you there, Rocky, and that's what I'd do if I were your dad. I'd use this beauty to start Sterling Custom Auto because *no* man could ever say no to her." Phil backed Mom and proved my Dad was right on so many levels.

"When Charlie brought her home for the first time, I about set her on fire. I was so livid with him. He spent our meager savings on her. He said she'd make it so we were comfortable and we could retire early." Mom shook her head. "I didn't want to be rich. I wanted a lifetime with him and my kids."

This time, my "Mom" was barely audible. I never knew my dad said that. He'd tell me it would give Mom the peace she'd need later in life. To live it happily and without worry. I was a kid and didn't know he wanted to set up Mom.

Max wrapped his arm around me, and I leaned into him.

His support meant everything.

"I tell him all the time now that he was right. The T-bird made us richer than he could ever believe." Mom smiled at me. "Our baby girl's dream of working with her dad every day doing something she loves, and our boy is grown and doing what he loves. Both happy and healthy —I'd say he was right." Mom turned back to the T-Bird and patted the hood. "Although sometimes I still want to scorch her."

My laughter was short and strangled between my tears.

"You won't do that because you'd have to burn down my garage," I told Mom and then looked at Phil. "But now you have the behind-the-scenes story of what started Sterling Custom Auto."

"In my opinion, that's the story you should post. Not the professional I-know-about-cars one you currently have up online." He raised his hand to stop my objections. "People want to know you're human and care about them." He cleared his throat. "And they want love. Your tale has it all."

At this rate, I would be a big bundle of tears. "I'll have to think about it."

Mom winked at me.

"She hasn't been out since Dad passed away." I looked up at Max.

His mouth dropped open, and his eyes popped in shock. "Seriously?"

"Serious." Sadness hit me as I remembered the loss of my father. "It's been seven years." I swallowed more tears. "Mom won't drive her, and I don't feel right taking her out without Mom."

"Ah, Raquel. I wondered why you didn't drive her." Mom's face wavered through my tears. "Well, I say we change that. I think it's time she reminds people she's hungry, don't you?"

"Totally." My mind spun as the possibilities of introducing her back to the world burst into my brain. Could I use her as a promo for the Wheldon contract? It was a way to give the haters the middle finger and remind everyone Sterling Custom Auto was here to stay.

My ringtone jarred me back to the present. "One second." I walked toward the barn door as Bruno's name appeared on my phone. He didn't usually call me on the weekends. He'd been running Sterling

Custom Auto with Dad since the beginning, so he was more than equipped to handle anything. But with everything that'd occurred lately, viewing his number on my phone didn't bring me happy joy, joy feelings. "Hey, Bruno."

"Rocky, sorry to bother you on the weekend." Dread slowly filled me as the worry in Bruno's voice penetrated.

"No problem, Bruno. What's going on?" Please don't let it be any more complications.

"Shit, I'm sorry, Rocky; I realized I forgot to run payroll yesterday since we weren't in the shop. So even if I run it tonight, we've missed the cutoff date for the guys to get it deposited on time. And I'm not sure how to pay them—is it considered non-pay? Or is it vacation time? I'm not sure how you want to handle this?"

My shoulders dropped, and the tension left my body at the simplicity of the issue.

"Don't worry about it, Bruno. As for the earnings category, leave it as regular work hours with SCA as the project build—don't deduct anything from their vacation, sick, or whatever hours. They didn't ask for the time off, so I'm not docking them for it. Run it on Monday, but don't have it directly deposited into their accounts. Instead, mark it as a manual check so we can still withdraw their deductions, and I'll just write the check and give it to them on payday." Phew, something that was an easy fix.

"All right, Rocky. I'll take care of it first thing Monday morning. I'll let you go so you can get back to your company."

"No problem, but how do you know I have guests?" I turned back to Mom and narrowed my eyes at her, knowing full well she'd been spreading Mom Joy across town.

He chuckled. "I think Martha already planned the wedding."

"Uh-huh. Of course, Mom has." She flat-out beamed. "Thanks, Bruno."

Before I could launch in on Mom, Cole said, "That's cool of you to treat your employees the way you do."

Of the Hudson bunch, Cole was the most quiet and watchful. He engaged in conversation, but he mostly sat back and observed. It didn't bother me because Ash was the same way in a more I'm devising a way to incapacitate you manner. So, Cole's comment made me wonder if I passed an unknown test.

"Thanks, but what happened at the shop wasn't the guys' fault, and they shouldn't be penalized for it, so it's really a no-brainer." I brushed it off.

"Yeah."

Vic bumped Cole's shoulder in reprimand. "So, it's undeniable you like speed. How do you feel about flying?"

"What do you mean?" I asked because I definitely enjoyed my last airplane ride.

Max slid his arm across my chest as he came up behind me.

"Have you ever flown a plane? Or gone up on a two-seater?" Vic asked.

"I've been in a two-seater but never flown a plane before." I'd love to go back up. "I don't have airplanes. I have high-speed cars."

"Would you guys stop playing twenty-one questions with Rocky?" Paul chided them. "Vic and Max own Hudson Flight School in Granite Creek. They're trying to determine if you can handle being up in the air."

"Well, Max already took me flying last weekend." My smile was unstoppable. "He says he's going to teach me how to fly." I bounced on my feet, jiggling Max in my excitement.

"Oh, dear God." Mom's concern bounced right off me.

Max hesitantly eyed Mom before he answered, "Once you complete all your lessons, you can fly it yourself."

That worked for me because I had plans to surprise Max with a blow job at thirty thousand feet.

"Really, Raquel? You don't think I have enough gray hair without you adding flying airplanes?" Mom tried once again to ground me.

"I'll pay for you to have your hair colored." I gleefully sidestepped Mom's worry.

CHAPTER TWENTY

Rocky

OUR JOURNEY BACK INSIDE THE HOUSE INCLUDED MOM CHASTISING Max for volunteering to feed my speed addiction and me smiling like the Cheshire cat because they were getting along as if they'd known each other for years, not just moments. Okay, the speed adrenaline played a big part too.

"Why don't you guys have a seat at the dining room table, and Mom and I will bring out the food." I interrupted Mom's plea to Max not to teach me how to fly an airplane.

"Or we can help you set the table." Cole made himself at home, grabbed some of the side dishes from the kitchen counter, and headed to the table.

It was like we all had dined a hundred times together. Everyone pitched in, and before I knew it, we were all seated around the table, comfortably chatting while eating Mom's delicious cooking.

During a lull in conversation, Cole turned to me. "So Max said your shop had some legal hassles recently. Something about zoning, traffic and parking, noise, and nuisance?"

I nodded and swallowed a bite of food. "Yes. My attorney and I are working on getting it nullified. It's been a pain in my…" I looked at Mom and smiled. "derriere."

Paul chuckled at my verbal save.

"I'll bet," Vic shook his head sympathetically. "Any idea who filed them?"

"No definite proof yet, but I have my suspicions. My lawyer and I are pushing the city council to reveal the source, but they've been stonewalling us." I stabbed my food with my fork in aggravation. "They recently switched from hard copies to digital and are having technical difficulties, so getting useful information from them is torture."

"It's a little bit outrageous," Paul chimed in. "A respected business like yours and the others that have been in that location for as many years as they have that are now being targeted in that way."

"It is incredibly frustrating." I couldn't wait until it was all done and over with. A bad memory in my rearview mirror. "By the way, Mom, I've got your new code ready."

"No rush, sweetheart. I'll grab that from you later."

"You're handling it way better than I would. You've kept your composure and grace under all these attacks." Max saluted his beer bottle at me while pride shone in his eyes. "I'm a firm believer in standing up for what's right, and you're doing it. Not only for your dad but for yourself."

"Thanks, but you haven't seen me when no one's looking." I winked at Mom. "And there's no way I'm going to let some bogus complaints ruin everything my dad built." I turned my hand to squeeze Max's, voice thick with emotion.

"I never knew your dad, but I imagine he would be mighty proud of you." Phil's kind words nearly brought tears to my eyes. Max's thumb stroking over mine soothed me.

"Without a doubt," Mom confirmed.

Cole raised his glass. "To standing up for what's right." Everyone echoed him and clinked glasses in my honor.

Overwhelmed by their support, I cleared my throat and said, "Enough about that drama. Please have more food." I busied myself passing dishes around, touched at how they'd embraced me. "But save some room for dessert."

The conversation shifted to safer topics after that as we finished up dinner. I was grateful when Max steered it toward funny work stories, allowing me to simply relax and enjoy the laughter and camaraderie flowing around the table. It was obvious the Hudson family were close, but they didn't exclude Mom and me. It was natural. It was right.

As we polished off our food, Paul turned to me curiously. "So when is that brother of yours coming home? I've heard his name mentioned a few times."

"Ash should be here sometime next week. He said he was wrapping a job up and would head here once he finished it." I sipped my wine.

"What line of business is your brother in?" Phil asked.

"He went into the military right out of high school, and right before he termed out, Charlie died. So, Ash headed back home to help me run the shop while Rocky finished her college degree at my insistence." She smiled at me. "At the same time, he opened up a private security firm with some of his friends from the service. His work takes him all over, and I'm not quite sure about everything he does," Mom answered.

"Yeah, I was nineteen when our lives changed, and I had another three years before I could get my degree. Ash loves the shop, but it's not his passion. I gave up trying to figure out a long time ago what exactly he does. I do know Ash has a strong sense of duty. I think losing Dad cemented his decision. The structure and purpose helped after everything kind of shattered." I smiled ruefully. "I think he also wanted the skills the military could give him faster than figuring it out alone. Plus, it connected him with his team."

"Either way, it's an admirable career," Phil noted. "You both must miss him with him being gone so much."

Both Mom and I nodded.

"Yes, but thankfully, technology makes it easier. We text, video chat, or just call weekly. More often, if Ash is not in the middle of something that requires his undivided attention," Mom said.

"It doesn't matter if he's here or not. He keeps tabs on me whether I like it or not," I mumbled.

That earned me knowing looks from the men around the table.

"Overprotective big brothers don't ever grow out of it," Cole said wryly.

Vic, Paul, and Max groaned.

I chuckled at their shared misery. "Too true," I acknowledged. "Even with Ash's brotherly vigilance, he has supported me in managing Dad's shop. I know he'll always see me as his baby sister, but he respects what I've achieved and believes in me."

"Of course he does. He's just like your father in that manner. Well, in every manner. Those two drove me batty with all the *'Be aware of your surroundings at all times.' 'Make sure to look in the backseat before you get in.' 'Lock your doors as soon as you get in.'*" Mom teared up as memories bombarded her.

I quickly gathered empty plates and dishes to bring Mom out of the past and into the present. If Mom started crying, I'd join her, and we didn't need that at our first get-to-know-you dinner with Max and his family. "I don't know about you all, but I could go for dessert."

"How did I know?" Max teased me as the Hudson men jumped up to help. "Let me guess. Is it chocolate?"

I stuck my tongue out at him. "No, it's not, but it's almost as good."

Mom's gasp made me backstep my response.

"I mean, it's waaaaayyyy better than chocolate." I widened my eyes behind Mom's back at Max at my fib. There really wasn't anything that tasted better than chocolate.

Okay, Max definitely inched past it.

"Now, I know you're lying." Mom playfully swatted me with the kitchen towel.

Paul chuckled at our banter while Cole and Vic's smiles were sadly happy. Of course, seeing that look on their faces made me want to deliberately spill my coffee on Delilah's pants the next time I saw her at Margie's shop.

"I do not lie." Stretch the truth a little, maybe, but not flat-out lie. "Your desserts are scrumptious." They really were.

Meanwhile, everyone helped clear the table over my mom's amused protests. Their thoughtfulness charmed me and Mom. The slight smile on her face was proof.

With the table cleared, I started brewing coffee while Mom pulled her freshly baked almond cake from the warmer. The warm, sugary scent filled the house, and my mouth salivated. It wasn't chocolate, but it was still good.

"Do you need any help?" Max asked, coming up behind me at the counter.

"I think we're all set." I turned and looped my arms around his neck. "Thank you again for suggesting this dinner. Your family is pretty awesome."

Max's strong arms encircled my waist as his forehead dropped to rest against mine. "Told you they'd adore you. But not as much as I do." He sealed his words with a soft kiss, and my heart attempted to gallop out of my chest.

He said he adored me. He said it. I wanted to do a cartwheel for joy, but I wasn't letting him go. Instead, I rested against him. The easy affection between us now felt natural. I wished we could stay wrapped up in our private bubble, but our families were only a room away. I reluctantly pulled back. "If we don't get out there soon, Mom will come barging in here to see if we're okay." No way he didn't hear the regret in my voice.

Max sighed but released me agreeably. "Yeah. Or it could be Paul." He shuddered.

I picked up the coffee and cups, Max carried the cake, and we returned to our families.

"You two were in there a long time." Paul leaned forward to grab a coffee cup and winked at me, the loveable jerk.

I glanced at Mom before I answered, "Not long enough."

Paul choked on his coffee, and his brothers laughed.

"Raquel Marie," Mom chastised me.

"He started it." I stood my ground like any sibling would.

"Paul Michael, apologize to Rocky." Phil's smile threatened to split his face even as he did his best to scold Paul. Phil clearly enjoyed our bantering.

"What? Why? I didn't do anything." Paul whined like all the babies of a family would do.

I smirked at him. "Ha! Finally someone besides me who will take the fall." Having Paul around was going to be awesome.

"No way," he protested. "I get to be the big brother for once."

Ah, that was so sweet. "Darn it. How am I supposed to say no to that?" It was my turn to whine.

Both Mom and Phil hid their smiles behind their sips of coffee.

"Well, if one of you would hurry up and give me grandbabies, then you could blame everything on the little rascals." Phil pointed out to his sons.

I groaned, knowing Mom would walk right through the door Phil opened.

"Oh heavens. Wouldn't that be lovely? It's not like we're getting any younger," Mom agreed with him. "I'm all for pursuing careers, but that shouldn't stop someone from having a family either." This time, she looked straight at me.

"Does anyone want more dessert?" I purposely looked at the Hudson brothers and ignored Mom.

"I don't think that's the dessert your mom is referring to," Paul mumbled.

"Paul Michael!" Phil reprimanded him at the same time us kids burst out laughing.

"Kids." Mom shook her head at our childishness.

Our conversation during dessert turned toward the restoration of the DeVille. "Even with the speed bumps, it's coming along beautifully," Max told his family. "You guys need to make time to come check out the work Rocky has done to it."

I was so freaking warm from all the happy feelings I felt that evening, but Max's words hit the hardest. From day one, he apologized for his misgivings of me as a female working on his vehicle. It didn't stop there. He made it known whenever he could that he respected the work my crew and I did for him. He stood by me and offered assistance wrangling all the balls I juggled. He'd been my silent support. So, yeah, his words wrapped my heart in a fluffy cloud of love endorphins.

"The engine overhaul is the most intensive part. We're pretty close to completing it. We're just waiting on some parts, and let me tell you, they were a..." I saw Mom's eyes narrow at me. "pain to find."

Paul chuckled.

"But once they come in, I know we'll have her purring in no time. As for the bodywork, that's almost done too." I nodded at Max. "I know last time I said all she needed was primer, but Clay has vetoed me on that and said she's not smooth enough yet. I..." I stopped talking when I noticed all five sets of eyes riveted on me. I looked at Mom and said, "I did it again, didn't I?"

She nodded. "I told you both at Coop's the other night that if it's not cars, then it's chocolate." Mom's smile was full of pride. "I think Rocky has proven this tonight."

I shoved a piece of Mom's almond cake in my mouth.

Everyone chuckled.

"It seems like you're ahead of schedule. Does that mean there's been a change in the completion date?" Phil asked eagerly.

"Well, I'd love to give you a definite answer, but I can't. I need to check with Bruno and the guys regarding our projects, schedule, and the reopening of the shop. I'm sorry. I wish I had better news. I know how excited you guys are to get her back." I crossed my fingers because, with my luck, anything was possible.

"It'll mean the world to have Grandpa's car brought back to life," Cole solemnly stated.

Phil leaned forward. "Well, I can't wait to take her for a spin once she's complete." His eyes glinted with anticipation.

"I got a confession to make. I was going to try to buy her off you guys when she first came in. Bella, my good friend, said I couldn't purchase every classic I came across. She's such a party pooper." I stuck my bottom lip in mock sadness.

"My goodness, Rocky. You do not need another car." Mom shook her head at me.

My hand shot up to my heart, and I gasped in fake outrage. "I can't believe you said that." I leaned toward Mom. "Take that back."

All the men chuckled at my dramatic acting at Mom's ridiculous words.

Mom shook her head at me again with a small smile on her face.

I purposefully turned my back to Mom and said, "My consolation was going to be that I would have the honor of roaring her to life." I dropped all my silliness, looked Phil in the eyes, and continued, "But if you would like, you can have that honor?"

The Hudson brothers sat immobile, breaths held, waiting for their father to respond.

Phil looked down at his hands circling his coffee cup, cleared his throat, and looked back up at me with moisture in his eyes. "I'd be honored."

Dammit.

I was going to make myself cry.

Mom stood with her empty cake plate and asked, "Does anyone want seconds?"

Bless my mother. Always there to get me through the hard times. She was just plain always there for me.

I raised my hand. "Is that really a question?" Sweets were a hard yes for me.

They all chuckled, but Cole and Phil stood up to help Mom bring out round two of the desserts.

Max used their distraction to lean into me, glided his hand along my leg to land at my thigh, and whispered, "I'm glad you love sugar. It lands in all the right places."

I reached down, squeezed his hand, and turned my head toward him. "Behave."

Mom, Phil, and Cole made quick work of handing out seconds. The conversation flowed as easily as before, and the familial intimacy saturated the dining room. I felt fortunate not only to have Max in my life but also to bond with his loved ones over my father's memory.

All too soon, the Hudson men had to get going. We moved to the front porch for a flurry of heartfelt goodbyes and promises to do this again soon.

Mom went inside to double-check everything was as it should be and gave Max and me a modicum of privacy. The Hudson men waited in their trucks and did their best to look elsewhere. Paul, of course, was staring at us through the front windshield with a huge smile and thumbs up, encouraging us to smooch.

The goofball.

Max ignored him and pulled me in close. "Thank you for an incredible evening and delicious food. I think our families got along great."

"You're welcome, and you better be prepared. Mom is going to mother the heck out of all of you now." I ran my fingers through his hair, not able to not touch him when he was this close.

"It might be awkward at first. We're not used to having a mom do mom things for us or to us," he admitted.

"If it's okay with you, I can share some of your mom's history with my mom and let her know to go easy on you guys," I offered. I didn't want him or his family to feel out of place around my mom or me. "But, just so you know. Mom is familiar with Delilah. We've run into her at Margie's coffee shop a few times."

"I trust you to share what you think you need to. We'll learn to adapt." He pulled me even closer. "I gotta go before Paul starts honking the horn or hollering out the window."

I gently wrapped my hand across the back of his neck. "Okay." Not really. I wanted him to stay.

Max leaned in and kissed me. It wasn't the panty-melting kisses he'd given me before, but it was pretty close. Although I had a feeling any kisses from Max would have that effect on me.

We held each other tightly, separating when Paul honked at us. "Call you tomorrow," Max said softly. With one more searing look, he headed down the steps to his waiting family.

I watched them drive away, my heart full. Bonding with the Hudsons over my father's memory made the evening especially poignant. With their affectionate support and Max's unwavering caring, I knew Dad would want me to embrace love fully again.

To fully embrace Max.

CHAPTER TWENTY-ONE

Rocky

IT'D BEEN ALMOST A MONTH SINCE THE HORRENDOUS BREAK-IN AND the whole complaints debacle. If I was being frank with myself, it seemed like my life started circling the drain about the time I dumped Carson. Not that I blamed losing him specifically as a loss. Just that everything got a little haywire around that time. Maybe it was my need to prove to my dad he made the right choice when he left his dream in my hands. So much so that I hyper-refocused on perfection instead of the principles my dad raised with me and didn't take a moment to appreciate the world around me.

Well, I definitely was now.

The small meeting room had a decently packed crowd. Businesses that also had multiple complaints against them were in attendance. Citizens of Feldspar who were concerned with other agenda happenings were there too. Everyone in our small town gathered to have their voices heard on what mattered to them.

And Max.

When I pulled up in the parking lot, I saw him leaning against his truck, waiting for me. It was too late. My heart was happily living in Maxdom and refused to listen to reason, to tread carefully and slowly.

I wasn't sure I wanted to anymore.

He was all kinds of good-looking, and I wondered if I could get him to be the cover model for SCA advertisements instead. Nope. My doors would blow wide open, and I'd have to hose down every floozy who wanted a piece of him.

The man definitely revved engines.

Just one look at him, and I wanted to pounce. My body screamed that Max absolutely deserved another good spin around the block. And my mind? It agreed too. It was my heart that was the problem. It wanted to keep him.

I glanced at him sitting beside me and wondered if Bella was right. Did I have too many barriers that I wasn't letting some sunshine in? Would I regret not taking this opportunity with Max? If anything, I knew I'd at least have fantastic sex with him.

"Stop imagining having sex with Max. You're steaming up the room," Bella leaned in and whispered.

I elbowed her. Max was sitting *right* next to me, and the little smile on his face told me he heard Bella too.

Mom, who sat on her other side, gave me the patented behave look.

I glared at Bella. She always got me in trouble.

"Where's Ash? I thought he'd be here," she leaned back in to ask.

I side-eyed Mom before I quietly replied, "He got here last week. He said he had something to do and would catch up with us later."

"Shhh." Mom shushed me. Not Bella.

So, I elbowed her *and* kept my eyes resolutely forward so I wouldn't fall victim to Mom's death glare.

Max coughed behind his fist to hide that he thought we were hilarious and avoid being in Mom's crosshair.

It also reminded me I sat in this small room, dressed in my professional business suit—for appearances and courage—and listened to the council members drone on about various issues. I prayed with every fiber in my being tonight would at least resolve one of my concerns—leaving Sterling Custom Auto exactly where it was, where it belonged.

But glancing at the clock told me fifteen minutes remained, and the probability of any resolutions seemed to slip away once more.

No. I knew with both the original and recent survey in Mr. Quincy's hands that he would have this nullified by tomorrow morning. They clearly showed Sterling Custom Auto was not in default of any zoning violations. Which I also hoped would invalidate the other violations as well. I just prayed this headache would end for me tonight.

"Now, onto the final item on the agenda: the possible zoning discrepancy surrounding the buildings in downtown Feldspar. After careful, detailed, and thorough investigation and discussion with the city council members and experts regarding zoning, traffic and parking, noise, and nuisance ordinances and its associations, the council has decided the original complaints are invalid and voted to retain all ordinances as they are. All in favor, say aye." Mr. Dixon turned to his left and right at his fellow council members.

I grabbed Max's hand and squeezed the life out of it as I held my breath, waiting for each council member to cast their vote, and when Mr. Dixon's gavel met the wooden block declaring the edicts would stand as they were—my breath left my body in one fell swoosh. All my pent-up anxiety, fears, and nausea exited my body in that one soul-altering pound. My eyes closed on their own accord, and the darkness allowed the image of my proud, smiling dad to soothe the remaining ache deep inside me. I didn't care that anyone could spot the tear sliding down my cheek.

Damn, it felt unbelievably fantastic to know beyond a doubt that the shop was safe.

"Raquel." A gentle, sophisticated voice sounded above me.

I opened my eyes and saw people exiting, but Mom, Bella, and Mr. Quincy stood before me. Max stayed in his seat beside me, holding my hand while Mr. Quincy scanned my face and followed the tear tracks down my cheek.

I wiped the elated evidence off my cheeks and slowly, oh so gratifyingly slowly, smiled at them.

"You're the shit, Mr. Quincy." I didn't care that my mother had repeatedly rebuked my shady public behavior in the last month.

Instead, I released my hold on Max's hand, stood up, and gave Mr. Quincy the tightest hug I could without hurting his aging body.

"Rocky! Really." Even with this win, Mom still reprimanded me.

Mr. Quincy's awkward pat on my back made me giggle. Mr. Quincy didn't do public displays of affection.

I stepped back and relieved him of his discomfort.

I didn't even care that my face hurt from my big, goofy smile. It felt unbelievably amazing to have won at least this hurdle.

"Very well then." Mr. Quincy's words showed his discomfort.

"Thank you isn't sufficient, but they're the only words I can find. Everything you've done for me? I can't express how much it means to me. So, thank you, Mr. Quincy." Those two little words never sounded so lame until I needed them to mean much more. But, in this context, they were immeasurable in their meaning.

Mr. Quincy's expression softened before returning to his natural state of professionalism. "I'll complete the outstanding paperwork by the end of this week and send that over for your approval." He hesitated for a split second before he said, "I'm glad you didn't settle." He nodded at Max.

"You're going to make me cry, Mr. Quincy." I teased him, wondering if my feelings were that apparent.

"Nonsense." His lips barely twitched at his dry humor.

"Congratulations, Rocky." Bella's smile was almost as big as mine.

"Thanks. It feels so good." I turned to Mom, wanting to witness her expression.

"Well, now that this nonsense is over, maybe my daughter can focus more on her manners now."

"Yes, ma'am." Mom's words would have given me the I gotta do better kid feeling, but I was too happy to let it penetrate.

"Excuse me. I was hoping to have a word with Rocky." Even Kevin's voice couldn't dampen my mood.

"Very well. Mr. Reynolds, please make sure your office sends over the appropriate paperwork. Good evening, everyone." Mr. Quincy bid his farewell.

"Me too. I'm working the graveyard shift tonight," Bella chimed in.

"Sweetheart, I have an early morning and must head out too. Do you need anything before I leave?"

"I'm good, Mom." I hugged and whispered in her ear, "I love you."

"I love you too, baby."

Mom left me standing with Max and Kevin. I was too happy to be worried about whether or not Kevin might throw another grenade at me. I turned to him and asked, "Sorry, what can I do for you?" I prayed it wasn't about the girlfriend thing again, or now that he couldn't pursue this avenue toward wifedom, he might venture down another path.

"I owe you an apology. In my pursuit to reach my life goals, I became blind to how that would impact others. Most especially the goals, ambitions, and personal beings of others. For that, I am deeply sorry."

My mouth dropped open. I never thought Kevin would realize what a rudimentary tunnel vision view he'd had. Much less apologize for it.

Next to me, Max watched in attentive silence.

Kevin smiled sheepishly at me, and just like that, I knew whatever girl he landed, she'd be so freaking lucky.

"I know my pursuits were relentless, but is it hard to believe that I'd figure out I was being..."

"Small-minded? Arrogant? Mayberryish?"

Both Max and Kevin chuckled at my description.

"That wasn't an admission to any of those qualities." Kevin's smile stayed firmly in place.

"Don't stop. This Kevin—the lighthearted, smart, and funny Kevin —that's the Kevin women want." My hand shot up. "Not me, but some other lucky woman." I smiled, hoping to lessen the rejection, and I bumped Max's arm, letting him know I was the lucky one.

"I know. I guess a part of me has always known," Kevin grudgingly admitted.

"Yeah, I'm just glad we're past the part where there isn't a require-ment to exchange wifely duties to dismiss the legal complaints," I sort of joked.

Kevin's eyebrows shot down. "What?"

I scanned his face and tried to figure out if he was messing with me. "You know, the go out with you, and you'd get rid of the complaints against Sterling Custom Auto? Or the how many times did you ask me to have conversations with you regarding it so we could come to an understanding?" The more I spoke, the more his face soured with hurt and affront. "Especially when I was served the traffic and parking, noise, and nuisance complaints you came in, again, pushing to have a conversation about it all." My stomach dropped the more Kevin's face reddened with insult.

"I would never use my authority to gain favor in any situation. And most importantly, I would never, *never* use my position to force any woman to date me or do anything else," Kevin vehemently refuted my assumptions. "I can't believe you would think I was capable of such a thing or that you think that low of me."

My heart clenched. Boy, did I fuck up. "I'm so, *so* sorry Kevin. I didn't know what to think. Your words and actions made me believe it was the only option. I mean, it all happened at the same time—your pursuit of me and the accusations to shut down Sterling Custom Auto. And since you're the Vice Mayor and the law would need to be changed, I thought you were using your clout to sway the voting." I tried to make him see it from my point of view.

He shook his head. "I couldn't and didn't understand why you responded the way you did when I approached you, but looking at it through your eyes I can see the misunderstanding. As for the other, it's pure coincidence because I am not the person behind the grievances."

"You didn't file them?" I asked for confirmation.

"No."

Shit. Who did? "I can't say it enough. I'm sorry I thought that about you." Because when he wasn't being uppity, he was actually a nice guy.

"Let's leave it in the past." He sucked in a deep breath. "Anyways, I'm glad it all worked in your favor and your shop was spared. Please know if you have any other problems, I'm always here to help." It was his turn to lift his hand. "I know you have an army, but I'd be honored if you considered me one of them."

Damn, when the man changed his stripes, he was all kinds of hot. It's just that I wanted a different type of hot sauce.

"Thanks, Kevin. I'm excited for a new and different friendship between us." I pushed my luck and said, "Now that the complaint has been squashed, is it possible to release the name of the individual who filed it? If not, do you have any word on all the forms I filled out a few weeks ago?"

"Unfortunately, I cannot release that information even with the grievance closed, and at this time, I do not know the status of your filings." He sincerely looked apologetic. "However, I will make sure to conclude this business with Mr. Quincy this week."

If he wasn't behind it, then who was?

"No problem. I'll follow up with City Hall and Mr. Quincy tomorrow."

"If you'll both excuse me, I have some things I need to complete before I take off." Kevin bid me and Max goodbye.

I turned to Max, ready to ask him back to my place to celebrate when his phone beeped with a text. He bent down to read the message as I stepped closer to him. His heat, strength, and scent seeped into me, warming me up.

He looked up from his phone to me, cupped my cheek, and said, "I want to take you up on your unspoken offer and celebrate with you."

I guess I didn't hide what I was thinking.

He gave me a quick peck. "But Paul just had it out with our mother, and I don't feel right not going and checking in on him."

That cow.

"I get it. Go. Make sure Paul's okay." I leaned into him.

He gave me another kiss.

"If it's not too late, I'll call you when I leave Paul's place," Max said.

"Okay. I'll probably be up for a while." I was too jazzed to go to bed.

We chit-chatted as we made our way to my car, where Max gave me a kiss I wanted to explore in more detail.

He pulled back and grumbled, "Dammit."

He could say that again.

I gently pushed back against his firm stomach and said, "Go to

Paul." Before I changed my mind and said screw Paul and definitely fuck Delilah and kept Max to myself.

Another quick lip touch and Max made sure I was secure in my vehicle before taking off to his.

I sat in my car for a few minutes and called the guys to tell them it was all right to return to work tomorrow.

I drove to the shop and thought at least I was down a few problems with the zoning issue resolved, and Kevin's romantic pursuit concluded. It was a relief to know I only had to focus on the break-in, the mystery woman, and the rumors. I texted Ash quickly, letting him know tonight's results, especially regarding Kevin's turnabout.

Mostly, I was thrilled my dad's shop was safe.

CHAPTER TWENTY-TWO

Rocky

I LAID IN THE MIDDLE OF THE FLOOR IN MY BARREN OFFICE AND surveyed the beams in the vaulted ceiling with a pile of chocolate wrappers surrounding me. I blindly patted the ground next to me and searched for another one to pop into my mouth while I conversed with Dad.

"Hey, Dad. So, as I'm sure you know, I encountered a few bumps with the shop. First, Kevin saw me as his June Cleaver, and I thought he tried to use his political clout to scare me into abiding by his plan by using the shop as bait. I thought it was more of a hostile attack. Fortunately, that was all a misunderstanding, and he put the kibosh on all that nonsense. Then some jerk hole decided they didn't like our decor and did something about it. I mean, I'll give the slimeball some kudos—the desk did need to be replaced. However, I would have gone about it a little differently. More the bonfire route, and I don't think I need to explain that one. Luckily, the damage to the shop was surface. Unfortunately, the vehicles, especially the DeVille, were harmed, putting us behind on our schedule. But I'm choosing to look on the bright side and thank the jackass for allowing me to do a top-to-toe cleaning, a necessary inventory take, provide the guys with an unexpected vacation, and replace the desk. I mean, I could have

done without any of the damage—besides the desk, or the insurance paperwork, or the police paperwork, or... Okay, going back to the bright side. Wheldon Luxury approached us to design a line of luxury automobiles. I was thinking of using the T-Bird as my inspiration. Mom agreed. I mean, how could it not be right? What do you think, Dad?"

My heart jumped, and my head swung toward the door when the chime rang through the eerily quiet building. *Who in the world would be ringing the bell at nine-thirty at night? Should I answer it? Was it the burglar coming back for round two? Call the cops?* It didn't matter. I was frozen in fear as I watched a huge shadow cup the glass door window, peer inside, and then back up to have another go at the chime.

I bolted upright and frantically searched for my cell phone. What did I do with it? Was it still in my purse?

"Raquel?!"

I turned back to the door and saw the figure cupping the window again.

"Raquel! Damn it! Answer me."

"Max?" I got up, walked to the door, opened it, and sure enough. Max was outside my office door. "What are you doing here?"

He ran his hands up and down my arms. "I thought I'd come see you instead of calling. Are you okay? Are you hurt?"

"Yes. No." I saw the worry etched on his face. "Are you okay?" I mean, he was the one outside my shop at night.

"Me? You were the one lying on the ground. I thought you were hurt."

My belly did a little flip, and my body remembered Max's hands were on me.

"Yeah, I was just..." I looked back at the barren office. "Communing with Dad. Do you wanna come in?" I stepped back as an invitation for him to come in.

"Your dad?" His eyebrows shot down in confusion as he stepped inside.

I locked the door behind him. I mean, it was nighttime, and there was someone out there with a not-so-good hard-on for me.

I shrugged. "Yup. After everything that's happened and with

tonight's win, I wanted to update Dad." As if conversing with your dead parent or any dead person was normal.

He surveyed the room and stopped at the chocolate wrapper outline of a person. "Do you have to act dead in order to talk to him?" He raised an eyebrow in question.

I burst out laughing.

"No, but I find it helps. Chocolate and cars. Almost everything my dad loved."

"You mentioned it before. So, it was his doing drawing you to the dark side?" Max asked.

I swallowed my suddenly dry mouth at the sensual fire in his eyes and forced myself to say, "Yeah. He'd munch on a piece of chocolate when he struggled with a car. Then, he'd hand me one when I started joining him. He told me it helped activate his thinking. So it became our thing."

"Is my feeding you all this chocolate," he pulled a bar from his back pocket, "activating your brain?" His eyes never left mine.

I struggled to think past the growing need inside me. But then, the fire in Max reached for me.

It fueled me.

It encompassed me.

It ignited me.

My eyes followed the movement of his eyebrow lifting in question and shot back down to the tiniest uptilt of his lips.

Biteable lips.

Suckable lips.

Lickable lips.

"Well?"

"What?" Focusing on his words while I watched his mouth move was challenging. His lips were indeed a work of art.

He waved the bar at me. "Does chocolate help you... think?"

I sucked in a much-needed breath and commanded myself to get myself together. I yanked my gaze away from Max's too-alluring mouth, grabbed the chocolate, and forced myself toward the garage bay.

"Why do you keep giving me chocolate?" I knew my shop didn't hide my obsession with it, but was that the only reason?

"One, it's kind of hard to miss that you enjoy it." His lips twitched. "Two, it's even harder to miss that it's a connection between you and your dad. Three, I knew you would need it with either of tonight's possible outcomes, and I forgot to give it to you earlier."

I was in serious trouble. Max had blown through all my reasons to stay away, and I had every intention of keeping him.

"I know your weekly scheduled visits got messed up after the break-in and the closure, but do you want to see the DeVille?"

"Sure."

"Come on. I'll show you."

The *click click* of my heels shouted through the cavernous building as I stepped next to the DeVille. With my Vanna White wave, I asked, "She's not as far along as we wanted. The recent damage put us behind, but she's coming along nicely. What do you think?"

Max did a slow perusal of the shop before returning to me. This time, his top-to-toe, back-to-the-top inspection stopped at all the right places and left me in a puddle of desire. He stepped closer, closing any space between us, and said, "Ever since I met you, I've imagined splaying you across the hood of the DeVille. It's driven me mad." He nipped my bottom lip. "I'm going to do that." Another nibble. "Tonight." He watched me, waiting for my decision.

"Ever since I met you, I've imagined fucking you—"

That was all the consent he needed.

In one quick squeeze, I was plastered against his solid body, and he laid the best, hottest kiss on me. My desire-filled breasts were squished against his firm chest. I sacrilegiously dropped the chocolate bar and locked my hands in his silky hair. No way was I letting him stop again.

The feel of him—firm, silky—amped my hunger even more.

And his taste? Categorically the best chocolate substitute in the world. I was never going back to chocolate after tasting Max. He was heady, warm, and addictive.

My body undulated against his—wanting more, needing more. With each tiny glide of my nipples against the barriers between us, my juices poured from me. It left a want deep inside me. I craved for Max to fill me. My body knew it was missing him. And no matter how much I rode his leg, it wasn't enough.

Max slid his hand down farther, and one long, thick, strong finger nestled between my legs and rested against my clit. My body readied itself at his move and automatically pressed down, wanting more.

Unconsciously, a moan escaped me at the thickness and weight of him near my intimate folds. I clamped my inner thighs to keep his hand there even while undulating against him.

Max knew I needed more. He moved the hand from around my back up and pulled my hair back, offering my neck and chest to him. An invitation he accepted. He kissed, nibbled, and sucked down my neck to my cleavage. All of it caused a frenzy of need in me.

Moans, whimpers, cries—all unintelligible—escaped me from the pleasure Max provided me.

Then he pressed his finger against my love button, and I begged, "More."

He slowly removed his finger, no matter how hard I squeezed my legs to keep him right there.

"NO!" I yanked my head up. "Don't stop!" I demanded.

With a slow but deliberate and torturous lick of the top of my breast, he lifted his head and looked up at me, and I froze.

Unhidden, Max scorched me with the molten desire that burned him up. His face was a mask of chiseled granite hunger, and his eyes were a storm of ravenous lust. His delectable lips were swollen from our kiss and glistened from our passion.

"Are you sure?" It was apparent he barely leashed his control. He forced his words out through clenched teeth. His immovable muscles locked in position. His desire banked.

"Fuck me, Max."

With my back to the DeVille, he undid one button at a time and parted my suit jacket, exposing my burgundy lace bra to him.

No way I was going to let him go slow. I dropped my arms and let my jacket fall. Immediately, I went to work on the side zipper of my pants and shimmied out of them when I saw his leather jacket and shirt joined mine, and then his strong hands were on his belt.

I whimpered and leaned forward to kiss his golden chest.

"Mmm." His taste was divine. Better than the finest chocolate.

With kisses and tiny nibbles, I meandered around his torso. I wanted to taste every inch of him. I needed it. I raised my hand and smoothed it across his chest, sliding over his broad nipple. .

His hands shot to my hair, and he growled.

I pinched his nipple between my fingers and flicked the other with my tongue.

His grip tightened. "You're being a bad girl."

I sucked his nipple into my mouth and rubbed the other with my fingers. I wanted him to let go. To lose control.

I wanted Max unconfined, unrestrained, and unleashed.

"Raquel," he warned me.

I kept up the torture but moved my hand down his delectable naked body and finally felt what I'd longed for. He was hard and wide, and the bead of pre-ejaculation topped him off like the most mouth-watering ice cream.

"Mmmm." I gazed up at him and slowly dropped to my knees in front of him.

He stood before me. Tall and erect. A god to be worshiped. And worshiping I was going to do.

I glided my hand up and down his penis and watched his thigh muscles clench and unclench. Then, just like a popsicle, I licked him from the base to the top and engulfed him in my mouth.

"Mmmm." My juices soaked my thong at the exquisite taste of him.

Up and down, my mouth went. My hand followed to milk more out of him. I swirled my tongue around the tip to savor every last drop.

"Enough." He yanked me up.

"I want more. You." A kiss on his chest. "Are." Another kiss. "Delicious." A nibble.

Max's rough hands slid up my sides, and goosebumps erupted. Seconds later, my bra was gone, and the weight of my breasts were in his hands. He squeezed, caressed, and pulled.

I held on to his shoulders, enjoying the feel of his calloused hands on my sensitive skin. I closed my eyes, savoring the feeling of him touching me, and licked him again. He was my new addiction.

And then I was up and splayed across the hood of the DeVille. My hair fanned behind me, my red lace thong and heels stark against the gray hood. And Max stood there—a naked Greek statue come to life.

I lifted my hands to him. "Come here."

"I've fucking dreamt of you like this since I saw you." A shake of his head. "No, not like this. Cup your breasts and open for me, Raquel."

Slowly, I smoothed my hands up my torso and cupped each breast. I molded them, squeezed them, and tugged on my nipples.

He was absorbed in watching what my hands were doing.

My left hand continued its torture, but I moved my right hand down. The closer I got to my pussy, the more I opened my legs for Max, and when my hand met my thong, I slid my fingers under it, and my legs opened wide for his viewing. Then, I moved my fingers through my juices and spread it more, hitting my clit.

I dug my heels into the hood and lifted my hips to get more.

"Fuck."

The word was barely out before I felt the snap of my thong, Max's hands on my butt, and his mouth on me. He clutched my ass and swirled his tongue around my fingers as I tortured myself. We moved in sync and amped the fire inside me.

"Max." The breath left me as I moved closer to my orgasm.

He hummed against me, and my body ached for release. I lifted my hips to get closer to him, to my release.

He pulled my fingers away and continued eating me.

I clamped down his head and moved with him, searching for but not getting the needed release.

He pulled away, and I grabbed him.

"Don't stop," I begged.

He bent down, sifted through his pants and wallet, and retrieved a condom.

My body readied itself even more as I watched him smooth the rubber on his engorged penis.

"Now that's how I envisioned you. Wide, wet, and ready."

"Max. Please." I lifted my arms to him.

He didn't make me wait. The warmth and weight of him felt like heaven. His hand between my legs ratcheted my need for him, and finally, I felt the tip of his cock skim my pussy. Slowly, he moved back and forth, inching himself further and deeper into me.

"Faster," I pleaded.

"I don't want to hurt you." He laid immobile, holding himself in check, and ensured I could take him.

I grasped his butt cheeks in both hands and dug my heels into the back of his thighs. Then, I stared into his eyes and demanded, "Fuck me."

Fire poured out of him as he pounded into me.

Fast, furious, and devastatingly hellish.

I loved every glorious single minute of it.

The girth of his cock stretched me wide. His fingers tugged my nipple to almost painful but divine euphoria. His hand on my buttcheeks tilted me up for his drilling.

Max unleashed.

My head thrashed back and forth with the ecstasy he gave me. My back arched as rapture filled me, and I offered my breasts as a gift. He accepted his righteous boon and sucked my breast as if it was the nectar he needed to survive.

Our rhythm was uncontrollable, frantic.

My hands wandered, not knowing where to touch, to hold. Unintelligible sounds poured from me. I was lost to what Max gave me and insane with it.

"Please," I begged.

His hand on my rear moved inward and up and gave me the lift I needed to be closer to him. I dug my heels in his ass and widened my legs for his impalement. His tongue whirled around my nipple and alternated between tugging on it with his teeth and sucking on it. Meanwhile, his finger met my anal star, where he spread my juices around and readied me for his combined assault.

He pulled his mouth away from my chest.

I willed my sex-drugged eyes open and saw him admiring me.

"Yes?"

I wanted Max in every way possible.

"All of me is yours."

I was wrong. He wasn't unleashed before.

Max ignited.

He plundered my mouth, and my uterus spasmed as I took him from the front and back. Each thrust of his tongue and cock jammed me back onto his finger. Each thrust stretched and filled me. With each thrust, he fucked me in every way possible.

"Come, Raquel." Max drove in as his thumb filled my rear, and his other finger pressed my clit.

He ignited me, and I exploded.

And I fucking loved it.

Coming down from my explosion, I opened my eyes to watch Max doing the same.

Magnificent.

He gazed at me and said, "By the way, the business suit is sexy. But the heels? Fuck me."

My body shook with laughter, and I immediately moaned, feeling Max shift inside me.

"That feels unbelievable." Max stared down at our union.

"Yeah, it does." In more ways than one.

Max's next kisses were slow, loving, and perfect. I didn't want to stop, but I could feel him softening and sliding out of me.

He slowly pulled out of me, and the withdrawal shot mini-storms through me.

Max smiled an I-know-I'm-the-man smile, and I didn't care. My body said he earned it.

"We can clean up in the bathroom in the back."

"Lead the way, Raquel."

"Why do you call me Raquel and not Rocky?" I asked.

"Do I?"

"Yeah. I don't mind, but I was just wondering why when most people call me Rocky."

"I guess I know you as Raquel, the woman. Rocky is too, but she's the car chick." His innuendo wasn't lost on me as he gave me a lopsided grin. "But it was Raquel, the woman who drew me in. It's the layers of the woman I want to unravel. Rocky just happens to be one of those layers. I want them all."

I'd never been so overwhelmingly consumed by a male partner.

Someone who gave me more than I knew I needed. Bella was right. I had so many barriers up that I couldn't recognize what was right in front of me.

Max.

And I wanted him to have all of me too.

"On one condition." I tapped his bottom lip.

"Anything."

The fact there wasn't a single second of hesitation from Max shattered any remaining barriers inside me.

"I want all of you too."

"Done."

Vindictive

I knew I shouldn't have left the violation matters in Kevin's incompetent hands. He touted that being the Vice Mayor was this all-important powerful position, so why in the hell didn't he use that so-called authority to shut Rocky down?

It was a simple task, and he fucking botched it.

It took too much of my control not to storm up to the podium and punch that weak pompous ass in the nose. It was obvious Kevin wanted Rocky. The way he puppy dogged his way around her was so damn sickening, leaving any and every ounce of his man card at her feet. And when Mr. Dixon announced the vote, Kevin's eyes never wavered from her. As if by doing this for her, she'd give him a chance.

The asshat of a loser.

And Rocky. That lone tear of relief—and it was fucking relief—when the ruling came through. Tore me the hell up. She wasn't supposed to be crying tears of joy or happiness. No, she was supposed to be bawling from the loss of having her treasured *legacy* torn out from under her. From facing everyone to knowing she couldn't keep what her father started going.

But this wasn't over, far from it.

By the time I was through with her, she'd lose everything.

CHAPTER TWENTY-THREE

Rocky

"I SLEPT WITH MAX, AND IT WAS *HAWT*." MY PASSENGER DOOR
barely closed before I blurted my admission.

"*What?!*" Bella screeched.

"Technically, he kissed me first." But I did participate—*with*
enthusiasm.

"Holy cow, Rocky! How did it happen? When did it happen? Tell
me everything," she twisted to face me, her knee on the seat, and
bounced excitedly. "And why are you just now telling me?!"

"Don't be mad I didn't tell you sooner. The first was in the cockpit
of Max's plane and then last night on the hood of the DeVille." I
chanced a glance at Bella, whose attention never left me. "I don't know.
One minute, we're discussing his mom, chocolate, and cars, and the
next, we're..." Not that I was complaining. "Although I think my suit
and heels had something to do with it."

An image of Max over me, in me, flashed through my brain.

I rolled down the window in hopes of soothing my suddenly hot
body.

"Tell me more!" she demanded.

So, I gave more information about the salacious parts of my sexy time with Max.

"OhmyGod!OhmyGod!OhmyGod!" Bella chanted nonstop after my detailed narrative of my heated exploits with Max last night.

On the hood of the DeVille.

"Breathe, Bella. I don't want to explain to Dean or Alex why you passed out." Nope, reciting my sexual escapades to any of the guys was not on my to-do list—*ever*.

Bella squealed instead. "I knew it! I told you he had the hots for you. And, by your recital of the... edge-of-the-hood spirited activities, he can deliver on his tooling." She wiggled her eyebrows up and down. "More than delivered."

"Oh yeah." Such an understatement.

"So, when are you going out with him again? Maybe we can go on a double date?" She moved at Mach speed.

I pulled into the parking spot in front of Harper's Corner and said, "Slow down, Bella. I'm already light years ahead of you, and I need you to keep me firmly planted on the ground. Because if this goes wrong, I don't think I'll get over Max as easily as I have any other guy."

The air in the truck cabin muted as Bella's excitement dampened.

"Ah, Rocky. I'm always here for you, you know that." She tapped my arm in solidarity and said, "But, I gotta say it: I told you so."

She jumped out of my truck on her parting words and rushed toward the front door before I could kick her.

She opened the door, waited for me in plain sight of all the diners, and thwarted my retribution.

I met her at the door and said, "Just for that, I'm not going to tell you about our family dinner."

I walked past her and greeted Emma, "Good morning," before Bella could respond.

"Good morning, Rocky, Bella."

"Good morning, Emma," Bella said and then elbowed me. "Don't think you're getting out of telling me." She warned me.

I ignored Bella and asked Emma, "How are you today?"

"I'm good, and you both?" She eyed us, knowing something was up.

"Oh, I can say the same." I smiled.

"Uh-huh." Bella received an elbow to her side for mumblings.

Emma eyed us and asked, "Everything okay?"

"Yup." More than okay but I wasn't going to share the details with Emma in public.

"One *tall* mimosa, heavy on the champagne."

"Um, I'll just have some orange juice." I gave Bella the stink eye. "Someone has to drive after this."

She winked at me.

Emma lowered her notepad. "I'm assuming this is in celebration of last night's council meeting or...?" Emma's eyebrows raised in question.

"Yes," I admitted.

Bella snorted on her withheld laughter, knowing my celebration last night was *waaayyy* more heated than Emma's scrumptious gourmet.

"I'm excited to be back on the job." I looked down at the grease under my nails from this morning's work.

Bella's snort was louder and more strangled. She would never let me live down the combustion between Max and me.

Emma's head shot back and forth between us.

"Sorry, Em. Bella's not feeling too well today." I kicked her under the table for good measure.

"Oowwww."

"Uh huh," Emma did not look convinced.

I ignored them and ordered, "We'll have your specials, or if you have anything special brewing up back there, we'll try it." Emma was always experimenting with her culinary creations, and she never disappointed.

"Sorry, not today. I've been so focused on fixing up my granddad's cabin that I haven't spent much time in the kitchen. I swear the house needs something else updated every time I turn the corner. I am going to Toole's in a bit to pick up more supplies." She rubbed her forehead.

"We can go," I offered.

Bella nodded her agreement.

"Really? I'd love the help and the company." Emma blushed.

"Ooohhh, do tell." I leaned forward, anxious to hear what caused the pink on Emma's cheeks.

Her eyes sparkled and her cheeks darkened as she rambled, "I swear Blake is stalking me. Every, and I mean *every* time I'm at Toole's, he shows up, which isn't a problem that he's there. No, the problem is that he follows me around asking what I'm doing, offering advice, help, whatever." She actually stomped her foot. "I may not have fixed a house up before, but that doesn't mean I can't figure it out. I'm not some little girl who needs some big, strong, hot guy to do it for me or tell me how."

I'm sure anyone who noticed me saw a huge Cheshire smile on my face. Our little Emma had a big ol' crush on Blake—a hot, MMA-strong, disciplined, and persistent fighter. Poor Emma didn't stand a chance.

"Yeah, that does sound horrible. I mean, how dare he!" Bella's back shot straight as she cried out in fake outrage.

Emma didn't catch on. "Right?! Women have been crossing tradi-tional gender roles for centuries. So you'd think the male population would catch on. Besides, there are so many tutorials online now anyone can fix anything." Her announcement cried exasperation at Blake's courting attempts.

"I don't know, Emma. I get confused sometimes with the online explanations. But I find that it's super fun when Dean uses tools with me." Bella's eyes danced with mischief. "You might consider letting Blake handle your tools sometimes."

"You're horrible!" Emma's hand towel hit Bella square in the face, as Emma's face turned the color of a ripe strawberry.

It didn't matter. Tears ran down our cheeks between our snorts of laughter, and I'm sure our faces matched Emma's.

I pulled myself together and said, "We'd love to help. I need to go by Toole's Hardware for some supplies for the shop anyway. So I figured I might as well turn this fiasco into something positive and finally reorganize the back office."

"Awesome. How about we go after you girls finish your lunch? I can get away then." Emma suggested.

"Sounds like a plan."

THE WALK to Toole's was just what I needed after I gorged myself on Emma's tasty food. And with every step we took toward the hardware store, the urge to unbutton my pants pressed down on me. It was more like my overstuffed stomach screamed at me to give it some relief.

"Hey, let's stop at Daisy's. I want to see how she's doing." I pointed to the flower shop.

The jingle of bells on the door sounded as we stepped in.

"Hey all," Daisy greeted us as she shoved some baby's breath in a vase.

We all returned our greetings, and I made my way to the counter. I leaned against it and said, "This is gorgeous. Someone is getting laid tonight."

Daisy's giggle was as soft as the flowers she was currently handling. "No comment." But then she winked at me.

"Oh boy. I bet you hear some great stories when people order." Bella leaned against the other side.

"Uh-huh. Even with our small-town gossip, there are so many more unspoken secrets out there," Daisy mumbled as she rearranged the bouquet.

The three of us stared at Daisy and didn't say a word. All of us wanted to know what hidden knowledge she knew.

She looked up at us when the silence continued, and we saw her mentally rewind the last thirty seconds. Her eyes slightly popped out, and she quickly defended, "Nope. Forget I said anything." She eyed me and did her best to change the subject. "I heard about your shop. Sorry that happened but congratulations on the win."

"Thanks and same to you, but you know that won't cut it." I wanted to know what juicy tidbits were happening around town that weren't related to me.

She ignored me and said, "Trent already came by for my security video, so I don't have anything to show you. I hope it helps though."

"Thanks, Daisy. I know Rocky and Bella understand you can't break client privilege. Otherwise, you wouldn't have any return customers." Emma bumped our shoulders.

Both Bella and I glared at Emma.

"Of course we do." Bella reluctantly relented.

"Yup." The number of panties we found in clients' cars reminded me of last night with Max on the DeVille, and my face blazed at the reminder.

Bella chuckled at my look.

"Ah, it sounds and looks like," Daisy pointed to my red cheeks, "Rocky's got a story of her own to share."

"Maybe it has to do with the hot customer she has. Sparks fly any time they are near each other," Emma helpfully added.

My mouth dropped open.

"Okay, time for us to hit Toole's." I pushed up from the counter and headed toward the door as their laughter trailed behind me. I looked back at Daisy. "Let's hit Coop's soon."

"You bet." She waved a beautiful burnt orange rose at me.

The walk toward Toole's was slow with all of our stops to congratu-late the other businesses on our win at Town Hall. They all even offered that they had already given their footage to Alex or Trent if they had anything to share regarding the break-in.

So, it was a bust, but not really. Maybe I could get Alex and Trent to let me watch some of the videos to see if anything stood out. It didn't hurt to ask.

Toole's Shop was a mixture of home maintenance, garden, and office supplies. It had a little bit of everything. The Toole family was super helpful and always ready to lend a hand with anything and everything. The whole family—dad, mom, son, and daughter—ran the shop together until Rose left after high school. There were rumblings about why she skipped town so quickly, but nothing was verified.

I was totally curious about it.

Rose and Trent were high school sweethearts. They were destined for the white picket fence, two-point-five kids—the whole works. And then, one day, they weren't.

Sure, Dusty was the logical, obvious conclusion, but I didn't think that was the only reason. As much shit as I gave Trent, he wasn't a cheater. He also wasn't big on sharing. So, curiosity, met the cat.

"Hi, Mrs. Toole. How are you today?" I asked.

"Doing great, Rocky. I'm sorry to hear about the break-in. How is everything?"

"Ehh." I shrugged. "That's why I'm here. I need some stuff to fix the shop."

"Do you need help getting it, or do you want to wander around?"

"I'm going to meander, thanks. Plus, Bella and Emma are picking up stuff too. We're going to help Emma with some renovations at her cabin."

"She's come in a few times. I don't know her very well, but I can't say I'm not curious about the changes she's making."

"Well, if her cooking is anything to go by, then I'm sure it'll be awesome." I winked at Mrs. Toole.

We were loaded with various supplies for our home projects, so by the time we hit Harper's, my arms felt like they would fall off.

"We should have driven," Bella mumbled as she dropped her bundle on the sidewalk beside my SUV.

"Yeah, I wonder why we didn't think of that? I mean, it totally makes sense to get in the car, pull out of the parking space, and then park it in the very next spot, then get back out to walk five feet to the next store."

Bella didn't miss my sarcasm as she flipped me off.

"Son of a bitch," I ground out.

"Umm..." Bella stammered.

"Seriously? What the fuck?" My language recall wasn't better than Bella's, but I'd had enough of getting knocked around.

"I take it this wasn't there before you got here?" Emma asked.

"No, it was not." My head swung back and forth as I scanned for cameras on Emma's building. "Please tell me you have surveillance equipment."

Emma's head shrunk into her shoulders. "No. It's low on my priorities. Sorry."

"Nothing to apologize for. Whoever decided to behave like a high school delinquent and key my car should apologize." I eyed the surrounding buildings and tried to remember which ones had cameras.

"I already called Alex. He says he'll be here in five and not to touch anything." Bella stepped next to me.

"I am seriously getting annoyed. What the hell? Not even on my worst day am I enough of a bitch to deserve the crap that keeps coming at me."

Bella gave me a side hug. "Of course not. This isn't about the type of person you are. All this stuff happening says everything about the type of person committing these atrocities. Definitely nothing negative about you." She tried to assure me.

"Then tell me why this idiot of a person keeps attacking me. I mean, why me? Why not you? Or Emma? Or Daisy? Or? Or? Or?" I wanted answers. If I knew what I did, I could fix it and stop all this B.S. from following me.

"I wish I had answers for you," Bella said as we watched Alex and Trent pull up. "I'm hoping my brother or Trent can give you some."

"Rocky, you're attracting a lot of bad vibes lately. Are you sure you haven't left anything out that we should know?" Trent asked as he walked up to us outside Harper's Corner.

"Yeah, I thought I'd keep you in the dark as much as I am." He was unaffected by the death rays I visually zapped him with.

He put his hands up in the universal please-don't-attack-me sign. "Just checking." He turned to Alex, eyebrows up to his hairline, with an expression that said, please help me.

"Walk me through how you found this," Alex requested.

"After Bella and I ate lunch at Harper's, we, including Emma, headed to Toole's for supplies. I left my car here while we walked over there because I wanted to stop at some of the stores to congratulate them on our win and ask them about their security footage. We just got back and saw this." I flung my hand out to point out the noticeable key marks on my vehicle.

"Do you have any cameras?" Trent scoped Emma's building out.

"No. It's on my list, but it's low in priority. I've got more hazardous items vying for preference." Emma mumbled, "And money."

"No problem." Trent's eyes roamed the neighboring buildings.

"I'm going to head inside and talk to some of your customers. See if they saw anything," Alex told Emma.

"I'm going to call the guys and see if they can get any prints off her car. It's a long shot, but with everything going on with you, I don't want to take any chances," Trent said. "Then I'll visit the shops around here and see if they caught anything."

I looked at the sky and wondered what I did to deserve this.

It didn't have an answer.

"Why don't you come inside too. You can have some pie while the guys do what they need to do," Emma offered.

"I'd love to, but I'm going to head back to the shop. I'll swing by later and pick my car up when they're done." I could follow Alex or Trent and learn what they did at the same time. But the thought of revisiting the same stores in less than an hour seemed invasive.

"Needless to say, Rocky, you need to be careful. If you think anything is out of the ordinary or something doesn't sit right with you —I don't care how inconsequential—call me or Trent as soon as possible," Alex ordered.

"You betcha." Right after I kicked whoever's ass needed it because I was beyond done with this bullshit.

"Not after you go exploring." Trent read my mind.

My eyebrows shot up, my eyes popped wide, and I squeezed my lips together to prevent myself from lying.

"Emma, call us the second you realize something is wrong. Don't wait for Rocky or Bella to figure it out. Don't go with them. Just call us," Alex demanded.

Emma's eyes widened as she nodded and looked between all of us.

"You're scaring her. Stop it." Bella smacked Alex's arm.

"Good. Then I know at least one of you will do the right thing." He kissed her cheek and walked away, taking Trent with him.

Brandie

It was a juvenile bullshit move. Some would even say it was childish, but I didn't care. It was the perfect payback for someone who adored cars.

More importantly, Rocky deserved it. She earned every single one of those metal machines scratched, smashed, and scorched to the ground.

After what she did to me. What she kept doing to me.

I was justified—even warranted—in serving her so much more.

Men were figuratively throwing themselves at her feet. One handed her a multi-million dollar auto contract. Others handed her high-valued cars to restore. Others gave her mind-blowing orgasms.

Oh, yeah, I heard all about it.

How if the opportunity arose, what they would do to her. How they'd splay her over the hood of one of her builds and fuck her comatose. How they'd choke every hole she offered with so much come. And how she'd beg them to fuck her.

And I knew, *knew* Max was filling her now.

I deserved to be filled by Max. I deserved to have my pussy pounded by Max. I deserved to walk around knowing Max owned my every orifice.

Not Rocky.

Not that bitch.

CHAPTER TWENTY-FOUR

Rocky

By the time I got home, I was exhausted.

Mentally burnt out.

I stayed at Harper's for hours while Trent, Alex, and the crime scene tech guys did their magic. They wouldn't tell what they found out or who they saw because they wanted to ensure it would all stick in a court of law.

Which meant they had a suspect.

Finally.

Everything in me wanted to shake the name out of them, but they had what Bella called their cop shields up, and no amount of battering against it would budge them.

So I stomped away and made my way home.

The whole time, I cataloged everything I needed to follow up on and prayed this would all end really soon.

So, seeing my brother sitting at my kitchen counter tapping away at his laptop didn't fill me with joy like it normally did.

"Wanna tell me why you haven't caught this fucker?" I demanded of him.

One dark, thick eyebrow shot up. "Hello. How are you?"

I blew out a breath. "Sorry. I've had enough of this shit. I want whoever is behind this caught, strung up by their privates, and electrocuted." I deserved at least that as payback.

"What happened?" Ash turned fully to me.

I updated him on *everything*—even the latest childish keying and the possibility that Alex and Trent might finally have a suspect.

"Wow. Seems like that smart mouth of yours finally caught up with you."

"Ha ha ha." I opened the cabinet, pulled out my stash of chocolate, and shoved a massive piece in my mouth.

"So, you have no clue who is behind any of it? You're sitting at square one with more piling on top? But with the likelihood of apprehending someone soon?" Ash summarized it all.

"Yup." But it came out "yyuummppp" because of the chunk of chocolate in my mouth.

Ash's mouth twitched in humor at the same time my phone rang.

I looked up at the ceiling and silently prayed it wasn't more bad news.

I grabbed my phone from my purse and saw Bella's name on the screen.

"Bella, I just left you."

"Shit, Rocky. I don't know how to tell you this."

My heart sank. "Tell me what?" I sensed Ash standing up next to me.

"Mr. Quincy's been in a car accident. He's at the county hospital. He's in pretty bad shape." Bella rushed to deliver the bad news as quickly as possible.

"I'm on my way. Has anyone told Mrs. Quincy? Who is taking her to the hospital?"

"I'm headed to her right now," Bella said.

"Okay, Ash and I will meet you at the hospital."

"See you then." Bella disconnected.

Ash was already packing up his stuff. "Let's go."

On our way, I texted Max to let him know I would be late for our date. Something he sprung on me while I waited for Alex and Trent to finish their preliminary investigation on my car.

By the time Ash and I arrived at the hospital, Max was waiting outside for us.

"How'd you beat me here?" I leaned into him.

"I was at Paul's." He bent down and gave me a peck.

I stepped back and did the introductions between Max and my brother.

"Do you know if Bella and Mrs. Quincy are here yet?" I asked Max.

"I haven't seen Bella, so I'm guessing no."

We turned just as Bella drove up to drop Mrs. Quincy at the curb.

We gave more hugs and introductions as Bella parked.

The second Bella joined us we guided Mrs. Quincy to the desk, where she told the attendant, "Hello. I'm here to see my husband, Theodore Quincy."

Mrs. Quincy was a soft-spoken woman with an even softer heart. She didn't raise her voice, get perturbed when waiting, or admonish anyone who did her wrong. Instead, she smiled the most grandmotherly smile in the world and kept on keeping on.

So, it was me who snapped, "Excuse me!" at Nurse Booby when she completely ignored Mrs. Quincy and continued gossiping to the attendant, who looked like they wanted a hole in the ground to swallow them up asap.

Her heavily kohl-lined orbitals shot lasers at me, but what she didn't do was stop gabbing. Instead, she glanced right through me and landed on Max and Ash. The flip switched right in front of our eyes. The bitchy customer service representative was replaced with the fakest I'd-do-anything-for-you-I-love-my-job-as-a-nurse persona, and the desk manager looked down at their feet.

Oh no, she didn't. "I'm talking to you. You *do* work here, right?" I jabbed a finger at her as the volume in my voice rose at the audacity of the cow.

Max slid his arm around my waist in a way I was sure was his attempt to keep me from flying over the counter, but Mrs. Quincy's frail hand grabbed my hand and kept me locked to my spot.

I looked down at her and apologized, "Sorry, Mrs. Quincy."

"I'm due that apology." My head spun back, and I saw her fire-red claws crossed over her barely contained bosom tapping impatiently and her equally red lips pursed at the slight she thought she incurred.

Bitch.

"I'm sorry to bother you, but I was hoping you could tell me where to find my husband, Theodore Quincy." The ever-pacifist Mrs. Quincy spoke before I could tell the overinflated blow-up doll where she could put her apology.

More eye lasers shot between us before she unfolded her arms and clicked on the computer.

"He's in the back with doctors." She purred at Max and Ash. Unable to decide which hunk she wanted. "I can show you to the waiting room, where you can wait for them."

My muscles tensed in preparation to launch myself across the counter, and Max's arm tightened around me.

"I'm sure his wife would love that." Max's hand bit into my side in his bid to hold onto me.

She froze at his rejection, then shot more lasers at me.

Ash actually chuckled.

I leaned back into Max's side, and I was sure my smile was purely I got the cat's cream, and you didn't.

"It's down the hall to your right. Someone will check in when the doctor has information to share." She sashayed her flat ass through the employee door, making it clear she was done.

Mrs. Quincy gently pulled my hand down the corridor even though I really, *really* wanted to follow Blow Up Barbie and pop her ego.

Dean met us at the door the second we crossed the waiting room threshold.

Dean bent down and kissed Mrs. Quincy on the cheek. "How are you doing, Mrs. Quincy?"

"I'm fine. Thank you for taking care of my Teddy," she said.

Dean saw Mr. Quincy's car flipped on the side of the road. Dean was on his way to grab Bella from the clinic for a late dinner. Thank goodness he was.

"Any time, Mrs. Quincy," Dean said.

"Dean, I don't think you've met Max." I looked at Max. "Max, this is Dean, Bella's hot guy that Paul talked about at Coop's."

They did that manly handshake and chin lift thing men do.

Of course, Ash and Dean added the back pounding and then promptly stepped to the side to converse about what I was pretty sure was all of the shit going on.

"Bella, it's nice to see you again, even under these circumstances," Max greeted her.

"Yeah, I can say the same." Bella couldn't hide the twinkle in her eyes as she replied to Max.

"Mrs. Quincy, why don't we have a seat over here while we wait to hear from the doctors." I guided her to what had the qualities of being the most comfortable chair in the room—wide with dense padding.

By the time we had her situated, Dean had returned to us, and Ash had headed out the door. I didn't even bother to ask. I knew he was going to look into it.

So, with Mrs. Quincy's permission, Bella and I moved to the other side of the room and made the necessary calls to various folks, letting them know what little we knew about Mr. Quincy's condition. So, it wasn't a surprise when numerous townsfolk came in to keep Mrs. Quincy company or to find out any news on Mr. Quincy.

But as time passed, it became flat-out excruciating, not knowing anything.

"Have you heard any news on Mr. Quincy? Find out what happened?" Max handed everyone coffee after running out to grab them and then sat beside me.

"Not really. No news on the CT scans, x-rays, or MRI. They ran a bunch of labs, but nothing on those yet, either. They're worried because he's unconscious and isn't responding to stimuli. So right now, it's a wait and see."

Dean tugged Bella closer to him. It'd been ten years since she'd lost her parents to a horrific car accident, so knowing Mr. Quincy was in almost the same position brought up horrible memories. Nevertheless, Dean wasn't leaving her side until he knew she was past the worst part, even if he wanted to be at the site investigating.

Max grabbed my hand and held it in his lap.

"I don't know Mr. Quincy very well, but he doesn't strike me as the type of man to let something like this keep him down." He gently squeezed my hand. "I have a feeling he's going to take his time waking up, and then he's going to jump out of bed and go back to kicking legal ass."

"He totally would too. However, I don't think Mrs. Quincy will let him do that anytime soon."

"What's he doing here?" Bella leaned into me and whispered.

"Who?" I turned to the door and saw Carson had approached Mrs. Quincy, who sat beside Mom. "I know Mr. Quincy does some business with Lodestone Financial, but I didn't realize they were close."

"Yeah, but if anyone from the bank were to be here, I'd think it'd be Carson's dad, not Carson. So, what's he up to?" Bella stared at them.

I didn't hide I was observing Carson and Mrs. Quincy conversing. Mostly, I watched Mrs. Quincy for any signs Carson was making her uncomfortable. She didn't need his type of insincere sympathy at any time, but especially not now.

"You two might want to cool it with your death glares. I don't feel like wasting energy to lock him down." Dean was the image of relaxed with one arm behind Bella's chair, the other on the back of the chair next to him, legs extended in front of him, crossed at the ankle, and his head tipped back, resting on the wall with his eyes closed.

"We weren't killing him with eye lasers," Bella flat-out lied.

He lifted his head from the wall, opened his eyes, raised one eyebrow, and silently called her on her bullshit.

She thumped his thigh.

At first, when Max's hand tightened around mine, I thought it was because he was commiserating with me, but his grip didn't lessen.

I followed his line of sight and saw Mom, Mrs. Quincy, Mrs. Dixon, and Carson huddled in quiet discussion. None of them paid any of us any mind.

I pulled our hands toward my chest and whispered, "What's wrong?"

My body unconsciously tensed at the look of disgust Max sported.

"Ah, I take it you've met the dick," Dean quietly muttered.

Bella snorted, but I knew it was more than that. Whatever interaction Max and Carson had left Max with a nasty taste in his mouth.

"Tell me about him," he demanded.

Then I braced. What had Carson told Max? That we previously dated? Was that enough for Max to dislike him, or was there more?

Dean straightened from his chair and faced Max. "Why don't you tell us what you're getting at?"

Max glanced at Dean and back at me. "You do business with the guy?"

"He's a customer." I squinted in confusion.

"Raquel, you're a brilliant businesswoman, but I have to say you working with him surprises me."

My eyebrows shot up, and my eyes bugged out. Hell, no, I didn't work professionally with Carson.

Never had.

Never would.

"Um, no. Dad and Mom believe in supporting the local community and joined Feldspar Bank years ago. I agreed with my parents and followed suit. I do *not* work professionally with Carson or his dad's financial institution."

Max opened his mouth, but before he could utter a word, a doctor asked for any relatives of Mr. Quincy.

Everyone shot to their feet, but Mom, Mrs. Quincy, and Mrs. Dixon steadily approached the physician. Carson, the dick, tagged along.

I wanted to know what the doctor was saying, but Mom would've had my hide if I instituted another public disgrace, so I kept my feet firmly planted where they were and watched. The doctor was serious but not apologetic. He didn't look upset or sad, just concerned, which I took as a good sign. The fact the doctor left with Mrs. Quincy and didn't stick around for a longer conversation could've meant it was either good news or not.

The best news was Carson left right after the doctor.

We met Mom halfway across the room.

"Teddy is stable but unconscious. The doctor isn't overly concerned with Teddy's broken wrist. He has a few bumps and scratches, which the doctor also isn't concerned with. It's the fact Teddy hasn't regained consciousness that Dr. Mendel is troubled with. Teddy's scans came back clear, leaving the good doctor baffled." Mom shook her head in disbelief. "I didn't want to remind him in front of Lizzie that Teddy isn't as young as he once was, so a little bump on the head would take a little bit longer to shake off. So, it's all good news."

Mom, she had such a way of thinking. A car accident with a giant tree was just a little bump that Mr. Quincy had to shake off. Bless my mother.

"Now, their children won't make it to town for another few hours, so I want you girls to head over to Teddy and Lizzie's house and make sure there are fresh sheets on the beds, deal with the laundry, stock their cupboards and refrigerator, prepare at least one breakfast and one dinner casserole, and do a quick but thorough cleaning. We don't want the Quincy family worrying about anything but making sure Lizzie and Teddy are cared for." Because all the above was making sure they were because Mom was on a mission. "Max and Dean, I want you boys to handle the outdoors. Make sure the lawn is cut and trimmed, and the bushes are as well, and..." She puttered out, not having a clue what yard work entailed. "Whatever else needs to be handled outside."

I seriously wanted to laugh.

"Yes, ma'am." Max may not have had a mother, but his dad had taught him how to appease women.

"Of course, Mrs. Sterling." Dean didn't hide his smile.

CHAPTER TWENTY-FIVE

Rocky

MRS. QUINCY HAD GIVEN US THE KEY TO HER HOME, AND WE SPENT the remainder of the evening there. The Quincy household didn't need the work Mom instructed us to complete. Only Mr. and Mrs. Quincy lived there since their children were all grown up with their own families. But, to meet Mom's mandates, we envisioned the entire home was a vacated derelict home filled to the brim with dust, dirt, and debris that wouldn't pass inspection unless we steam cleaned the curtains, bleached the bathrooms, sanitized the kitchen from ceiling to floor, and deloused the beds. It didn't need it but we cleaned to Mom standards and left with the most enticing scents of lasagna and garlic bread still in the air.

So, by the time I got home, I was exhausted from good old-fashioned back-bending housework, and the only thing I wanted to do was luxuriate in a hot shower, fill my belly with some good food, and Max. I hoped he was up for doing most of the work because I was pretty pooped.

But, the universe only allowed us a partial shower—and let's just say I had a reserve of energy showering with Max—because my freaking phone would not stop ringing. Instead, as soon as it stopped, it'd start back up or chime with a text alert. So, finally, after what felt like the fiftieth buzz, I snatched the phone up and noted both Alex and Bella had left me back-to-back calls and messages.

Dread immediately filled me, and the room swayed as I thought Mr. Quincy didn't make it.

"Bella?" My voice cracked as I prayed she wouldn't break my heart.

Max's arm wrapped around my waist and held me steady.

"Rocky, is that water I hear?"

"Yeah, I'm in the shower. Now tell me why you and Alex have blown my damn phone up for the last five minutes."

"Okay, why don't you get out of the shower first? I'll be there in ten minutes to pick you up."

"What? Why? What the hell is going on, Bella?" Even though I was standing in a steaming shower with Max's heat at my back, chills raced up my spine.

She blew out a breath. "Darn it, Rocky, I don't know how to say this."

I leaned back into Max as my blood raced toward my feet, leaving me lightheaded. "Just say it, Bella."

"There's been a fire at your shop, and neither your alarm nor your sprinkler systems went off." The words left her mouth at the speed of a race car.

Time stopped.

No way Bella just informed me that my shop had a fire with *no* alarm warning and *no* sprinkler assistance. How in the hell could that be?

"Max is here, so we'll meet you at the shop." I didn't wait for her response. Instead, I turned in Max's arms and blurted, "My shop is on fire. We gotta go."

He didn't delay. He yanked the water off, and we raced to dry ourselves off and get ready.

I was hanging on to my nerves by a thread so the fact that my first time having shower nooky with Max was interrupted because of a fire in my business pushed me closer and closer to hysteria.

Besides the phone call I made to Ash, who told me he'd tell Mom, letting him know about the current situation, it was an eerily quiet ride to town.

After I told Max the horrible news, he closed down. Then, he went through the motions—collected our sandwiches, chips, and drinks for the road. He ensured I had everything I'd need to await the destruction. But, once that was done, it was like all the sound in the world had been sucked into outer space.

All the precious moments we shared—gone.

I didn't even have the original grumpy Max anymore.

Shit. The food I scarfed down on our way threatened to come back up.

We drove around the corner, and I saw the fire trucks lined up. Firefighters handled the massive fire hoses and drenched my shop as billows of fire and smoke lit the sky. And all the blood raced from my head to my feet for the second time that night.

Max shoved my head between my legs as he parked on the side of the road.

"In through your nose. Out through your mouth," Max ordered.

My door opened. "I'm so sorry, Rocky." Bella rubbed my back.

I pulled myself up and stared at the red flames and gray smoke dancing out of the shop, and I thought *this wasn't a little fire. This wasn't a prank. This was fucking real damage. This might genuinely be the end of the shop.*

I turned to the side, bent down, and wretched the sandwich Max had just prepared. But my stomach didn't get the memo to stop. Instead, it did everything to rid itself of the ridiculousness surrounding me.

Bella pulled my ponytail back and handed me napkins and a water bottle. "Take some deep breaths, Rocky."

I did as directed, but the smell of burnt rubber, chemicals, and the ruination of my life filled my nostrils, and I gagged again.

Max stood next to his truck and stared at the burning building. His blank mask was still in place, and my stomach revolted once more.

Shit, I needed to get my nerves under control.

I got out of Max's truck and stood numbly in front of my shop, stunned as firefighters worked to extinguish the blazing inferno. My business, my livelihood, my father's legacy was ablaze. Someone destroyed all the hard work he and I poured into it over the years in one act of hateful vengeance.

Hot tears spilled down my cheeks. I had poured my heart and soul into this business for years. Watching it burn felt like losing a piece of myself.

"Are you doing okay?" Bella side-eyed me.

"No, I am not." I laced each word with fire. "I am going to nail this son of a bitch to the car lift by his balls and let him hang."

"While I don't think Alex and Trent would personally mind you getting your licks in before they arrest whoever, as police officers, they'll have to refrain you from attempting such activities." Bella tried to lighten the mood.

"How did this happen? Again? I changed all the codes, and I recently serviced the sprinkler systems too." I shook with so much barely contained fury.

Because if someone destroyed my dad's shop, I didn't think I could survive that.

Alex approached, his face grim.

"I've got some bad news," Alex said. "It looks like arson."

The confirmation sent a fresh wave of nausea through me. This wasn't an accident. Someone intentionally targeted and destroyed my livelihood.

Alex squeezed my shoulder. "We'll find who did this, Rocky. You have my word."

"Was everything destroyed?" I managed to ask through the bitter taste in my mouth.

Alex exchanged an uneasy look with Bella before he gently said, "I'm afraid the damage was extensive. The fire burnt most of the interior and contents beyond recognition."

The fire burnt most of the interior and contents beyond recognition.

A wounded noise escaped me as I absorbed those words. All Dad's tools, the projects we were restoring, the irreplaceable mementos on the walls... gone. It was like losing a part of him all over again.

Bella wrapped her arms around me as I shook with sobs. She didn't offer platitudes, just held me close as I grieved.

After a few minutes, I took a shaky breath and wiped my eyes. When I looked up, Max's gaze met mine. His stoic mask had slipped, and regret and sadness crept around the edges.

He stepped toward me hesitantly. "Rocky, I..."

But Ash and Trent strode over before he could continue, looking ready for war. "We did a walk-through with the fire marshal. It's definitely arson—they used an accelerant. Disabling the alarm and sprinklers was amateur in appearance—quick and dirty, but effective." Ash's eyes bored into mine, filled with anger. This was as much his loss as mine.

"They completely shut the valves off," Trent told Alex grimly. "And the backup battery is dead—looks like it was punctured or disconnected before the fire." His eyes met mine, flickering with anger. "They wanted to inflict maximum damage—quickly."

"Rocky..." Max choked out. "The DeVille..."

My heart dropped. I had almost forgotten about Max's Cadillac. The gorgeous classic that Max and his brothers wanted restored for their dad. Now nothing but a melted, twisted lump of metal.

"Sorry, Max." Trent barely shook his head. "It looks like it was the point of origin."

Max let out a choked guttural cry, and his entire frame solidified as grief encompassed him. I moved to comfort him, but he recoiled from my touch.

"This is all your fault," he ground out. "I told Paul we needed to move it to another shop. I should have stood my ground."

I reeled back as if he had struck me.

Ash stepped forward, his body barely held in check. "Careful. I know you've suffered a loss, but taking it out on Rocky isn't the answer."

"How can you say that?" I cried. "You know I would have protected that car with my life."

Max's face contorted in anguish. "But you didn't, and now it's gone because of you."

I shook my head helplessly. This couldn't be happening after everything Max and I had shared.

"There was nothing I could do," I said, my voice breaking.

"I don't want to hear your excuses," Max said. "That car was irreplaceable. I was going to give it to my dad to honor him and my late grandfather. Now it's just a melted hunk of metal, like you never even cared about *its* legacy."

His words cut me to the core. I knew how much that car had meant to him, painstakingly restored it as an homage to his dad and late grandfather.

Max clenched his jaw, and I heard the grinding of his teeth.

I tried to touch his arm. "Max, please, that car meant everything to me too. I did everything I could to restore it to its former glory—"

He stepped away from me. "Well, it wasn't enough. The one thing I asked you to do, and you failed me completely."

Numbness spread through my body. "I'm sorry," I choked out through sobs. "I never meant..."

But Max didn't hear me. He turned his back and strode away, the wreckage of my dreams smoldering behind him.

Another billow of fire shot up and I sank to the ground, rubble digging into my knees. I barely registered the screech of tires as Max left. Then Bella was kneeling beside me, speaking in an urgent tone I couldn't comprehend.

Bella gripped my shoulder, and her eyes searched mine with concern. "Rocky, are you okay?"

I just shook my head mutely. How could I be okay? My business was destroyed, and the man I loved blamed me for his most precious possession being reduced to ash...

I covered my face with my hands as fresh waves of hysteria rose in my chest. The violation I felt was staggering. Not just my shop and Max's car, but all the blood, sweat, and tears I had poured into my business—my passion and livelihood—now just char and ash.

The night wore on in a blur. Bella and Mom—who left Mrs. Quincy's side once she heard about the fire—stayed by my side the whole night, a steady, comforting presence. Ash, Trent, Alex, and Dean made pit stops throughout the night with updates, fresh coffee, and warm blankets. Lastly, the fire marshal completed his inspection and confirmed that someone had deliberately set the fire to do maximum damage.

"It's a clear escalation," Alex said gravely. "First petty vandalism, now arson and destroying lives. We'll do everything to make sure they don't get away with this."

But their assurances barely registered through my fog of devastation. I could only see Max's brutal and unforgiving eyes as he blamed me for failing to protect his precious heirloom.

Mom drove Bella and me to my house when the guys flat out stated there wasn't anything for me to do, especially since the fire department said I wouldn't be allowed anywhere near it for a few days or weeks. She didn't leave me. Of course, she wouldn't. She'd make sure I was okay before ever taking off.

My gut twisted at the loss we endured—our tie to Dad ravaged by the fire. I silently thanked the heavens above that the T-bird wasn't at the shop but safe and sound in my garage at home.

That night, I lay restless. Nightmares of my shop consumed by raging flames and Max's accusing face filled my sleep when it finally came.

So, in other words, I slept like shit.

Vindictive

Rocky wasn't laughing now, was she? No, she was vomiting her guts out and bawling like a baby.

Yes!

Oh, and Max was pissed too. Whatever he said to her upset her. No, it ravaged her.

I thought her precious legacy being in smoke would do the job, but Max delivered the uppercut I meant to give her. It was a bonus I didn't know I needed.

If only she listened to me, none of this would have happened. But instead, she made me do it, and she deserved all the grief she was going through. She should have stayed with me. She should have given me the contact. She should have obeyed me.

But since she didn't, I couldn't let her get away with it. So I had to stop her.

Everyone was so focused on the Quincys that I jumped at the opportunity to cover more of my tracks and deliver more punishment to Rocky. Fire was the perfect tool to accomplish both.

Rocky fell to her knees as Max stormed away.

This was perfect!

No more fucking shop. No more fucking Max. No more fucking Rocky sitting on her high horse.

Finally, the bitch was getting what she deserved.

CHAPTER TWENTY-SIX

Rocky

MOM AND BELLA DROVE ME BACK TO THE SHOP A FEW HOURS LATER.
The early morning sun peeked over the horizon as we approached
Sterling Custom Auto.

The million and one thoughts that bombarded me earlier were
gone. None of the usual daily tasks clamored at me to complete. None
of the *who could have done this* bounced around. None of the *how I disappointed Dad bulleted out*. None of the *how could Max not be who I thought
he was*.

Nothing.

My brain was eerily silent as I walked around Sterling Custom
Auto. I wasn't allowed in the building yet but I did my best to see
inside. Some firefighter investigators sifted through parts of ash.
Others would huddle together, pointing at something. Even Alex,
Trent, and Dean meticulously went through every square inch—burnt
or not. Ash ignored the authorities and did his own investigation.
But my brain flatlined to a blank black screen as I stopped at the
curb.

"I got you another *café* from Margie's. I thought you'd need the jolt of espresso over milk." Bella thrust the coffee cup in my face as she stood beside me.

"Thanks." The sip I took hit my system and reawakened my dormant thoughts. I asked Bella, "Am I bitch? I mean, really, truly a bitch? Because what could I have done that would have caused anyone to want to exact such a vengeful act on me? The list I created for Alex and Trent was short and pitiful. I laughed when I finished it." I pointed at the shop. "But this? There is no one I can imagine that I pissed off enough to do this."

"You are *not* a bitch. This is *not* on you. This says everything about who they are. About how juvenile and demented they are. What it does not say is one damn thing bad about you." Bella's tone left no room for argument.

"Max doesn't agree with you." I couldn't hide the pain behind my words.

"Well, men *are* stupid." She shoulder-bumped me. "I'd love to give him an excuse, but all I want to do is kick him in the butt for being such a jerk because there is no reason to hurt someone you love."

Love.

There was no hiding from it.

I loved Max.

I thought he loved me too.

I blinked back the tears pooling in my eyes. I wasn't as sure as Bella. Max made it pretty clear he was done with me.

Mom wrapped her arm around my shoulder. "Bella's partially right. It takes men a little longer to put two and two together concerning women. As for Max, he was out of line. He was mean and hurtful; for that, he owes you an apology in conjunction with lots of groveling. Lots of both." She gently squeezed my shoulder, making sure she had my attention. "However, I will point out he was sucker punched at the news of the loss of the DeVille, and since I'm gathering that they believe this vehicle is the foundation of their family's love, it was a double whammy for him. But what truly got him was not the harm to the DeVille or the tarnishment of what he believes is the root of their love; it was the realization that he had it forever. That it's not an item, but the people he loves and love him in return."

She lifted my chin and looked into my eyes. "This building is not your father. Your father's love for you is not over there in the rubble. He'd love you even if you decided to sell it all and start a goat farm. Max is a lot like your father. He loves you and is terrified because he hasn't had the best experience with it."

"I don't know." My voice cracked as I used every tool I had to keep from breaking apart again.

"You'll see. Your mom is right. Now suck it up because the guys are heading this way. You don't need them thinking you're a fragile girl." Bella barely shoulder-bumped me.

I snorted. They'd never think of us any other way. We were their sisters. To love. To protect.

"Do you think they found anything?" Would they let me in on it?

"Between the four minds coming at us, I don't know how that's not possible." Bella didn't move from her spot next to me.

"How are you hanging in there?" Ash asked me.

"The shock is wearing off, and anger is definitely seeping in." The pain was a whole other matter. "How are you?" This was his shop too. He worked alongside Dad almost as much as me.

"Oh, I'm fucking pissed."

"I know it's a trying time, but do I really need to remind you all of your language?" Mom looked between us.

Ash bent down and kissed Mom on the cheek as his way of apologizing.

"Please tell me you got something." I looked at the remaining trio. "Or did you guys?"

"Why don't we head back to the station where we can have a private conversation and get some things in motion?" Trent stated more than he asked us as he headed toward his truck.

Everyone shuffled to their respective vehicles and headed back to the police department. I was bouncing out of my skin with the need for answers by the time we reached Alex and Trent's desk, who had already pulled out chairs for Mom, Bella, and me.

I didn't want to sit. I wanted to run out and strangle whoever had been messing with me. But I sat anyway as Dean poured more coffee for everyone.

The warmth of the hot coffee in my palms reminded me to stay calm in order to get this S.O.B.

"The police auto technician finished inspecting Mr. Quincy's car this morning. Someone did a piss poor job of hacking through his brake lines, and there were multiple puncture wounds on various hoses. It presented as someone who wanted to do damage but didn't know what to do to cause maximum results." Alex dropped the bomb on us.

"What is Mr. Quincy working on for you?" Dean asked.

"The only thing Mr. Quincy is working on for me is finishing the zoning crap and reviewing the Wheldon contract." I stilled at the thought of Mr. Quincy getting hurt because of me.

"What makes you think Theodore's accident has anything to do with Rocky?" Mom's usual sweet perkiness was nowhere to be seen.

"Lily called me to tell me that he had reached out looking for me the day before his accident about a matter related to you. He told her it wasn't urgent and he'd catch me some other way. It wasn't until she heard Mr. Quincy had been hospitalized that she got a hold of me," Dean said.

"Poor Lily. She's probably beating herself up thinking if she told you sooner maybe she could have prevented this somehow. She's always so on top of everything for you at work." Bella's concern was genuine for Dean's assistant. "Did you find anything at the wreck site?"

"Nothing. Not even his briefcase, which Mrs. Quincy stated was not at their home, and Mr. Lewis confirmed Mr. Quincy left the office with it the night before the accident," Trent continued, making me feel like shit that my crap harmed Mr. Quincy.

"Let's break this all down. First, we have the zoning complaint, which we still don't know who filed. We also have the missing part and business card with a mysterious female employee we still can't identify. Next came the break-in that targeted the photo and DeVille, showing us that this is personal and linked to Max but no suspects. We also have rumors from the online reviews casting Sterling Custom Auto in a negative light that tracks back to false accounts. Rounding all this off is your vehicle being keyed to shit, again, with no suspects, and now the fire where the DeVille was targeted again." Ash looked at us. "Am I missing anything?"

"Nope." I asked Trent and Alex, "Or is there something you didn't tell me?"

"No, that's all of it," Alex agreed.

"How is Max connected to all this? How did he hear about the shop?" Ash grilled me.

"Max didn't know anything about us. Paul was the one who found Sterling Custom Auto, signed the contract, and brought the DeVille in. When Max learned I was Rocky and not a man, he wanted to pull the DeVille. And, as far as I know, he is not connected to any of the other stuff." Just talking about Max shot a pain through my heart.

Mom squeezed my hand, knowing I hurt.

"So, you're the connection for all of it," Ash stated in his no-nonsense way.

"Clearly." My sarcasm wasn't hard to miss.

"We've got two people working here," Alex said.

"That's my thought too. Female and male," Ash continued.

"What? How do you figure?" Then it hit me. *Badhorsey*." That is such a girly thing to say.

"Exactly. Some of the stuff swirling is non-violent but petty. Like the missing card and part, the keying of your car, and the rumors. Something a female would do." Ash raised his hand to quell my objections. "I know women can be brutal, but statistically and psychologically speaking, this is female. The other shit fits a male's psyche."

"By the way, the missing part and business card nabbed by the mysterious woman is the same person who started the online rumors about Sterling Custom Auto." Trent shifted through papers on his desk before he pulled one out and looked at me. "Do you recognize this woman?" He handed me the photo.

"How do you know it's the same person?" I mumbled as I studied her. Both Mom and Bella leaned into my sides to look too. She had long auburn hair that gleamed from a recent keratin treatment with perfectly applied makeup that screamed sexual invitation. She was someone you wouldn't forget meeting, and she struck me as familiar, but I couldn't place her. I looked back up and said, "Something about her is tugging at me, but I can't put my finger on it. Should I know her?"

Trent and Alex shared a look.

"You've seen her before, but you haven't met." Was Trent's cryptic reply.

I squeezed my eyes together in confusion. "Um, what?"

"That's Brandie Morgan, also known as the woman Carson fu..." Alex looked at Mom. "The woman you caught Carson with."

"That makes sense. She looks skanky." Bella scrunched her nose in disgust.

I saw red. "That bitch. Why would she do that? It wasn't me who screwed her boyfriend. *She* fucked *my* ex-man on *my* desk and then did this?" I shook my head. "Nuh huh. What is wrong with her?" I twisted my head and said to Mom, "Sorry, but I think I should be given some grace under the circumstances."

Mom shook her head and smiled at her feet.

"Did she key Rocky's car too?" Bella asked no one in particular but everyone at the same time.

"I believe so. We'll find out for sure when we bring Brandie in." Alex said. "On top of that, we're finishing the last security video from the day at Harper's. Hopefully, it ties it all up for us."

"Is she still with Carson, or did she move on?" Bella asked everyone.

"She is," Trent answered. "And she's also Carson's alibi for everything."

My brain kicked in. "Ash, Mom, did either of you check the footage for the night of the fire?" I had been too stunned by everything. My brain had not functioned properly to remember to check.

Both Ash and Mom said no.

An eerie calm descended on me. I stood up, walked over to Alex's desk, and said, "Can I use your computer?"

"Sure." He closed various files and apps down before moving the keyboard to me.

I pulled up the video from the fire with a few clicks as everyone gathered around Alex's desk.

I fast-forwarded to thirty minutes before the destruction started and saw a man walking toward the shop.

"He's got the same gait as the vandalizer," Trent mumbled.

The dick went straight to the valves and power source and didn't mess around. He yanked and cut whatever he could to get it all to stop. Then he stomped to the front door, smashed the beautifully etched window, and opened the door.

The alarm didn't blare with the power out.

Even without the power, the camera had some leftover juice and captured the asshole before it died.

Carson.

"Motherfucker," Ash ground out.

"I want to remind you of your language, but I can't seem to bother," Mom mumbled as she stared at the image of Carson on the monitor.

Dean walked over, saw the jerk's face on the screen, and said, "I see you figured it out."

"What do you mean?" Trent asked.

"He's behind the zoning complaint." Dean waved his phone. "My contact did a little digging."

"Well, I think you guys need to bring Brandie and Carson in for questioning." Because if they didn't, I'd hang them up by their fingertips and use them as target practice for my new nail gun.

Alex grabbed my hand. "I'm sorry, Rocky, but we'll have to question Max about all this."

My stomach plummeted as new pain slashed at it.

"Yeah. I know." That meant I'd have to see him again.

"Wait. Max hinted at the hospital that he might know Carson or that you had business dealings with him. What was that about?" Bella said.

"I don't know. Unfortunately, the doctors came in, so we didn't get to finish the conversation." I looked over at Bella. "You don't think they know each other, do you?"

"Max gave me the impression that he didn't have a high opinion of Carson," Dean answered for her.

"So how does Max know Carson? And why did Max seem perturbed by him?" I asked anyone in general.

"Let's find out." Both Alex and Trent turned to their desks.

CHAPTER TWENTY-SEVEN

Max

"Do you want a beer?" Dad asked.

"Got anything stronger?"

Dad stopped his trajectory toward the refrigerator, turned back to me, and said, "I gotta say I'm not liking how you're starting this." He then resumed his course but instead hit the cupboard where he stashed his whiskey. He pulled it down and two tumblers.

After he poured it, he brought the tumblers and the bottle to the kitchen table, where he sat next to me.

I picked it up and downed it.

I needed all the fortification I could get.

Dad raised his eyebrows and refilled my glass. "What's going on?"

I took a deep breath as I stared at my dad. This was a conversation I had put off for years, but it was time. I wanted Rocky in my future, and I needed to do everything I could to get her back and keep her.

Starting with my mom.

"I think it's time we talked about what happened at my eleventh birthday party," I said quietly.

Dad sighed and nodded. "I wondered when you would come to me about it. Your brothers and I have had several conversations, but you never wanted to talk. That day changed all of us. You more than any other."

I thought back to that sunny Saturday. All my friends were in our backyard for my big one-oh birthday party. Everyone had just sung Happy Birthday, and I was about to blow out the candles on my airplane cake when a long black limousine pulled up the curb. The front door opened, and out stepped my mother, dressed to the nines with a small suitcase in her hand.

"She didn't even look at me," I said bitterly. "She just walked right by as I sat there stunned and confused with my party hat on. She got right into that limo and drove away without a backward glance. Why didn't she wait until after the party?"

"I know, son. I was just as shocked as you. I had no idea she planned on leaving that day. I thought we were working on a future together," Dad said. "If I had known what she was up to, I would have stopped it. I would never have let her ruin your birthday. Never."

"I know, Dad. That's the one thing I never doubted: you doing right by any of us." I took a sip and swallowed hard. "I found out from the kids at school that she left us for some rich guy. That she was just a... gold digger."

After all these years, the pain and the humiliation was still there. The sting was less potent but still poisonous. Because my friends had watched my mother abandon me on my birthday and trade my family in for a richer one. The gossip at school was vicious.

"Max, I wish I had words to take it all away, but I don't. Delilah always wanted the nicer things in life, and she found a way to get it." Dad tried to explain.

"Finer things? You mean not family? Because that's the finest thing you can ever have." I downed the rest of my whiskey.

"On that, we agree." Dad finally took a sip. "Unfortunately, your mother wanted material things for which she didn't have to work. I wasn't able to provide that for her."

"I started hating women after that day," I confessed. "Or at least, not trusting them. I saw how easily Mom tossed us aside for money. And I wondered if all women were capable of that."

My dad nodded gravely. "I know. You started building up walls. Closed yourself off from getting close to girls."

"Can you blame me?" I asked. "I didn't want to end up like you—betrayed. Blindsided."

"I don't blame you," Dad replied. "What your mother did that day... it was unforgivable. Selfish and cruel. She hurt you deeply; I know that pain has stayed with you. But your mother is *not* the example to base women on, and you shouldn't stop yourself from sharing the love you have to offer because of her. You have too much goodness in you to keep it to yourself."

I dropped my gaze, staring at the whorls on the wooden table but only seeing Rocky's face. The pain that slashed through her at my cruel words. My throat tightened with emotion.

"So... I guess I haven't let anyone get too close," I said gruffly. "Haven't let myself really care about a woman." Except for Rocky. "I date, but keep it casual. As soon as things get serious, I... I end it."

It was the truth. I feared if I let myself love someone, they would only leave me. Just like my mother did so callously, without looking back. The pain of losing someone I cared about terrified me. So I pushed them away just like I did Rocky.

"But keeping folks at a distance hasn't made you happy, has it?" Dad asked me gently.

I let out a harsh laugh. "No, not really."

"Son, I can't believe you've held onto all of this for all these years." Dad squeezed my shoulder.

"It was during my birthday party when she left us." So how did he think it wouldn't stay with me?

"Shit, Max." He let go of my shoulder and shook his head. "Your mother leaving had nothing to do with you or your brothers. It didn't even have anything to do with me."

I stared at him in disbelief.

"Mom never hid why she left. We were too much work. You didn't make enough money. We weren't enough for her." Those words were permanently engraved in my brain at the age of eleven.

"True. Delilah did say all that. But what she meant was that she was a selfish bitch who wanted to be catered to hand and foot while living off someone else's hard work. It wouldn't have mattered if she didn't have any kids or never married. If your mother had to lift a finger to pitch in for *anything*, she would have thrown a fit. It had nothing to do with us and *everything* to do with her."

Dad stood up and paced back and forth.

"Max, her leaving was the best gift she ever gave us. Don't get me wrong. I loved your mother, but I saw the petty in her. I thought my love and our family would be enough to make her happy. I knew better, but I still wished because I did love her. But when she did go, I was more upset because I *wasn't* upset she left. I sighed in relief because her toxicity wouldn't be around to taint my beautiful boys. I didn't want her brand of venom to color you or your brothers' view of the world or women." He ran his hand over his head. "I thought I made it clear in my actions with you boys that she wasn't the average or normal female. I hoped you all would find a woman who would love you and your family as much as I did and do. I didn't notice this was tearing you up so badly."

"You never dated or remarried after she left." So if he wasn't still in love with Delilah, why didn't he find another woman to spend his life with? He had so much to share.

"With you loveable little monsters?" A short chuckle escaped Dad. "I didn't have the time. I made sure you boys were fed and clothed. I made sure I never missed any of your events. You all ran me ragged from one thing to another. So how was I supposed to find time to date?"

"I thought you did that to keep us out of trouble?" Could it be that I read the entire situation wrong all these years?

"Well, yeah. My mom swore I gave her every gray hair she ever had, and here I had four of me. No way in hell was I going to go gray early," he joked.

"I thought all these years that you've been holding out for Delilah, and I couldn't figure out why when she's..." Bitch came to mind, but one look at Dad's face and I knew he wouldn't let that fly. He was allowed to cast evil words upon Mom's character, but he taught us boys that she was our mother no matter how much she wasn't in truth.

"Max, my bachelorhood has nothing to do with your mother. All joking aside, I was too damn exhausted at the end of the day to muster up the energy to tangle emotionally with another woman. My sons filled me up in a way that was right for me at the time." He threw his hand up. "I don't care how old you are; I will never discuss my base needs with you."

"Thank God," I teased Dad.

"Now, tell me why you're here with me and not with Rocky?" He cut to the chase of the matter.

"I fucked up." Boy, did I.

"How?"

It was my turn to pace. "I saw the shop on fire. It wasn't a little bonfire. It was a full-on take on everything in its path inferno. The firefighters were doing their best. Water was everywhere, but it wasn't putting a dent in it. The whole time, I kept thinking that was it. The DeVille was toast." I rubbed my hand over my face. "I knew there was no way Raquel could salvage it after that hell pit and that you'd never get the one thing that truly made you happy."

"We've already established that I had everything I ever needed to be truly happy, and it wasn't the car."

"Yeah, now, you did." I shrugged. "But in my mind, the DeVille was the only time I ever saw you smiling. And after your heart attack, I needed you to be that again. Light. Carefree. Alive. To remember there are things, people here to fight for."

"Max." Tears pooled in Dad's eyes.

"So, with the blaze of fire shooting out of the shop, I felt like someone kicked me in my teeth. How would you be happy if the one thing you needed was no longer around? And, with one thing after another going wrong in getting that damn thing fixed, I just felt... betrayed." I picked up my pacing. "Raquel wasn't supposed to do that to me. She was supposed to be different."

"She didn't do that to you. She *is* different," Dad reprimanded me.

"I *know* that. I do. I just..." I ran a hand over my head in frustration. "I don't even know." And in doing that, I fucking hurt her.

"What did you do?" The fear in Dad's words made it so they were barely audible.

I stopped pacing, stared unseeing down at my feet, and felt pain slash through me at the memory of Raquel's expression. She'd been through one hit after another and kept getting back up. Not once did she back down from the curveballs thrown at her. But last night, she unraveled when she saw her father's legacy up in flames. The sobs that racked her wrenched at my soul.

But I wasn't there for her when she needed me. No, she was down, and I fucking kicked her while she was there.

"I accused her of not caring about our legacy and not doing everything to protect my interest. That she only cared about her dad's shop and that I should have transferred the DeVille when I had the chance." The image of Dad's disappointment was another kick to my gut. "You don't have to say it. I know she's not like that. I fucked up."

"If I thought it would make things better, I'd hunt your mother down right now and shake the ever-living tar out of her for the damage she caused you." He shook his head. "She is not all women. She is not what love is. She is not what you deserve. So promise me right now you're over the bullshit your mother did."

I shook my head. "I can't promise that. But I can promise I'll do everything in my power not to let it harm my future. Again."

Raquel proved to me what women truly are.

Givers.

Lovers.

Fighters.

More importantly, Martha demonstrated in her actions with Raquel, Bella, me, all of us what true mothering was. The woman took care of everyone around her regardless of biological ties. She taught Raquel those same values. I just ignored it. "How do I fix this, Dad?"

"You grovel. You beg. You plead. You do not give up," he ordered. "And use that damn plane to show the world you mean it."

"I don't think it's going to be that easy. I..." My cell phone rang and cut me off. "Just a second, Dad. It's a Feldspar number." It was another kick to the gut as my mind raced with possibilities. "Hello?"

"Hi. Is this Maxwell Hudson?"

"Yeah. Who is this?" Because I did not recognize the deep masculine voice on the other end.

"This is Trent Cooper, Feldspar Police Detective. I have some questions regarding an open investigation and need you to come down to the station as soon as possible."

My stomach plummeted. "Yeah. I can be there in ten minutes."

"Good. I'll see you soon."

I disconnected and looked at Dad. "The police need me to come down. They want to ask me some questions."

Dad stood up. "About what? Do you need a lawyer?"

"I don't know, but I'm guessing it concerns the fire and the DeVille." I grabbed our tumblers and placed them in the sink.

"Leave the cups. Let me grab my keys, and we'll head out." Dad was already moving toward the hallway.

"You don't have to go with me. I'll call you after." I didn't want to add any more stress to his heart.

I met him at the front door.

"You're not going to go have a conversation with the police without me."

The determination stamped on his face told me he wouldn't budge because that's what dads did. They stood by their children.

No matter what.

CHAPTER TWENTY-EIGHT

Max

I SAT IN THE HARD METAL CHAIR WITH MY ARMS ON THE METAL table across from Alex as he questioned me in the small interrogation room. Fluorescent lights hummed overhead, adding to the tense atmosphere. The limited interactions I previously had with Alex were nothing like the one I was experiencing now.

"Let's go over this again," Alex said, studying his notes. "You claim you picked Sterling Custom Auto randomly to restore your grandfather's vintage Cadillac DeVille."

I sighed. "I already told you, my brother Paul researched auto shops, and Sterling had top ratings for quality restoration work. That's why we chose them."

Alex leaned forward and narrowed his eyes. "Come on, Max. We both know this has to do with Carson, Rocky's ex. You two have a history, don't you?"

Scrubbing a hand over my stubble, I shook my head. "Look, I've spoken with Carson a handful of times. I didn't even know he used to date Raquel until later."

"But he warned you away from using her shop, correct?" Alex persisted. "Told you Rocky was bad news?"

"Yes, Carson did say that," I said. "I ran into him a few times at Margie's coffee shop. He, in not so many words, basically told Paul and me that Raquel's customers were dissatisfied with the quality of work she produced and that this poor craftsmanship lost her a lucrative contract."

Alex nodded as if this confirmed his suspicions. "So Carson poisoned you against Rocky. Tried to sabotage her business."

"Maybe," I reluctantly admitted. "But honestly, I didn't give much credit to what Carson said. I could tell he had an ax to grind with her." It was my hangup with my mother that made me doubt Raquel.

"Yet you still chose Sterling Custom Auto," Alex said. "Interesting."

I shrugged. "Not really. I trust my brother. Plus, the work Raquel did on the DeVille proved Carson was wrong. She knows what she's doing. I don't know Carson's deal, but he clearly had ulterior motives."

Alex scribbled some notes, then looked back up. "What about Brandie Morgan? How do you know her?"

I hesitated. Surprised. I hadn't expected her name to come up. "Brandie? What about her?"

"How do you know her?" Alex's disposition hadn't changed.

"We met at a bar about two months ago. Ended up back at my place for the night." Not my best decision.

"Just a one-night stand?" Alex raised an eyebrow.

"Basically. But then she kept texting me after, showing up at my work unexpectedly. She wanted more. I didn't. She was looking for someone to keep her in the lifestyle she wanted." Now that I said that out loud, Brandie was my mother.

"Which you weren't interested in," Alex said.

"Absolutely not." Not with her. "Brandie seemed a little..." I searched for the word "...unstable. I cut things off quickly."

Alex reviewed his notes again. "Unstable enough to be involved in threatening behavior?"

My eyes widened. "Wait, you think Brandie was behind the attacks on Rocky and her shop?"

"We have evidence suggesting both Carson and Brandie were

involved," Alex confirmed. "Brandie seems to have an obsessive grudge against Rocky, possibly because of her past with Carson."

I sank back into my chair, stunned. I had written Brandie off as a hookup gone wrong. But clearly, there were layers I hadn't uncovered.

"I didn't know Brandie and Carson knew each other. She also never mentioned Rocky during our short times together," I said. "I had no idea any of them knew each other. Well, besides Carson and Raquel."

"You should know we are bringing Carson and Brandie down for questioning. We have evidence of their wrongdoing, but that doesn't mean they won't get out on bail. They've proven they don't mind getting their hands dirty, so be careful. Watch over Rocky and keep her safe." Alex nodded and closed his notebook.

A chill went down my spine at the thought of Raquel being in more danger.

"I appreciate the warning, and I'll keep her safe," I said grimly.

I stood up, eager to get back to Rocky's side. To have her forgive me and give me another chance. I was tired of letting fear hold me back from love. What happened with my mother wouldn't dictate my future anymore.

Raquel was different–I knew it. And I was ready to leave my past behind and fight for a chance at real happiness with her.

It's too bad I almost ran into Brandie on my way out of the room.

"Max? What are you doing here?" She looked at me, then Alex, then back to me.

"I'd ask what you're doing here, but I already know." I shook my head. "Good luck getting out of this one."

She smiled the smile of a woman who was used to using her looks to get out of everything. "I don't need luck."

"Let's go." Trent pulled Brandie by her arm down the hall to another interrogation room.

I didn't wait to see anymore.

I needed to win over the woman I loved.

Brandie

Men.

They were all the same. Show them a little cleavage, a sexy smile, and *bam!* They were opening doors and their wallets right up.

This one though. He was tall, dark, and handsome but with a serious no-go written all over him. His type was always more challenging initially, but they always came to heel in the end.

Even though this one handcuffed me to the table, I knew I'd walk right out of there. I always did.

Time to get to work.

"I'm Detective Trent Cooper, and I will be asking you some questions. But before we begin, Brandie Elizabeth Morgan, do you understand your rights as they have been explained to you earlier when Officer Ramsey arrested you?"

I leaned forward to give him a better view of my breasts. "Would you mind explaining them to me again?" Guys loved to think they were more intelligent than women and loved mansplaining things to women.

"Certainly."

The whole time he rambled on about my rights, he never once looked down at my tits. He kept his eyes solely on my eyes. A warning shot up my spine.

"Do you understand?" he repeated.

"Yes." I nodded and tilted my head, giving him my lost puppy eyes. Guys loved a damsel in distress, and it helped that my hair slid across my nipples.

Not even a flicker.

"All right. You worked at Sandstone Auto Supply, but it says you left earlier this year. Why?" He looked from his paper back to me.

To my eyes.

Both his question and inattention shot another sliver of warning.

"I was offered a better opportunity." Although Carson wasn't proving to be the financial provider he said he was.

"Which is?" Trent maintained his professional persona, which meant I had to up my game.

I licked my lips. "Well," I smiled the-I-got-a-secret-smile, "I'm an independent contractor." Still nothing from him.

"What services do you provide, and who is your current customer?" Trent asked.

"When you say it like that, it sounds—naughty." I slightly bent my head and looked at him from under my eyelashes. Guys liked women to be coy.

"Let's cut to the chase, Brandie," Trent said evenly. "At this time, you do not have valid employment. You are, however, sleeping with Carson Humphreys in order to have a place to stay."

Shit. None of my usual ploys deterred Detective Cooper from his mission.

"If you already knew, why were you asking?"

"You know what else I know?" Trent stared at me.

I shook my head. The blood in my veins rushed a little faster at the calm composure he kept, not wanting to know what he knew.

"We have evidence connecting you to multiple events in relation to Sterling Custom Auto and Raquel Sterling."

I wasn't sure what that meant, but it didn't sound good. But no way was I going to take the fall for Carson or Rocky.

"You have no proof I did anything." I kept up with my lie.

"We have proof tying you to these crimes." He paused as my stomach revolted at his comment. "And we know your... partner, Carson, was also involved."

Fuck this. "Carson didn't make me do anything! I chose to help him get back at that bitch, Rocky, for myself."

Trent raised an eyebrow. "Oh? And why exactly were you so eager for revenge against Rocky?"

Sneering, I examined my long pink nails. "She had it coming. She got me fired because I hooked up with Carson on her precious desk. What a prude."

"I see," Trent said, making a note. "So you were angry at Rocky because your employer terminated your contract after you were caught having sex on your employer's client's desk with the client's then-boyfriend? That gave you a motive to target her business."

"I mean, it was humiliating getting canned like that. But Carson was the one obsessed with getting back at Rocky. I just went along for the ride." I gave a careless shrug. "I mean, she didn't do anything to help me out."

Trent studied me shrewdly. "Here's the thing, Brandie—we have surveillance footage placing Carson alone vandalizing Rocky's garage. But you lied and gave Carson a fake alibi when we first questioned you."

"I, uh, I must have misremembered," I stammered. Carson told me he disabled the alarm.

"Is that so?" Trent asked calmly. "Because I think you were deliberately lying to protect Carson. Which means you two are in this vendetta against Rocky together."

Pausing, Trent slid the damning photo of Carson across the table. Then he slid a paper toward me with the bad reviews I wrote, linking my account to them. Then he slid another photo of me at Rocky's garage, shoving the part and card in my purse. Then another of me jamming my key in her car. I stared at it all, my mouth agape, the bravado draining from my face. No amount of sexy was going to get me out of this.

"So I'm going to ask you again," Trent continued. "Why are you and Carson so intent on destroying Rocky's business? And don't lie." He pointed at the papers on the desk. "We have the evidence."

I was silent for a long moment, my lower lip trembling as I tried to find a way out of this. He patiently waited as I pulled myself together.

I burst out angrily, "Fine! Carson needed Rocky to use him—his dad's bank—for the loan she would need for the Wheldon contract. He was in trouble with his dad, and she was supposed to be his ticket out of the dog house. But she wouldn't do it. So Carson wanted to get back at her." I crossed my arms with a huff. "There, happy? I just went along to piss off Rocky for getting me fired over some stupid office hookup. Plus, she got her hooks in Max. It's like she can't give a girl a break."

"What does Max have to do with this?" Trent tilted his head to the side. "Carson took it far enough to commit multiple crimes, and you became an accessory by helping cover for him."

"Max was someone I had on the hooks, but once he started seeing Rocky, he wouldn't give me the time of day. It's like that bitch can't share." Anger seethed under my skin.

Trent slid a pen and legal pad across the table. "So if you want to help yourself now, write down every illegal act you committed and the ones Carson committed against Rocky and her shop."

I eyed the pen hesitantly. "And if I tell you everything, you'll get me a plea deal? No jail time?"

"I suggest you worry more about being truthful and less about deals right now," Trent replied firmly.

With a heavy sigh, I scribbled on the pad, my handwriting big and loopy. I always thought it was pretty. Trent observed silently.

I filled out two pages' worth before I pushed it over to Trent. He reviewed the list—breaking and entering, vandalism, false online reviews, stealing auto parts and business card, and the fire. A damning account of the harassment campaign Carson and I had unleashed.

Trent closed the file and looked at me. "This will help if it's all true. But no promises until we verify your story."

I nodded glumly.

"So why Carson?" he asked. "Sounds like you two never had a real relationship. What kept you tangled up with him in all this?"

I laughed harshly. "Um, have you seen his house? He's loaded. I was just biding my time, getting what I could, until I could find somebody richer." I looked down at my manicured nails. "Too bad Rocky had to overreact and get me fired. Who knows, maybe I would have already moved on."

CHAPTER TWENTY-NINE

Rocky

BELLA AND I WERE SITTING ON HARD PLASTIC CHAIRS IN THE POLICE station waiting for... everything.

I didn't want to be there. I wanted to rewind the last twenty-four hours and start over.

No Mr. Quincy hospitalized.

No fire at the shop.

No Max gutting me.

I just wanted to be wrapped up in his arms again.

Instead, Alex and Trent made sure their t's were crossed and their i's dotted, so when they nailed Carson and Brandie to the wall, there'd be no way they'd get out.

Alex, Trent, Ash, and Dean stated they had enough evidence to put Brandie and Carson behind bars and end their Rocky Reign of Terror. They just wanted Brandie and Carson to confess so they could wrap everything up nice and neatly.

That's why Bella and I were there.

I wanted to see Brandie and Carson handcuffed and marched down to a cold, drab cement cell.

Trent stated they finally received video surveillance from the surrounding shops that confirmed Brandie and Carson were near Sterling Custom Auto for all relevant events.

On top of that, Trent pulled Carson and Brandie's fingerprints from the previous pile they found at the shop. That in itself wasn't incriminating enough, but their locations were. There was no reason Carson's prints would be on any of the tools. He brought his car to have it worked on, *not* do the work himself. Plus, his slimy fingers were on the alarm panel post-break-in. Something I confirmed with the guys when I told them I *never* gave him that kind of access and that he hadn't been to the shop since the morning he stormed out, swearing I'd regret not taking him back. Something I did *not* lament over. My repentance was dating the asshole to begin with.

As for Brandie's prints on my desk—anyone and everyone's prints could've been there. It was out in the open. Luckily, my security footage showed her swiping the card and the part—right where the tech guys lifted her prints. More importantly, Ash pulled video history proof of Carson and Brandie's past interaction on my desk, proving a solid connection.

Lucky me.

So, in Alex and Trent's bid to make sure all their evidence lined up, they had brought Brandie in for questioning—hoping to get a confession out of her. Carson was a little more difficult to find, but they weren't giving up.

"It's almost over." Bella shoulder-bumped me.

"Yeah." In more ways than one.

"What did your mom say when you called her?"

"She used a curse word," I snorted at the memory.

"What?" Bella twisted in her seat to look at me.

"Yup. Mom said, *"I always knew that boy was a no-good little turdball."'"* More laughter bubbled out of me as Bella's mouth dropped open in disbelief.

"Turdball? She actually said it?" Bella demanded confirmation.

I nodded, unable to speak due to my laughter.

Bella joined me.

And that's how Carson and Brandie found us—laughing our butts off because mom said the word *turdball*. Carson because Alex marched his ass in, and Brandie because Trent relocated her to the cells in the back.

"What the fuck are you laughing about?" Carson yelled at me while Brandie said, "Why aren't you crying?"

"Enough," Alex barked at them.

Bella and I stood up to face the terrible twosome.

"I'm laughing at you." I pointed to Carson. "And I've met my quota of the day for tears."

"How is that possible? I screwed your man while he was with you, stole from you, hindered a major business deal, and keyed your car. All this while spreading rumors about your atrocious business dealings. On top of that, you wear greasy, ugly overalls while working with cars, and your manicure is chipped to all hell. So what could you possibly have to be happy about?" Brandie actually stomped her foot like the teenage nitwit she was proving to be.

I smiled even bigger. "Thanks for the confession. It'll go great with the evidence."

Trent waved the notepad in the air. "Signed, sealed, and soon to be delivered."

"You stupid bitch." I was pretty sure Carson was referring to Brandie, but I'd been wrong a lot lately, so who knew?

"Watch your mouth," Ash warned him.

"I couldn't figure out why someone who said they were business partners with Raquel would go out of his way to speak poorly of said business. It wasn't until I saw you storming out of the last council meeting that it hit me. You *needed* Raquel's business, but you *wanted* Raquel under your control. Something you knew you were never going to get from her," Trent said.

"All you fucking had to do was introduce me to Wheldon and give me the fucking loan for the luxury line. But, no, you just had to follow your dad's *legacy* and stay with the local fucking bank," Carson fired at me.

I opened and closed my mouth. "The Wheldon contract wasn't even a possibility when we dated."

"You didn't know that, but I did. It isn't hard once you know the right people to... lubricate." He sneered at me. "Tracy runs the mail room at Wheldon Luxury and loves spy movies. So when I dangled the possibility of being the first Mrs. Humphreys, she jumped at the chance to help her future husband succeed." He leaned toward me, a psychotic fever in his eyes. "She liked sucking me off. She liked taking my cock whenever and wherever I wanted. She wanted to please me."

Ash stepped in front of me. "Back off."

Carson leaned back and continued, "I kept telling you to switch your accounts to me. But you wouldn't budge. How do you think that represented me? When the woman I'm sleeping with doesn't bank with me?" He leaned toward me again. "I'll tell you. My dad wanted me to bring in high-value clients, and I couldn't even bag the woman I was banging. You made me look weak. Incompetent."

"I am so glad I never let you touch me bareback." I shivered at how lucky I was that I didn't end up in a health scare from being with Carson.

"And Max?" He glared. "How many damn hints did I have to give him for him to take his precious DeVille and run? Delayed timelines? Nope. Vandalism? Not enough. Fire? Did that do it?" He shook his head in disgust. "No? All because I'm sure Rocky will drop to her knees and suck—"

Carson's head swung back from the force of Ash's punch.

I wrapped my arms around him and tried to yank him back from Carson. Meanwhile, Alex placed himself between them and pushed Carson backward.

"I want to press charges on that shithead. Everyone here saw Ash swing at me unprovoked." Carson tried to lift his cuffed hands to the side of his face.

"You told me you wanted to get back at her because she got me fired," Brandie accused Carson.

"I did not get you fired," I bit out from my position behind Ash.

"Yes, you did. I lost my job after I fucked Carson on your desk. If you hadn't said anything, I'd still be working there."

"You lost your job because you were screwing the company's male

customers to find yourself a sugar daddy instead of selling their prod-
ucts. Carson just happened to be the last one you did on their dime," I
countered.

"Don't knock my sales tactics. Men will do anything for you when
you have your mouth around their cock."

She had a point—just the wrong one.

"Apparently not enough," Bella mumbled.

"Clearly, I was giving the wrong person a blow job. I should have
blown you instead." Brandie licked her lips as she ogled me. "Even Max
didn't want seconds, so what does your pussy have that these two
wanted it so badly? Why your honey and not mine?"

My hands spasmed around Ash's shirt. She'd been with Max?

"You slept with him while you were taking my dick?" Carson swung
his head toward Brandie.

She shrugged, not worried at all. "A woman needs options."

I ignored Brandie and her disillusionment and asked Carson,
"How'd you get into my shop? I never gave you the security codes. And
what about Mr. Quincy? What'd he do to you?"

"That's bugging you, isn't it?" Carson smirked. "It was really simple.
You tie everything to your dad and that shop, so I had a few dates to
guess it right." He shrugged. "It worked. Everything else I targeted.
The desk because you wouldn't let me bang you on it. The picture
because you wouldn't shut up about it. The chocolate because you ate
it more than me. The DeVille because you fucked him on it."

I tensed at him mentioning my adventure on the DeVille with
Max. How'd Carson know about that?

His laugh was evil. "It doesn't take a genius to figure it out. You two
have been eye-fucking each other for weeks. How many times did I
mention that I wanted to bend you over one of your cars and..."

"Shut your mouth," Ash cautioned.

But Carson was on a roll and not to be deterred. "Then I heard
that too-good little shit, Kevin, talking to Mr. Quincy about his
concerns regarding me. How he was worried that I might be targeting
you in my misjudgment of my situation. How he knew I filed the all
the complaints to throttle Rocky's business. How he knew the pressure my dad was putting on me to perform, or he'd fired me. Fire me!

His son. No way in hell. Mr. Quincy voiced Kevin was right to come to him and that Mr. Quincy was going to gather all this information and hand it over to Dean for validation before he handed everything over to the police," Carson all but shouted. "I had to move fast to stop him. He may be old, but the prick doesn't drag his feet. I hacked at his brake lines, stabbed at anything under the car I could reach, and followed him to make sure he didn't make it to Dean's."

"You asshole. Mr. Quincy never hurt a fly." My voice was barely over a whisper with my contained outrage.

"He hurts people all the time. The difference is I got my hands dirty, and he doesn't," Carson argued uselessly.

"Please tell me that's enough to lock him up?" Bella asked.

"Oh yeah. Thanks for making our jobs easier." Alex tugged on Carson's arm while Trent guided Brandie away.

Ash turned back to me. "How are you doing?"

"I... I'm relieved to know that all this was happening because people were just screwed up and not because I was truly a witch." I shrugged. "Mostly, I'm glad it's over." Now, I had to see to getting my gutted shop back up and running.

"Are you headed over to the shop?" Ash continued to stare at me, knowing I was doing everything I could to forget that Max tore my heart out.

"Yes. The fire marshal called me earlier and gave me the clearance to go in. I'm going to call the guys and see if they want to join in on the cleanup. Do you have time to help?" I didn't always know how long Ash could stick around. His work always pulled him away at odd times.

"Yeah. I'll meet you there. Are you going to call Mom, or do you want me to?" He was the best big brother ever.

"I'll let you share the good news." I turned to Bella and Dean and said, "Thank you both for being there for me. I know that sounds lame, but thanks."

Bella playfully shoved me. "Shut up. Like I'd be anywhere else."

Dean just gave me one of those manly chin lifts.

I exited the police station, thinking I should feel relieved that all this crap had finally settled, but my mind kept circling back to Max.

How did I get him so wrong?

Was I so weak that a few kind words and gestures from him that I fell on him like a kid in a candy store?

And why did it hurt so damn much?

CHAPTER THIRTY

Rocky

THE OVERPOWERING STENCH OF SMOKE AND CHAR ASSAULTED MY
senses as I surveyed the post-fire destruction at Sterling Custom Auto.
My eyes watered against the haze that lingered, and my heart ached as
I looked through the ravaged garage. The fire left behind a gutted,
charred mess. Twisted, melted metal and piles of ash were all that
remained of some of our finest restoration projects.

The classic Mustang I had been working on for weeks was now an
unrecognizable, charred hunk. Tools and equipment lay in puddles of
water, damaged beyond repair from the fire crew's efforts. Scorch
marks blackened the walls and beams, which creaked under the strain
of holding up the remaining structure.

My heart clenched to see my family's lifelong business reduced to
this hollowed-out, barely standing skeleton. I felt the loss of each
classic car and cherished project like a physical blow. But I was determined to rebuild, no matter what it took.

"Alright, team, let's get cleaning," I said bracingly to the guys gathered amidst the destruction. I tried to inject confidence into my voice.
"I want to start getting the shop functioning again as soon as possible."

They fanned out silently, shoveling sodden debris into wheelbarrows and hauling away scraps of wood and insulation. The only sounds were the slosh of water and the crunching of ashes underfoot. Morale was understandably low after the devastating fire.

I joined in, ignoring the ache in my back as I lifted a heavy chunk of drywall. I had to show strength as their leader, especially for Sterling Custom Auto to rise from these ashes. Besides, I needed the strength to keep myself from falling apart.

"Rocky, do you mind if we put some music on? I brought my little speaker," Clay yelled across the building to me.

"Sure." Anything to raise everyone's spirits.

Including mine.

Mostly, I didn't want to hear the sounds of loss that surrounded me.

"You know we're going to get this place up and running in no time." Bruno tried to cheer me up.

He was right, and I needed to suck it up and get over my pity party. "Yeah." I looked at the guys working. "Make sure to save anything that we can salvage. We'll do another freaking inventory when we finish disposing of the garbage. We will need to examine all the builds to see what damage they incurred and develop a game plan to get them back in shape."

I got various versions of *"Sure thing"* and *"You got it"* from them all.

I stood next to the DeVille, and my heart twisted as I thought of Max and his beloved family heirloom. It had been one of the classics lost to the inferno. I vividly recalled admiring its Venetian blue paint job and perfect chrome details before the fire ravaged it. I had promised Max a complete, flawless restoration. Now, the beauty was a mess. But I was still determined to rebuild it. I wouldn't let Max or his family down. Not again.

Because even if Max no longer returned my feelings after everything that had happened, I still loved him. I had tried to deny it and protect myself, but it was useless. My heart belonged to Max, whether he wanted it or not.

I gazed outside through the opened bay doors, and my eyes landed on the shiny blue Thunderbird parked out front, gleaming in the sun.

The car that started it all. Mom and Ash encouraged me to bring the ol' gal today. To let the world know nothing could keep Sterling Custom Auto down. I wanted Mom to drive her in, but Mom insisted it had to be me. She said that as much as the T-bird was a representation of the dreams Dad had, I was undeniably the same. So, I drove her in with my head held up high and parked that beauty front and center of Sterling Custom Auto. The vintage car's proud form inspired me even through smoke and tears. Now, it stood as a symbol of the shop's fighting spirit. Just like that old T-bird, Sterling Custom Auto would shine again.

I would see to it. I would make sure I continued my father's legacy.

The rumble of tires on gravel interrupted my reminiscing. That familiar blue truck made my pulse quicken as it pulled up alongside the Thunderbird.

Max.

Uncertainty swirled through me. So much lay unspoken between us. My heartbeat raced, but I braced myself as I watched Max hesitantly approach, his eyes taking in the destruction.

"Rocky, I'm so sorry about the fire."

"Thanks." Was that the only thing he was sorry about? I shook my head to get those thoughts out of it and tried to ignore the ache in my heart at his nearness. "I'm just glad no one was hurt."

"How are you holding up?" Max asked gently.

Blinking back tears, I glanced around at the ravaged shop. "Honestly? It's devastating. But I can't let Carson win." I wiped a hand across my soot-streaked face. "I'll be okay once we rebuild. It's just hard seeing everything my dad worked for destroyed."

Max nodded. "If anyone can bring this shop back, it's you," he stated firmly. "You're one of the most passionate, hard-working people I know. You're also the strongest person I know, Raquel."

I stared at him. What was he getting at?

"If you give me the contact information for the shop you want the DeVille transferred to, I can get that situated by the beginning of the week." Seeing it go would kill me, but he made it clear I wasn't the right shop for the job.

He shook his head. "No. I don't want it moved. It's in the right hands. It's always been."

My breath caught at the sincerity in Max's eyes.

"You know I've had time to think about things. I don't blame you for questioning my business acumen when it looked bad. I mean, anyone would have." It was the lack of faith in our bond, in our love, that hurt.

He shook his head. "I should have trusted you," Max said firmly. "My past made it hard for me to believe you truly cared. But these last week apart made me realize..."

He broke off, emotion glimmered in his eyes.

My stomach rolled at the hope. I hardly dared believe this meant what I hoped.

"Realize what?" I asked tremulously.

"You know I also came to say I'm sorry. For everything. For ever doubting you. You didn't deserve that. You didn't deserve any of this or my lack of faith in you." His eyes never left mine.

I swallowed the emotions that vied to pour out of me. Ever since Max left, I had prayed he would come back apologizing and begging me to forgive him. So I didn't want my lovesick heart to jump at the first sign it might actually be happening.

"I..." I didn't know what to say.

Max's hand found mine and gently squeezed. The warmth and strength of his grip brought me comfort even through my swirling emotions.

"I can only hope you'll forgive me. I don't deserve it, but I will fight for it. I'm going to prove to you that I deserve you." Max met my gaze. "Because I love you, Raquel. I tried to bury my feelings and be practical. But losing you made me see what matters. And the fact my dad kicked my ass. Because it's you, it's always been you."

He didn't wait for me to answer.

He gestured to his truck. "I have something else for you. A surprise."

I followed him around to the truck bed. My breath caught at what lay inside: the framed photo of my dad kissing my mom over the hood of the Thunderbird, the one Carson had stolen.

"The police recovered it in Carson's things," Max explained. "I thought you should have it back where it belongs."

Tears prickled my eyes as I cradled the photo. "I can't believe you have this. I was heartbroken thinking it was gone forever."

"Only temporarily borrowed," Max said, a small smile graced his lips.

"He was an ass, but I think he groveled enough, don't you?" Ash said as he strolled by us with a load for the dumpster.

I chuckled. Leave it to my brother to break it down succinctly.

Max stared at me, hope in his eyes.

And love.

"Ye..." I didn't finish because Max wrapped me in his arms and kissed me.

It was the best kiss ever. Better than any other one he'd ever given me. We only pulled apart when the guys started catcalling and whistling at us.

I didn't let him pull too far away. I kept him close, looked into his eyes, and whispered, "I love you too."

So, of course, Max had to kiss me again.

We didn't part even when the guys hollered at us.

Because we loved each other.

It wasn't until Ash said, "I'm going to shoot someone." that we stopped.

I giggled against Max's mouth.

"How about we hang the photo where it belongs?" he asked.

Together, we carried the framed picture inside the ravaged garage. Finding a clearing on the wall, Max hung the photo in its rightful place of honor.

"There," he said. "Your dad is watching over the shop, as he should."

EPILOGUE

Margie

EVERYWHERE I LOOKED, MY FRIENDS WERE BEING LOVED UP.

Bella and Dean.

Rocky and Max.

Don't get me wrong. I was happy for them. They both deserved it.

But it was sickening to be around when your only option was your overused and not as good as the real thing B.O.B.

I pushed that gloomy thought out of my head as I hefted the large tray of pastries out of my van, inhaling the sweet scent of freshly baked Portuguese goods. Rocky had asked me if I wouldn't mind catering today's event. More like she threatened to disown me as her friend if I didn't show up with my coffee or sweets.

As if she could stay away from my chocolate desserts.

Emma emerged from her SUV beside me, laden with trays and catering dishes. We exchanged excited smiles.

"Hey, Emma!" I greeted her.

"Hi Margie." She pulled another tray onto her cart. "I'm so excited for Rocky. She worked so hard to get the shop back in order."

"Me too. At one point, I drove over here with *Salame de Chocolate* just to make sure Rocky was still alive. I hadn't seen her in days," I joked.

"Me too! Except I had chocolate cream pie."

We both giggled as we finished setting up the food and drink stations.

As the owner of the local bakery and coffee shop, I felt honored that my friend had chosen my food and drinks as one of the suppliers to cater this event. My friend had rebuilt her entire auto shop after that devastating fire. Not only that, but she had landed the huge Wheldon Luxury Auto contract. This party was to celebrate it all–the rebuilt shop, the big new client, and the completion of the DeVille's restoration for Rocky's man, Max.

Emma and I hurried to set up the food and drink stations before the guests arrived. I had to pause to admire the gleaming shop, rebuilt even better than before. Classic cars were parked out front, polished to perfection. And there was the iconic blue Thunderbird Rocky's father had restored all those years ago to start Sterling Custom Auto–still striking as ever.

Emma and I shared a look of pride for our friend. Rocky emerged from the shop, beaming but with wet eyes. I could only imagine the emotions she must be feeling, seeing her family's legacy rising like a phoenix from the ashes.

I was beyond honored to be a tiny part of this special day.

"The place looks great. Rocky did an amazing job," Emma said as she rearranged platters.

"Yeah. She practically lived here trying to get it back into shape."

"I don't know anything about cars, but these are gorgeous. So shiny and pretty." We looked around at all the spotless vehicles parked in and out of the garage.

"I agree. Rocky sure makes them pretty," I agreed with Emma.

Guests filtered in shortly after, oohing and ahhing over the rebuilt space. I recognized many of Rocky's employees there to celebrate their revived livelihoods. Rocky's mother circulated through the crowd, accepting hugs and well wishes. She paused by the vintage T-bird, patting it fondly. This place meant so much to Rocky's whole family.

Even Rocky's brother, Ash, was there. He spent so much time away that I wasn't sure he would have been able to make it.

I kept busy handling the bakery table, refilling empty platters, and pouring cups of coffee. But I glanced up when Rocky called for every-one's attention. This was the big moment—the reveal of the rebuilt DeVille for Max and his family.

She gave a touching speech about how this restoration project brought her and Max together. How the fire tried to destroy connec-tions and dreams but ultimately only made them all stronger. I dabbed at my eyes as Rocky unveiled the gleaming red DeVille. Max looked at her—the car and Rocky—with such love and gratitude that I knew he was a keeper.

Cheers broke out, along with joyous manly back pounding from Max's family. They hugged Rocky, overwhelmed by her dedication and skill in restoring their precious heirloom. That was why I adored small towns, I thought warmly. We rallied around each other in hard times. We celebrated victories together.

The party rolled on cheerfully. I took a well-deserved break, sipping Emma's delicious punch.

"Is that the secret punch?" Paul eyed the cup in my hand.

Man, he was so freaking handsome and so out of my league.

"I wish someone spiked it, but I'm working." Not true. I had added a shot of Portuguese liquor to my coffee.

"Ah." He took a sip from his cup.

"The DeVille came out nice. I never should have doubted Rocky, but when I saw it after the fire, I thought it was toast." I smiled up at him. "Your dad seemed happy when he saw it."

"Yeah, we all thought it was over." He shook his head. "I'm glad it wasn't. Dad is overjoyed. I haven't seen him that happy in a long time."

I'd only seen Paul joking, so his sad tone caught my attention. I didn't like him being down, so I leaned into him and whispered, "If you don't tell anyone, I have some *Macieira* if you want to add it to your drink?"

He looked down at me, and I thought I could get lost in those eyes forever.

"What is that?"

I pushed in closer, lowered my voice further, and said, "Portuguese brandy."

He smiled. "I knew you had the good stuff."

We made our way back to the van, and I saw Rocky circulating through the crowd, but I noticed she kept glancing around as if looking for someone.

"I think Rocky is looking for your brother." I pointed to her across the forecourt.

"Uh-huh." His smile was all kinds of wicked.

I poked him in the side. "Give it up, mister. What's he up to?"

He mimed sealing his lips.

I never got it out of him, even on threat of holding the brandy hostage. Some time later, when placing empty trays in my van, I heard excited gasps from the party. I hurried back over to Bella and Rocky, who were staring up at the sky.

"Oh my God! No, he didn't!" Rocky gasped.

"What?" Bella asked as she crammed her neck left and right, trying to catch a glimpse of what Rocky referred to.

"I'm going to kill him," Rocky muttered.

"That'd be a shame. From what you've told us, you should at least keep Max tied to your bed." I wanted a hot man bound to my bed.

"Hahahaha!" Bella whooped.

"Move over. Let me see what Max's done." I peered over Rocky's shoulder and saw a plane flying by with a banner. "What does it say?"

"*Join the mile-high club with me?*"

Across the garage, Paul stared at me with a naughty smile on his face.

Yes, I'd love to join the club.

The End

www.ingramcontent.com/pod-product-compliance
Lightning Source LLC
Chambersburg PA
CBHW031211260626
47169CB00007B/2019